LEECHING

THE

SIRENS

BY

T. M. PRINCE

LITTLE RED LEAF

FOR THE OTHER 38; AND SOMEONE
I USED TO KNOW.

Little Red Leaf

Salt Lake City, Utah

First Edition: September 2015

All of the characters, organizations, and events portrayed in this novel are
either products of the author's imagination or are used fictitiously.

ISBN-13: 978-0996520690

ISBN-10: 0996520694

Library of Congress Control Number: 2015914559
Little Red Leaf, Salt Lake City, Utah

Printed in the United States of America

10 9 8 7 6 5 4 3 2

CONTENTS

ONE

TWO

THREE

FOUR

FIVE

SIX

v

LEECHING
THE
SIRENS

1

THANKS FOR THE THREE-DAY WEEKEND MLK JR.

Mrs. Shawsen, pacing. A brusque military clack on the flagstones of the kitchen. A muted staccato thump on the rug in the living room. A smart, nervous tattoo on the polished floorboards in the entrance hall. High heels at home. A house on a corner lot was an excellent vantage point when you were expecting company, and Mrs. Shawsen was expecting company; eagerly, and apprehensively.

Mr. Shawsen was waiting too, but he wasn't pacing; he sat quietly in the den in front of the computer, as if he was working. But he wasn't working, he was counting; tracking his wife's fevered footsteps across the various floor surfaces. After he'd counted her eighth lap of the house, he took a deep calming breath and called out:

"Darling, you don't need to be so anxious. Why don't you just give her a call on her cell phone?"

"Certainly not. Not while she's driving. My daughter isn't about to join the statistics for cell-phone related accidents. Besides, she never answers her phone; not when the call's from me."

Mrs. Shawsen stopped pacing, and viewed the figure in the small hall mirror. A slender, stylish figure, for sure, but she didn't like the crow's feet gathering around the eyes of the woman who stared back at her. She lifted expert fingers to her temples and carefully stretched the skin until it was smooth again: *we can do something about that.*

Mr. Shawsen sighed a sigh of small relief, broke the silence.

"Our daughter will be here soon. Meantime, why don't you find something relaxing to do while you're waiting? All that pacing is making me nervous, so it can't be doing you any good."

He took off his spectacles and wiped them, absently, with a small white cloth, swiveled around in his chair and looked out the den window at the soft haze of snow drifting across the mountain sky line, muted colors dappled with white. His round, reassuring face was topped by hair just starting to grey in places; a comfortable face, comfortably aging. Mr. Shawsen, husband and father; Dr. Shawsen, trusted psychiatrist. He was proud of his profession and his reputation, but his real pride lay elsewhere, in his family; his lovely wife and his beautiful daughter, Jessica. Pride and joy, he thought to himself: *men are, that they might have joy.*

The somber walnut surface of his desk was broken up by photos in assorted frames. Photos of his family and photos of his wife, but especially photos of Jessica, a young life frozen into snapshots. A tooth held proudly in a tiny hand, a big smile in a sea of freckles; the same smile, with a few less freckles, on the face of a high-school girl, the hand now proudly proffering a diploma. Bittersweet reminders that his baby was growing up, had grown up into a beautiful young woman. She was halfway through her sophomore year at college, and he still hadn't gotten used to the idea of her living away from home. He knew she had her own life to live, but he hated the idea of anyone taking his baby away.

...

Jessica changed gear as she slowed for the freeway exit, on the familiar cloverleaf that led to a pleasant little Colorado city; Mountain Valley. The white Mustang's V-6 hummed a throaty rumble as it changed down, a bass accompaniment to Jean Valjean's hymn to freedom resonating from the car's speakers. She smiled at the curious symphony, and surveyed the interior of her little mobile kingdom with a warm glow of well-earned pride. Hard work was worth it; straight A's and a part-time job in retail, plus a big hand from her Dad, and here she was at the wheel of the car of her dreams. OK, maybe it wasn't the latest model, but the '01 was still pretty cool, and the money she'd saved would come in handy in the coming years.

She coasted the bend of the weather-worn two-lane blacktop and saw the rounded archways and bulbous brickwork of Mountain High, sitting heavy and squat behind the waist-high walls and fractured landscaping, random rocks and flowing water a contrast to the ungainly solidity of the school buildings. Jessica never passed it without a shiver of regret; bad memories tainted the good, however hard she tried to suppress them. She'd kept in touch with hardly any of her classmates; most of them had faded from memory already, and only Shannon remained, a rock among the drift of superficial relationships.

The curving blacktop took her away from the uncomfortable mix of memories and to the foothills at the other side of town. She passed a small gas station and came to a four-way stop, crossed it and drove by the church she and her parents had walked to every Sunday for as long as she could remember. Nearly home; she felt herself tensing a little, preparing for two different kinds of homecoming.

She had to concentrate at the intersection after the church, to avoid bottoming out on the low-set gutters. When she looked up again, there was the house, standing apart in the spacious yard, a split-level three-story house that looked like six, with a four-car garage; *home is where the heart is*, she mused, sincerely and at the same time a little wryly. Parking in the cobbled driveway, she hefted two large bags of laundry out of the trunk and tottered up the steps to the porch, reaching unsteadily for the doorknob as her baggage swayed precariously around her.

"Jessie, I didn't realize you'd got here. Let me take your clothes to the laundry room." Mrs. Shawsen put down the copy of *Cosmo* she'd been pretending to read as Jessica stumbled through the door. She took the clumsy bags from her daughter, glad of something to do with her hands.

"Thanks, mom," said Jessica: "Oh, wait." She unzipped her sweater and added it to her mother's burden.

As the sound of high heels receded toward the utility room, Mr. Shawsen emerged from the safety of the den. His daughter's voice had lured him from his sanctuary.

"I guess the magazine didn't fool you either, huh? She's been pacing for the last hour, at least." He peered over his spectacles, waiting for the little girl's smile to appear in the face of the well-groomed young woman in front of him.

4

There it was. Jessica's face lit up as she threw her arms around him. "Hi Dad. I guess you and Mom are really excited about the cruise."

"We sure are. A little burst of sunshine after the winter gloom is just what we need. Freedom for a couple weeks. Actually, I was planning on one week, but your mother insisted, and I guess she's right. We do have to leave kind of early; the flight is at 7 am, and we need to give ourselves time for the TSA parade." He grinned ruefully.

Mrs. Shawsen came back into the room, hands probing for any signs of stray hairs after her brief exertion; there weren't any. "Come here, sweetheart."

Jessica turned to her mother with open arms; Mrs. Shawsen grabbed her daughter's arms in mid-flight and examined her critically. Jessica's hair was full of strays, her hair tied into a loose ponytail that drew her hair back casually from her face.

"You look pale, Jessie. Are you OK, or are you still doing the vampire thing?"

"Mother, I have fair skin, always have. So do you, except you cook it regularly."

Mrs. Shawsen smiled warily and clumsily pinched Jessica's cheek. "I'm only kidding, sweetheart. And I couldn't go on a cruise without a tan, could I? I might burn under all that tropical sun."

"You're safe enough, mom; you won't burn at noon on the Equator."

Mrs. Shawsen patted a little hint of seasonal fluff around Jessica's waist, and the air thickened between them; Jessica's eye twitched, and Mrs. Shawsen's lips tightened. Mr. Shawsen took his cue and changed the subject.

"So ... are you staying the night here, Jess?"

Grateful for the escape route, Jessica turned to her father. "Thanks, but I'm meeting Shannon later tonight, in Denver. She has a three-day weekend too, so we can spend some time with each other. Plus it'll be a shorter drive back to college for both of us."

"Denver, huh; so what's in Denver?"

"Nothing special. Just a friend of Shannon's who has a place where we can crash. We plan to catch a movie and grab dinner somewhere. I haven't seen Shannon for a while, so there's a lot to catch up on."

Mrs. Shawsen pressed out the non-existent wrinkles in her skirt and sat with her back straighter than the straight-backed chair. "Jessie, sit down and tell us how the new semester is going. Are you still thinking about taking that engineering major?"

Jessica relaxed onto the couch across the room, beside her father's worn recliner. "I don't know yet. I'm almost finished with my generals, and I've really enjoyed my art history minor, but I don't know if anything really excites me just yet. I'll see how it goes."

"And ..." Mrs. Shawsen paused for just a second before she ploughed back into uncomfortable territory. "Have you ... met anybody?"

"I'm, uh, focusing on classes right now. One of my classmates, Ashley, got engaged last semester, and with all the excitement she nearly failed all her classes. I don't want that to happen. And besides," she smiled at her father, "I doubt I could be as lucky as you were, mom."

Mrs. Shawsen tried an historical tack. "Whatever happened to that nice boy you introduced to us? What was his name again?"

"Eric."

"Yes, Eric. He was a real catch. Nice boy, outdoors type, athletic …"

Jessica finished for her. "Studying to be a doctor. I know. After he graduated he moved to Utah to take up a residency. And …" Jessica let the story drop, hoping the subject would follow it.

Mrs. Shawsen wasn't good at hints. "If you find a good husband, you don't have to worry too much about your own career. You can focus on yourself, and your family; your children, you know. You're not getting any younger, sweetheart. Just make sure you don't leave it too late and end up with some creep; you had enough of that at high school."

Children? You mean grandchildren. And who's not getting any younger? Jessica fumed, but kept her thoughts to herself. Mr. Shawsen saw another cue and took it. He stood up and clapped his hands briskly.

"So who's up for a late lunch?"

Jessica responded gratefully. "Works for me, I drove straight through lunch. I'll just go change my clothes and I'm ready." She made a break for the stairs and the safety of her bedroom.

Mr. Shawsen turned to his wife, a plea in his eyes. "Darling, can we keep things positive? I'd kind of like it if Jessica came back once in a while."

"You're right, I know. I don't want to scare her away, in case we never see our grandchildren."

"It's not just the grandkids' thing. Jess doesn't need reminding of bad stuff right now; she has enough on her plate with college."

The hangers in Jessica's closet took the brunt of her frustration. She rattled them furiously to let off steam, and they clattered like worried mothers as she fished for clothes that didn't live there anymore. She loved her mother, but it was hard to like her, especially when she tried to mold her daughter into a perfect woman she had no intention of becoming. Jessica's tomboy life had ended at puberty; as much as she had enjoyed her mother's increased attention, it had worn thin over the years, decayed into nagging that felt like a constant put-down. She knew it was more about her mother making herself feel good than making Jessica feel bad, but that didn't make it any easier to live with.

She opened a drawer and pulled out a sweater, a swirl of autumnal colors that reminded her of a favorite Chagall. Then she paused in mid-step and looked around her room. Every time she came here it felt like stepping into a museum, a personal time capsule that had petrified the moment she graduated from high school. Everything in the room was a reminder: books she used to read, trophies from the junior swim team and the high school dance team; a Jessica she had left behind.

Well, not everything. The framed print of Jesus, dressed in quiet white, arms extended, with the quote from Matthew 11:28-29 that was imprinted on her heart: *Come unto me, all ye that labor and are heavy laden, and I will give you rest. Take my yoke upon you, and learn of me; for I am meek and lowly in heart: and ye shall find rest unto your souls.* There was the poster from *Les Misérables*, still a favorite with her. But the rest?

She looked at the montage of photos that spiraled out above the mirror, each arm of the spiral a different part of her life; junior high, high school, family vacations, church activities. Above them all stood her graduation photo, relegating the images below to the prison of the past. It was poised as if for flight, to college and beyond into the firmament of her new and unknown life. Unconsciously she twisted the silver ring on her right ring finger, staring at the montage and simultaneously at nothing at all.

When she focused again, she was staring at a break in the chain of high school dance photos, the blank space that represented the Sweethearts Ball from her junior year. *That's why it gets to me when mom calls me sweetheart*, she thought, twisting the ring a little faster. Just before the break in the chain was a photo of Jessica in a lilac dress, holding hands with a tall, blond, muscular boy. His dress suit was a dark purple, with a black tie, and he towered over Jessica. After the blank space she was dressed in light blue, beside a boy closer to her own height. He had light brown hair with frosted tips, combed forward and spiked a little. His clothes didn't match hers at all; a smooth black dress shirt with a white tie. The longer she looked at him the less she wanted to; she tore the photo off the wall and stuffed it into a nearby desk drawer.

A photo from another arm of the spiral caught her attention; the only year she had been on the cheerleader team. She liked this one even less, and she tore it off the wall and stuffed it into the drawer along with the badly dressed dance date. As she pushed the offending images to the back of the drawer, her fingers grazed the wrinkled edges of a photo that had been crushed and flattened back into shape more than once. She withdrew her hand as if she'd been stung, then paused, her teeth grazing her lower lip, and jerkily forced her hand back into the drawer; this was the photo that used to hang on the wall, the blank space in the chain. She turned the crinkled paper over in her hand, and stared unseeing at the image on the other side.

"Jessie, we're ready to go."

Jessica heard the sound of her mother's voice from downstairs and another world. "OK" she answered absently, as her fingers ran tentatively along the edge of the forbidden image.

2

POWER ASSERTING WOLVES

A string quartet played softly out of the darkness; islands of hard light punctuated the cavernous gloom. The music struggled to fill the space, faded in and out as Stacey struggled to stay conscious.

Naked and trembling, she sat constrained on a hard wooden chair, her skin cold and clammy despite the beads of sweat that ran from her forehead, melding with the tears coursing down her cheeks. The bruise on her face drummed a dull ache, a pulsing accompaniment to the pain in her arm and shoulder, fading now into a cold, terminal numbness.

Forcing her swollen eyes open, she looked down at her captive form. She was tied at the shoulder and wrist to the hard edges of the chair, plastic zip ties locking her arms in an extended position. Slow trails of bright blood flowed from the points where three hypodermic needles nestled in her pale flesh, grim clinical leeches draining her of energy, of life.

Her dulled senses registered a vague feeling of panic that grew as she focused on it. She could feel her heart race and hear her labored breathing, a rasping echo in the hollow chamber. Instinctively she reached with one bound arm to free the other, to remove the ugly, threatening needles, but the ties allowed her very little room to move, and her hand grasped feebly at nothing in the cold air.

Her left leg was strapped to the leg of the chair but her right was free, the only limb she could move; she tucked it up onto the chair seat, to shield her exposed form, preserve her ruptured modesty, from his gaze. A tiny gesture of control, the only resistance she could offer.

The halo of harsh light in front of her sharpened his silhouette, darkened his form into a solid shadow. Stacey couldn't see any more, didn't want to see any more, but she knew what was there. He was there, in that mask, a monster wrapped in white bandage. The mask had terrified her at first, had seared itself into her nightmares the whole week of her captivity. But terrifying as it was, the mask wasn't the thing that scared her the most. It was those dark, staring eyes, the only sign of expression in his masked face. Sometimes, like now, they held her with a cool calculating iciness, the cruel eyes of a master watching his slave; but sometimes, when he lay on top of her, a wilder darkness burned in them.

Stacey's eyes began to close again, the world around her sank into a blur, and she struggled to focus again; she feared what would happen if she allowed herself to sink into the darkness now. Her head nodded, snapped back upright; she forced her parched mouth into speech.

"I'll do. I'll ... do what. What you want. Be good ... I'll be good. Just ... just, please, stop. Be good."

The silhouette paused, turned towards her, turned back to the apparatus beside him, and turned to her again. A shard of light glinted in his eyes, skidded off into the darkness around them. He turned away again, ignoring her, torturing her with his silence. He hardly ever spoke, except to issue curt instructions, and once to tease her with hope – "I'll take you to Rachel, soon"; the only other sound he made was when ... those rasping animal noises. As her head dropped in defeat, a sob escaped her.

The sound of his weary sigh made her struggle upright again. "Be good, huh? You're not so good at that, are you?" he inclined his masked head toward the bruise on her face. "Though I have to say, you were - better than I expected." She sensed a twist in the mask, almost a smile.

"I can ... will ... be better."

"No, I don't think so, Stacey." Another sigh, weary, almost resigned. "No, this is the last one, the final piece. Once I've finished it, we're done. Yeah, we're done here."

"Here? Where's here? Where am ... are we?"

"Same place, Stacey. Same place you've been all week."

Stacey looked from side to side, futile glances into the dark, as if she might finally see something she recognized. Her tongue rolled weakly over cracked lips.

"I'm ... really ... thirsty. Cold. And thirsty."

"I know," he said dismissively as he drew close to her, examining her with a detached professional gaze. He bent down beside the chair to pick up the beaker from the floor, the beaker that held the blood that he had siphoned from her arms. It was full. He put an empty beaker in its place. Then he paused and put the full beaker back on the floor.

"Hmm, looks like we have a clot here."

He pulled the needle out of her arm, roughly, and walked off into the darkness. Somewhere behind her, Stacey could hear drawers opening, the sound of someone sorting through a disordered pile of things, the sound of plastic wrapping being torn off. Footsteps, emerging from the darkness; his masked form looming back into view.

He had a new needle in his hand, a longer one. He scanned her arm, an experienced eye. He found what he wanted, among the chaotic pattern of bruises on her pallid arm. "Here." With a swift, practiced motion, he jabbed the needle into the flesh of her lower arm.

"We'll use an artery this time. It'll speed things up a bit, get it over with."

Stacey looked down at the new stream of scarlet coursing through the tubing, heading down into the empty beaker on the cold concrete floor. She heard the first drops hitting the beaker, then the sound muffled as more blood swirled in.

"Clepsydra; you know that word, Stacey? A kind of clock the ancient Greeks used. Means water thief. As the water flows out, time flows on. Funny, you have a kind of hour-glass figure. I guess you could say time's running out, huh?"

He walked back to his spot in the hard pool of light, took something in his hand. Stacey heard the sound of a brush grating against coarse paper; the music's stopped, she thought. Time's running out. She watched as he dipped the brush into the beaker in his left hand, brought the brush back to the paper.

"Rachel."

Stacey's voice surprised her. In the silence it was like the whisper of a ghost in an empty hall. "Where's ... where's Rachel? You said ... "

"Soon." His reply was clipped, irritated; don't bother me now.

"Where is she?"

He stopped painting, and stepped back to appraise his work. After a while he looked over at her, as if he'd just remembered she was there. "Rachel."

Stacey, she thought; I'm Stacey. "Where?"

"She's still there. Same place she's been the whole time. Your whole time, Stacey. Sleeping." The dreamy tone of his voice hardened suddenly. "Sleeping in the septic tank."

Stacey's breath died in her throat. He took up his brush and made a few touches, finishing touches.

"You'll see her. Soon enough."

He walked over to the other side of the room and flicked a couple of switches. Harsh florescent light flooded the room. Stacey squinted around her and realized she was in a big basement, concrete walls and strip lighting; a workspace, or a garage. He walked back toward her, turning off the spotlights that had punctuated the dark. He took a small flashlight from his pocket, lifted her chin and forced her eyelids open with a casual thumb. He waved the flashlight back and forth across her eyes, calculating.

"Soon enough, Stacey. You're almost there. Look."

He went back to the easel, and turned it around so she could see the painting. Standing beside his work, he held out an arm and gestured toward the painting.

"Well, what do you think?" he looked at the painting for a moment, returned his cold gaze to her. "Hmm, even in this state you're still kind of ... beautiful."

Through a thin veil of tears, she stared at the image before her; her weeping self, naked and exposed, a sacrificial victim in a cold hard chair, sunken eyes staring back at the viewer, devoid of hope. Her hair was a deep lustrous red, more deep red at her center; the rest of her form was depicted in faded pinks and sepia, the colors dimming even as she looked on in quiet horror.

"Enjoy it, Stacey. This is the most vibrant it will ever look. Soon it will fade, like an old master."

"It's ...let me go, please. I won't tell, I won't. I don't even know who you are. The mask ... please."

He walked toward her, calm and confident, final. Kneeling between her legs, he cupped her chin in his hand, and leaned in until his face was just a few inches from hers. His voice was mocking, quiet.

"Go? Go where, Stacey? There's no going back. If you had kept your mouth shut in the first place, you'd never have ended up here. Rachel either. As for letting you go, well," the mask rippled slightly as a hint of cold laughter blew through it. "I am letting you go, finally."

A faint flicker of hope stirred inside her, then died as she stared into his eyes. He grasped the mask, and slowly raised it over his head. She stared at him in bewildered recognition; *you*. Sorrow gave way to despair. He kissed her, softly, almost tenderly, moistening her parched lips, and whispered.

"Say my name."

His name escaped her lips in a low sob. He smiled, and stroked her hair, held her face in his hands, hands that trembled just a little.

"You're mine, Stacey, all mine. But I'm letting you go. To Rachel."

He stood up and folded his arms, gazing down at her. His face betrayed a hint of anxiety, a touch of remorse too remote to feed her hope. Stacey began to drift in and out of consciousness, struggling and failing to hold his gaze. She heard him say something else, but she was unable to make out the words properly, something about more needles. She gathered her little remaining strength and forced out a few words.

"I ... be good."

Her head fell slowly onto her shoulder, looking up at him as her eyes filmed over. A spotlight flicked on, illuminating the painting. He walked away and turned off the fluorescents. The cavernous room descended back into darkness, the spotlight on the painting the only island of light. He came back and stood behind her, stroked her hair again.

"I'll leave you with your final portrait."

Music flooded the room again; not the serene tones of a string quartet, but the frantic clash of a discordant orchestra. Stacey dimly felt him hold her head upright, and then he forced the mask down over her face. Through the orchestral din she heard his footsteps as he walked to the far side of the room, opened and closed a metal door; the crisp jangling of keys in multiple locks, then his footsteps, fading into the distance. She was alone with the harsh music and the cruelly beautiful painting. The music subsided into the sound of lapping waves and the forlorn cries of seagulls. As her head sank onto her chest, the room gradually quieted into silence.

3

FICKLE ELEMENTS

OF AMBIANCE

Jessica was glad of the drive to the restaurant; it gave her time to get over the troubling images she had found in her bedroom. She parked in front of Riverwoods and went to meet her parents outside the big double doors.

The pretty young girl at the hostess desk was dressed in the Riverwoods staff uniform of black pants, a dress shirt and vest, and a light green tie flecked with yellow. She greeted them with a big smile and said, "Welcome to Riverwoods. Will it be just the three of you?"

"Yeah, just us," Mr. Shawsen replied.

"Very well. Come right this way."

"Could we get a table next to the fireplace?" Jessica wanted to take her favorite spot.

The hostess changed direction and pulled out a chair at the table nearest the fireplace. "Will this be okay?"

"Perfect, thank you."

They took their seats and the hostess handed them each a menu.

"Here you go, folks. Your server will be right with you."

As he flipped through the menu, Mr. Shawsen said, "Funny, I thought that Carlisle's was your favorite restaurant."

"No, I stopped eating there ever since … since high school." Jessica cleared her throat uncomfortably.

"Oh yes, of course, sorry Jessie, I forgot." Mr. Shawsen changed the subject quickly. "Let's see, you've been here before. What would you recommend?"

"Well, most of the times I've been here it was for dinner. But they do a great turkey avocado sandwich." She flipped through a few more pages of the menu. "Their pizzas are delicious too, and though I've never tried it, I hear the bison burger is pretty good."

"That sounds good. I think I'll order one."

A broad-shouldered young man dressed in the same uniform came to their table. He offered them a big smile and greeted them warmly. "Good afternoon, folks. My name is Josh and I'm your server today. Would you like to hear about our specials for today?"

"No thanks, Josh," said Mr. Shawsen. "We already know what we're going to order."

"Excellent. Can I get your drinks order first?" Josh turned to Mrs. Shawsen.

"I'll have a coke, a diet coke, with lemon."

"And for you, miss?" Josh glanced up from his note pad toward Jessica.

"I'll just have water, thanks."

"Same for me," Mr. Shawsen added.

"Okay, diet coke with lemon and two waters. Now, what would you like to order, ma'am?"

"I'll have the garden salad with Italian dressing, on the side."

"Okay, and you miss?"

"Can I get the BBQ chicken pizza with a baby spinach side salad and ..."

"Sweetheart," her mother interrupted. "Don't you think the salad would be enough?"

Jessica's cheeks burned. She glared at her mother as the server looked back and forth between them, waiting for the tension to subside before he wrote down the order.

Mr. Shawsen cleared his throat and tried to rescue the situation. "Don't worry, my dears, this is my treat. You can both order whatever you want."

"No, I meant ..."

"Yes," Mr. Shawsen replied before leaning toward his wife and continuing in a whisper. "I know exactly what you meant, Carol. Now can we get on with it?" He sat back in his chair, glanced at the server, smiled at Jessica and said, "Go ahead and order what you want, sweetie. My treat."

Jessica tried to push her mother's comments to the back of her mind, and continued with her order.

"Um, yes. The pizza with the baby spinach salad." She gave Josh a chance to write it all down and then added, "And with the salad can I replace the blue cheese with feta, and can I get the dressing on the side too?"

"I got it." Josh made a note of the alterations and then turned to Mr. Shawsen. "And for you sir?"

"I hear good things about the bison burger. Would you recommend it?"

"Oh, it's the best. When I've finished my shift I plan on ordering one to take home with me," Josh replied enthusiastically.

"That's good enough for me. I'll have the bison burger."

Josh took the menus and made to leave. "I'll be right back with your drinks and the salads. Enjoy."

As they ate their lunch, Jessica tried to direct as much of the conversation as she could toward her father and his plans for the future. She knew he had been saving up and investing for a few years so that in the near future he would be able to cut back on the number of patients he saw each week. If all went well, he intended to retire early and spend his days traveling the world with his wife.

"So you could say this cruise is a kind of preview for what I hope we'll be doing when I retire."

Mrs. Shawsen squeezed her husband's arm. "I am just so excited. I can't wait to get away from this cold, depressing winter. Just think, in about sixteen hours from now we'll be in the air, heading for the sunshine."

Jessica finished the last of her pizza and turned back to her father. "So you'll be gone for two weeks?"

"Actually no, the cruise itself is two weeks, so along with the flights it'll be a little bit longer than that." He took a drink of water to wash down the last of his bison burger and sighed contentedly. "Plus we may spend a bit of time in Florida before we head back home." He glanced toward his wife and gave her a broad grin.

"Florida, really? Oh, there are so many wonderful things to see in Florida," she gushed excitedly.

"How about Miami, or Orlando?" He offered a few hints to feed her excitement.

Jessica shared her parents' excitement. "That sounds like a whole lot of fun. You'll have to email me some pictures, I can't wait to see them."

"And there's something you might appreciate, Jessie. I was looking into the various art museums in Florida and I found out that just about ten minutes away from Orlando in Winter Park, at the Morse Museum, there's an exhibition of a certain statue by an American sculptor you may have heard of."

"Who is it? Who?" Jessica was feeling giddy with excitement.

"Hiram Powers," her father answered with a smile.

"You mean the Greek Slave? You're actually going to see the Greek Slave in the flesh?"

Mr. Shawsen began to recite. "Naked, yet clothed in chastity she stands;

And as a shield throws back the sun's hot rays,

Her modest mien repels each vulgar gaze.

Her inborn purity of soul demands

Freedom from touch of sacrilegious hands,"

Jessica continued the poem in a hushed voice. "And homage of pure thoughts.

Call her not Slave;

Her soul command what servitude would crave,

Nor feels the pressure of those iron bands."

Mrs. Shawsen broke in with more than a tinge of disgust in her voice. "Ugh, who wrote that?"

"It was a poem from the *Knickerbocker* Magazine, dear. I'm not sure who wrote it though, someone with the initials R S C."

"What kind of magazine is that?" Asked Mrs. Shawsen, perplexed. "I've never heard of it."

"That's because it isn't *Cosmo*, right mom?" Jessica joked.

"It's actually an old New York magazine from back in the mid eighteen hundreds," Mr. Shawsen told her.

"And there's that beautiful poem by Elizabeth Barrett Browning too," added Jessica. "From God's pure heights of beauty against man's wrong."

"Well, I don't care how poetically it's been described. Naked is naked. I don't know how you can stand to look at them, even when they have leaves covering their, uh, areas." Mrs. Shawsen could barely contain her feelings.

"Mom, that's what makes Powers' sculpture so significant. It shows that the nude body can be perfectly modest without masking itself in any way. And there's plenty of other art works that show –"

"So what, you're telling me we should all be walking around the place naked?"

Josh reappeared just in time to catch her comment. He and Mrs. Shawsen both blushed as he made a polite noise in his throat and asked, "So, did we save some room for dessert?"

Glad of the break in an awkward conversation, Jessica picked up the dessert menu and started to say, "Yeah, can we get -?"

"Oh, sweetheart. Do you really think that's necessary?"

Jessica had about reached her limit. She leaned over to her mother and hissed her frustration. "Are you trying to embarrass me? I cannot believe you would have the nerve ..."

Over the harsh exchange of rasping whispers, Mr. Shawsen looked up at the server and said, with an embarrassed shrug, "I guess we'll just have the check, thanks."

When Josh hurried off to print out the bill, Jessica and her mother continued their exchange in normal voices. "I don't mean to be critical of you, sweetheart. I just want to help you look your best, is all; especially if you're thinking of becoming a modest nude." Mrs. Shawsen's feeble attempt at a joke went down like a lead balloon.

"So I can find myself a nice husband? Look, mother, I don't need your help, or anyone else's, to find someone I like. Maybe when you went to college, for the whole semester, all the women were only looking for an MRS degree. But the fact is, nowadays, we all need an education, and right now that's where my priorities lie. I'm not ready to give up my freedom just yet."

The server returned and laid the bill on the table. "Thank you for coming in," he said, before rushing off in relief to take another table's orders.

Mr. Shawsen paid the check and they got ready to leave. Jessica hustled into the parking lot and stood by the door of her car, gripping the collar of her coat a little too tightly. "Thanks for lunch, dad. I really do have to be going now."

"Are you sure, Jessie? You're welcome to stay at the house until you meet up with Shannon."

"No, really, I need to get going. I have a couple hours' drive ahead of me to Denver." Talking to her father, even with her mother standing beside him, helped Jessica to calm down.

"So Shannon doesn't go to UNC?"

"No, she goes to the University of Colorado, down in Colorado Springs."

"It's too bad you two didn't get to go to the same school."

"Yeah, I know. But we still get together during the summer vacations, and for this rare weekend. Anyway, I need to get going." She gave her father a big hug and said, "See you soon, dad. Thanks again for lunch." She opened her car door, and was about to step inside when she turned and gave her mother a hug too. "Bye, mom. Have fun on the cruise. Take lots of pictures."

"I will. Bye, sweetheart."

Jessica started the car, and waved to her parents as she drove out of the restaurant parking lot.

"I didn't mean to nag her, Blaine. I just ... well, she has hardly dated anyone since what happened in high school, and I, you know ..." Mrs. Shawsen turned to her husband in appeal.

"I know you mean well, Carol, but you mustn't push at her so much. She's a strong young woman and she'll push right back. She's kinda stubborn, just like her mother." He smiled, and gave his wife a comforting hug.

"Besides, let her enjoy school and her friends while she's still young. She's grown up too fast as it is, and she deserves a break." He kissed her on the forehead and turned to the car. "Let's get back home so I can finish packing."

4

A WOLF AMONG DOGS

In the high desert basin the wind gets in everywhere. The halls of the fine art department at Uintah State University seemed to shiver in anticipation as the north doors opened, and a slender figure, dressed in a three-quarter length black coat, stepped in out of the snow. His coat, along with his jeans and shoes, were old and worn, and gave him a slightly vagrant appearance, which the grey scarf wrapped around his face did nothing to dispel. Only the portfolio case and sketchbook held tight in his numbed fingers marked him out as a student.

He headed for the stairs to the second floor, whipping off the scarf as he did so to reveal a sharp nose reddened by the cold, and a narrow chin damp with condensed breath. He counted his way down the corridor past the doors on the left, until he came to the one marked with a plaque that read 'Professor Stephen Foster'.

He knocked and waited until a cheerful tenor voice answered, "come on in". In the office he came face to face with a tall, elfin man in a shirt two sizes too big for him. Professor Foster was standing beside an easel that held a half-finished urban landscape: Vernal's famous bank building against a backdrop of industrial architecture.

"I won't make tonight's class, so I brought you my drawing assignment."

"Okay, good. Put them over there on my desk." The table Professor Foster pointed to was less a desk than a dumping ground for abandoned art materials. His student put the drawings down gingerly among the paint spills and half-empty oil tubes. As he turned back to his painting, the professor shrugged apologetically and said, "I can give you full credit for the assignment, but I'm afraid I'll have to dock you for missing the class."

"That's fair. It's just how the holiday weekend panned out work wise for me. If the university had given us the long weekend, there wouldn't be a problem. By the way, is there any chance I can make up the credits somehow?"

"You could go to one of the Art Guild's figure drawing classes on a Wednesday or Friday evening. Michael Vance will sign your attendance, and if you bring the drawings you make to my next class, you're home and dry."

"Thanks, Steve, I appreciate it." The student turned to leave, but Professor Foster threw a question after him as he headed for the door.

"Are you ready for the painting critique session Monday?"

"Gonna have to be."

"You'll be fine, don't be anxious. Remember the first session will be an anonymous critique, so you don't have to stand there and defend your work against all-comers."

"That should make it slightly more bearable." The student looked visibly relieved. "Well, I guess I'll see you Monday, Steve."

"You relax and enjoy your weekend." Steve turned away and looked critically at his work, and in a moment the student was forgotten, which suited him just fine.

He jogged down the stairs and traced his way through the maze of corridors in the arts faculty. He was occasionally distracted by the paintings and drawings hanging in the student display cases, but when he got to the photography department, he sped up again; he didn't get photography, why merely use a machine to capture an image when you could capture the subject and create the image yourself?

A light dusting of snow crunched under his feet as he left the arts building, wrapping his scarf back around his face to keep out the keening wind and the insistent cold. The computer lab was only a few yards away, but he was shivering by the time he got there.

PC s to the left, Macs to the right: no contest. He sat down at a spare Mac terminal half hidden from the rest of the room by a clumsily large potted plant. With a quick glance over his shoulder, he opened his student email account and checked his inbox. Then he opened another account, his fingers tapping out a nervous rhythm as he waited for it to load. He typed a message, sent it and closed both accounts before printing out a detailed road map, carefully clearing all history on the terminal, and shuffling out of his seat. All done.

He hustled across the parking lot to where a black Intrepid was backed into a corner lot, its roof and hood blurred with a dusting of snow. Cold fingers fumbled in a pocket for some keys; he cleaned off the door lock with the keys before jiggling them into place with shivering hands. After a frozen pause, the door reluctantly agreed to open and let him in.

The engine groaned when he keyed the ignition and he revved it until the gas got the trick and the defrost kicked into life. He sat there as the engine idled and waited for the windshield to clear and the interior to warm up a little. The falling snow was grey through the tinted windows, like a dust storm turned suddenly cold.

He studied the road map he had printed out as the car, and he, slowly thawed out. He traced out his route with a sketching pencil, writing the exit numbers in large print so he could see them more easily when he was driving. The light in the car changed, and he looked up to see that the outside world had become visible again. Turning on the wipers to clear the rest of the windshield, he reached for the CD player and pressed play. Feeling the tires make a slight skid on the snow-littered ground, he set off to the sounds of Bach's Cantata no 140, 'Sleepers Awake'.

5

Books, Boys, and Bread

Jessica's white Mustang slowed to a stop at the traffic light just before the freeway on ramp. With the three-day weekend it seemed like everyone was headed out of town; the cars were backed up for a block and a half. Jessica shifted into neutral while she fumbled for her purse. Digging through its contents in search of her chap stick her fingers brushed a corner of the crumpled photo she'd found in her old desk drawer. She took the photo from her purse and smoothed out the wrinkles on the thigh of her jeans before scrutinizing the image again. There she was in a silky red dress, blushing uncontrollably; her date had literally swept her off her feet when he picked her up in his arms for the picture. She stared at the faces, their smiles frozen in time, and her mind wandered back to her 11th grade year.

...

Jessica fumbled through her high school locker, trying to get the text book for her junior biology class out from underneath a pile of other books. The narrow locker door prevented her from simply sliding it out, so she lifted the stack with her right hand and deftly rotated and removed the biology book.

She dropped the stack with a *slam* back onto the bottom of the locker.

"Hey Jess," said a familiar voice. "You should stand all your books vertical instead. It's a lot easier." Liam Hobbs was one of those people who always knew the right way to do stuff, thought Jessica. Clever, but irritating; like he was always the one in control.

"Oh, thanks." Jessica took all of her books out of the locker and restacked them vertically inside. "You're right. That is better. Thanks."

"So Jess, have thought any more about modeling for me?" Liam gestured toward the primed wooden panels he carried in his left arm. He had the long arms and slender body of a swimmer, which added to his air of confidence.

"Um . . . I don't know. I still need to figure out my schedule. Also, I was wondering, what would I be wearing for this?"

"I don't know, Jess; I hadn't really thought about it. We could try a few things and see how they work out." Jessica couldn't help feeling slightly threatened by the tone of his voice; what 'things' did he want to try?

"Okay . . . well, is it alright if I think about it some more and get back to you?"

"Sure. I'll check with you during lunch?"

"Okay." Jessica was feeling uncertain about the whole thing, and she didn't really like the feeling that Liam was pressuring her for a decision. There was more to it than a simple yes or no.

"Alright, I better get to class. See ya Jess."

"Okay. Bye."

"Hey, hey girl." Shannon had an inquisitive look in her eyes. "You've been getting some attention lately. So did he ask you out?"

"No, he wants me to model for him for a portrait assignment he's doing in his art class."

"Aww, how romantic . . . an artist and his muse," Shannon gushed. "Are you going to?"

"I don't know. I'm worried he might want me to model nude."

"Just tell him it's clothed or nothing at all."

"You mean no modeling at all. *Nothing at all* sounds the same as nude. Anyway . . ." Jessica quickly changed the subject, "How come you're so chipper today?" She closed her locker and they walked down the hallway toward their next classes.

"Well . . . did you check out the new banner in the commons area?"

"The one about the blood-drive?"

"Oh my gosh! Not that one, Jessie, no." Shannon brushed her curly red hair behind her ear and did her best to look shocked. "I meant the Sweethearts Ball banner."

"Ohh, that banner? Yeah, I saw it."

"Well, so what did you think? Isn't it, like, just perfect?"

"It looks great; perfect publicity for the Valentine's Dance."

Shannon's face lit up, and the books she was cradling bounced along with the extra spring in her step, "I know right? Me and the Activities Club spent, like, hours cutting out all the hearts and gluing the lace around the edges. Plus this one girl, Meredith, is really good at calligraphy, so we had her write the words 'Sweethearts Ball 2009' in big red letters."

"Well, it's really good. You did a good job," Jessica assured her. "You know, you should actually join the activities club instead of just helping out now and then. It's obvious you really enjoy it."

"You're probably right, but I don't know if I'd have enough time for everything. I mean, there's the dance squad. Plus I want to try out for the cheerleaders again."

"No, Shannon. The Dance Squad is so much better than the cheerleaders. I'm so glad I quit the cheerleaders last year." Jessica grimaced at the memory. "I got so tired of all the drama and the jocks . . . *hitting* on me."

"They still do a little with the Dance Squad. Plus, I wouldn't mind a little extra attention from a couple of the guys on the football team," Shannon said with a grin. "You think Jared will ask you to the Sweethearts Ball before your painter guy does?"

"Which one, Scott or Olsen?"

"I meant Jared Scott. So, who's Jared Olsen?"

"Olsen is on the wrestling team and I could care less about Jared Scott. Ever since I quit cheerleading he hasn't been very interested in me anyway." Jessica tossed her hair dismissively, as if to remove irritating football jocks from it. "I'm telling you, Dance Squad is much better. So as far as quarterback Scott goes, I don't think I'm on his top ten to ask, which is fine by me."

"Well that's his loss. What about Jared Olsen then? You said he's on the wrestling team. Maybe you could . . . help him practice," Shannon giggled at her own joke, but subsided when Jessica didn't join in.

"Oh my gosh, Shannon, I hardly know him. The only reason I know he's on the wrestling team is because I sit behind him in Algebra 2."

"So if he asks me you won't be mad?"

"Sure, since you two haven't actually met and the odds of him asking you are about the same as being struck by lightning. So no, I will not be mad."

They came around the corner to the commons area. There, hanging from two of the columns in the large open room, was the extravagantly saccharine banner: 'Sweethearts Ball 2009'. Shannon pointed at the banner like she'd never seen it before. "Look!"

"I know. It looks really good." Jessica glanced around the commons area; in the distance she could see a couple different groups of guys talking to one another as they looked at her and Shannon, then shifted their eager gaze toward the other girls in the room.

"Feels like the banner should say 'open season'."

"I know. It's so exciting, though. There's a guy in my history class I'd kinda like to ask me, or one of the football players . . . or even a wrestler maybe," She winked at Jessica.

The bell rang; students dispersed and hurried to their classes. Jessica and Shannon found themselves alone under the banner.

"See you at lunch," Jessica said and headed downstairs to her Biology class.

"Bye, Jess." Shannon waved over her shoulder and went the other way.

. . .

Thomas King rushed up the stairs. Under his arm he carried a couple blank canvases and in his other he held a biology textbook. On his back was a large bag crammed to bursting with art materials. Paintbrushes stuck out the top of one of the side pockets and the main pocket was so full the two zippers weren't able to close anymore. He wore a paint-smudged shirt with matching paint-spattered pants. His light brown hair was spiked up with gel. Despite his appearance, Thomas tried to make himself inconspicuous as he walked the corridor; he tried hard not to make eye contact with the other students he passed in the hall. When he finally spotted a few familiar faces he breathed a sigh of relief and jogged to catch up to the small group of junior guys who were just leaving their lockers.

"Hey guys, wait up," he called, a little out of breath.

The three guys paused and one of them turned to greet him, without too much enthusiasm.

"Oh, hey Tom," said Jake. Jake Larson had light brown gel spiked hair, with frosted tips. So that's how you do it. Thomas winced as he thought of his own amateur effort to look cool.

"Cool hair, Jake. When did you do that?" Thomas asked.

"Over the weekend."

"It's cool. I really . . ."

Jake ignored his comment and turned to his companions. "So like I was saying Nick, if you and Rob can . . ." He turned back toward the other two as they walked down the hallway. Jake, Nick Brown, and Rob Riley walked side by side down the hallway, Thomas following as closely as he could behind them. He had known the three guys since his freshman year of high school, but it wasn't until he'd gotten his driver's license that they had started hanging out with him. Thomas could live with the exploitation; he was just glad to have a small group of friends for a change.

As he walked down the hall behind them he could only catch a few bits of what they were saying. He tried to walk up beside Nick on the right, but ran into oncoming traffic, and had to settle for a place behind him. Peering over the guys' shoulders he caught a glimpse of a small ceramic item in each of their hands.

"Are those pipes?"

They all stopped and moved to a corner in the hall. Standing in a circle they showed off their designs.

"You make those in Ceramics?" Thomas asked.

Nick sneered; he liked Thomas about a whole car's worth. "No, we made `em in gym."

"Yeah, we finished them this morning. Mrs. Siggart is having us all make whistles, but with some minor adjustments ..," Jake said, waving his hand proudly around the pipe he had crafted.

"It's too bad you guys had to transfer to the morning Ceramics instead of the afternoon. Then we all could have been in the same class."

"Yeah, we needed to . . . uh, retake our history class from last term," said Jake.

"Oh, I didn't know you guys were in history last term," said Thomas.

"Dude, wouldn't it be sweet if we could make a bong?" Rob said, tilting his head back and peering out from under his green beanie.

"You know Mrs. Siggart won't fire those. Anything that looks like a pipe is smashed and thrown away," Thomas told them. "What would you use them for anyway?"

The three glanced at each other. "They're for smoking this, uh ... all natural herbal stuff my cousin told us about. It's good for the nervous system." Rob's answer made his friends smirk knowingly.

"Really? What kind of herb is it?" Thomas' question turned the smirks into sniggers.

"It's um, a kind of clove cigarette type stuff." Rob glanced toward Nick for approval.

"Well if it's already in a rolled-up cigarette then why use the pipes?" asked Thomas.

"So we can be *creative* and get some use out of this Ceramics stuff. Duh," Nick was doing his best to make Thomas feel small. He turned to his friends and continued. "Ceramics was so much better when Mr. Schulquist taught it."

"Dude, I know," Rob replied. "He didn't care what we did. He'd either nap at his desk or be busy working on his own pottery."

"These pipes won't last very long. My brother made one last year and it broke while it was in his backpack. So we'll have to make more again later." Jake spoke with the voice of world-weary experience.

"I could probably make one that doesn't look like an obvious pipe." Thomas saw an opportunity to get himself some cool points.

"Yeah, you're pretty artsy, obviously," Nick said as he pointed towards Thomas' paint stained clothes. He was about to sneer again, but suddenly thought better of it. "Make us some artistic pipes, Tom."

"Um, okay, sure. I ... I think could do that."

"Dude, you wanna go in with us on a bag?" asked Rob.

"How much is it?" Thomas tried to imagine how much a 'bag' was.

"Well, how much cash you got?"

Thomas set down his textbook and canvases, pulled out his wallet, and counted the bills inside it. "I've got twenty five."

"That's close enough." Rob glanced away from Thomas toward Nick with a smirk on the side of his face.

"Well, I need some for lunch, so how about twenty?"

"I guess. You'll just get a little less than the rest of us." Rob turned back to Nick and managed a stage whisper, "… and we get an extra five bucks."

The bell rang, and all three boys stuffed their ceramic pipes back into their pockets. Rob and Nick turned to head off to their classes. Jake called out, "Later guys."

"See you at lunch," Nick and Rob replied in unison.

Thomas and Jake walked around the hallway corner and then down the stairs toward the Biology classroom. Thomas lagged behind Jake, who had quickened his pace; his arms and his bag were full to bursting, and he struggled to keep pace. "Hey, Jake. Wait up."

Without turning around Jake just waved for Thomas to catch up. Out of all three of the guys Jake was the friendliest to Thomas. They all treated him a bit rudely, though Thomas tried to pretend it was just friendly sparring. But Jake at least didn't ignore him most of the time. A few awkward strides and Thomas was walking next to him again. Jake asked, "Why do you carry all of your stuff around with you?"

"I don't want to take up more space than I should in the painting classroom's dry wall, and most of my paintings can't fit in my locker. Plus it's at the other side of the school from your lockers. This way I can hang out with you guys more between classes."

"Well, you should at least put some of your books in your locker. Or else you might get spina bifida or something," said Jake as they walked into the classroom and took their seats just in time for the class bell to ring.

At the front of the classroom their teacher, Mr. Wright, stood up and began calling roll. He was a middle-aged man with grey hair that circled the sides and back of his head, leaving the top completely bald. On his lip was a matching grey mustache, and he wore owlish, round-framed glasses. After he'd finished calling out names he set down the roll and addressed the class. "Alright, quiet down. Today everyone will get into the same groups you had last week and we will team dissect a crawfish."

A hand went up at the back of the class. Mr. Wright peered over his glasses, pointed and said, "Yes, Ryan?"

"Couldn't we do frogs instead? Crawfish seem kinda lame."

"I agree, Ryan. Frogs would be much better, but the school budget only allows us to use crawfish. Now go ahead and take your things over to the lab tables and we'll get started."

Thomas gathered his things and walked with Jake over to the lab table where they had sat the previous week. Jessica Shawsen was getting out her textbook and notepad. She sat at the right side of the table near the small sink. She glanced up at Thomas, flashing a tiny awkward smile before looking back down at her textbook. Thomas came and cautiously sat down in the middle, next to her.

"Hi Jessie."

Before she could reply Jake chimed in, "Hey Jessie, how was your weekend?"

"Hi Tom, Jake." "Weekend was fine; too much homework to fully enjoy it, as usual."

Thomas placed his blank canvases on the table and set his backpack on the floor.

"Dude, your pictures are taking up the whole table," Jake said. "Here switch places with me and you can set them off to the side."

"Oh, I can just move my stuff and stay…"

"Nah, don't worry about it. Just slide over and it'll be fine." Jake hung his bag on the back of the chair that Thomas was sitting in; Thomas reluctantly moved over to the chair at the other end of the table.

At the front of the class, standing behind his own lab table and now wearing a white lab coat, Mr. Wright had everyone open their textbooks to page ninety-nine and review the chapter on crawfish anatomy.

Toward the end of class most of the students started cleaning up early in preparation for lunch. Jessica was genuinely interested in the assignment and continued to examine the crawfish. Having done most of the actual dissection, she had the crawfish and tools on her side of the table, along with the notes she had taken. Both Jake and Thomas were leaning towards her trying to see the organs. Jake had spent most of the time copying Jessica's notes and trying to look down her shirt. Thomas had his sketchbook out, and after copying the drawing in the textbook he started drawing as he watched Jessica remove various organs.

Mr. Wright called out to the classroom, "If you haven't already done so, start cleaning up and hand in your notes at my desk."

Jessica put the crawfish in the garbage and placed the tray and tools into the sink. As she washed her hands, Jake leaned toward her and glanced down at her notes. "Hey Jessie, how do you spell that science word for the crawfish's brain?"

"You mean the *encephalon*?" she replied, pointing to the word in her notes.

Thomas chipped in. "It's labeled in the textbook too."

"Yeah, I know Tom, but I already put my book away and ..." Jake paused and looked over toward Thomas' side of the table. "Dude, where's your notes?"

Jake had piqued Jessica's curiosity, so she looked over as well. Feeling the weight of both their eyes on him Thomas looked down at his sketchbook and said, "These *are* my notes."

"They're just pictures. I don't know if you'll get credit for that," Jake chided.

"I labeled all the specific organs though."

Jessica reached over, touched the corner of the sketchbook, and asked, "Can I see?"

"Sure."

She turned the book so that she could see it from a better angle. "Are these *my* hands?"

"Yeah, they're *supposed* to be. But they didn't turn out as good as I wanted," Thomas fidgeted with the pencil in his hands, wishing he'd kept his notebook to himself.

"No, they look good. You're a pretty good artist." She held her hand out. "Here, I'll take all our notes to Mr. Wright."

Thomas tore the two pages out of his sketchbook, picked the little ruffled edges off, and handed the clean edged papers to her. Jake too presented his notes, which bore an uncanny resemblance to Jessica's.

She walked off towards the door next to Mr. Wright's desk. Something made her slow her steps, and she found herself taking another look at Tom's drawings. Momentarily lost in the images of her hands, she absently brushed at a strand of hair that had fallen over her face, then set the papers down on Mr. Wright's desk. She wandered out of the classroom, half in a dream.

Thomas saw Jake hurry to catch Jessica up outside class; he gathered his things together and hustled out to join them. He caught up with them just in time to hear Jessica saying, "Yeah, sure. I guess I can go get some free bread with you guys."

"Cool. Let's go to the commons area real quick and get Nick and Rob, then we'll walk over," Jake replied.

"Is Tom coming too?" she asked.

"Oh, yeah, Tom too."

It was a routine during lunch that Thomas and the three guys would walk over to the Crumb Bakery and get a free slice of bread. Actually they hadn't invited him to go with them, he just tagged along.

The air outside was crisp and dry, what little snow remained on the surrounding lawns arranged into crunchy piles of dirty, white ice. It hadn't snowed for the past week so the streets and sidewalks were clear and dry. Halfway to the bakery they cut through a large parking lot and walked pass the drive-thru window of a local bank, waving at the cute college girl teller.

Nick and Rob walked in front, scheming how to get their pipes fired without being caught. Behind them Jessica walked with Jake on one side and Thomas on the other. After a few moments of silence, Jessica looked over at Thomas and asked, "So, what kind of art do you normally do? I mean I know you're a painter, but I've never actually seen any of your finished paintings."

Thomas was caught completely off guard by Jessica's interest in him; his reply was barely more than an embarrassed murmur. "Um, yeah mostly drawing and painting. I don't carry my finished paintings around too much. Don't wanna ruin them. I've been focusing more on painting this year than I did when I was a sophomore."

"Are any of these guys in your art classes?" She nodded toward Nick, Rob, and Jake.

"Nah, most of the people in the class are seniors."

"Why are there so many seniors in a junior class?"

"Actually, it's the other way around." Thomas blushed a little as he continued, "It's really a senior class and I'm one of a few juniors that were admitted into it."

"Well, that must mean you're very good to jump ahead to the higher classes. I'm excited to see what you can do. The most artistic I can be is when I sometimes doodle in my diary . . . nothing like what you can do."

"Thanks. I sometimes do a diary too." He felt like a real jerk for being so tongue-tied. "I mean journal, well not really a written journal, but more of a sketchbook with notes."

"I guess it's made me think differently about modeling."

Thomas was so bewitched by the sound of Jessica's voice, and the fact she was talking to him, it took him a moment to realize what she'd said. He pointed toward her hands. "I think you're a great model." His stomach churned as he blushed.

"That's only because I didn't know I was. But I guess it wouldn't be that hard to just sit there, right?"

Thomas thought of the idea of having Jessica model for him for his painting assignment and swelled with nervous excitement. After a moment of silence Jessica asked, "So, what do you like to paint most?"

"Um, in class we usually have all these boring still-life assignments we work on. They mostly consist of these hollowed out replicas of different objects like fruit and such. But when we get to do a choice painting I'll do some animals or skeletons . . . like anatomy or something . . . Oh! I've also got some comic book characters that I painted on the walls of my bedroom."

"Well, you're really good. I like your drawing of the crawfish and my hands."

"Thanks. I have a hard time drawing people, but I've been making myself practice more. The portrait assignment we're doing is going to be a challenge."

"After seeing your drawing in class I'm pretty sure it'll turn out great." She looked over to Jake and changed the subject. Thomas felt crushed. "I guess if your shirt is anything to go by then you like to ski?"

"Oh yeah." Jake was so confident with her; Thomas almost hated him for it. "My friends and I try to make it up the mountain a couple times a month at least."

"I did some skiing when I was in junior high. Lately I've been trying out snowboarding. Have you done any snowboarding?" She glanced at both Thomas and Jake.

Thomas had nothing to say, so Jake answered, "Nah, I tried snowboarding for a while. But since they came out with the twin tipped skis I've stuck with skiing."

"That's cool."

They were only a couple buildings away from the bakery now. Jessica turned back to Thomas and started to say, "So have you ever painted any...?"

Jake quickly interrupted, "I also play the guitar. Oh, and during the summer, when there's no snow, I do a lot of skateboarding."

47

"Oh, really? I play the violin. It's kinda like the guitar, but not really." She gave Thomas a wry grin, which almost made him feel better.

Inside the bakery, Thomas went to the front of the line to select his bread. The three other guys stood glancing over the menu, pretending that they might actually buy something. Jessica followed behind Thomas and was greeted by the man behind the counter. "Hello, Miss. Can I interest you in a free sample?"

She looked at the bread that Thomas had in his hand as he sat down at a nearby table, setting his canvases on the floor beside him. "Oh, yes. Thank you. I'll have the same one he had." She compared the appearance of Thomas' bread with those on the table and read from the labels by each loaf of bread, "The sunflower honey oat?"

"Can I get you anything else?" asked the man behind the counter as he cut a thick slice and handed it to her.

"No, thank you," she said with a smile as she buttered the bread and then walked over to where Thomas was sitting. She sat down and looked over at him, only to find him staring at her with a dreamy expression on his face. As their eyes met, his gaze quickly darted back to the slice of bread in his hand. She smiled awkwardly and glanced around the room, taking a sudden interest in the menu on the far wall. They both sat quietly eating their bread as they waited for the others. After a few moments, their eyes met again; they smiled shyly and both looked away.

The walk back to school was quiet; Thomas had things to think about, and everyone else had their mouths full of bread.

When they reached the patio entrance to the cafeteria at the back of the school they parted ways.

"Thanks for inviting me along, you guys," Jessica said, looking directly at Jake and Thomas. "I'll have to get bread there more often, see ya." She jogged over to the table where Shannon and a couple other friends were sitting.

"Alright man, let's go ask your cousin about that bag," Nick said to Rob. It took Thomas a moment to register that they were leaving. "See you later guys."

"Oh, yeah see ya ... later Tom."

Shannon waved from across the room to get Jessica's attention. She was about to head over to Shannon and her other friends when Liam stepped in front of her, blocking her way, and asked, "So, have you made a decision yet?"

Jessica was caught a little off guard, like someone had just found out one of her closest secrets. "Um, yeah sure. I figured you knew I was planning to from when we were talking earlier."

"Great. I just wanted to make sure. Meet me in the painting classroom after school. It's usually empty so we won't be interrupted." Liam gave her a knowing smile and turned to leave. "See ya then." Jessica couldn't tell what Liam was thinking; his face was a mask of confidence and command.

Jessica called out after his retreating form. "What should I wear?"

But Liam was too far away to hear her voice. Jessica went and picked up a tray and got her lunch, trying to figure out why her confidence had just left the room with Liam. As soon as she sat down with the others Shannon began interrogating her. "So who were those guys? Where did you go? Which one do you think is cute?"

"Shannon, seriously." Jessica rolled her eyes, shook her head, and smiled, "They're just some guys in my Biology class that asked if I wanted to get some free bread at the Crumb Bakery. That's all."

"So what, they all got together and asked you to go to the bakery? Come on, which one was it?"

"The one with the spiked hair and the long sleeve shirt. His name's Jake."

All the girls at the table glanced around; at the cafeteria doors, they could see one of the bakery guys struggling to open the door and balance the awkward pile of canvases in his arms. He wasn't doing too well.

"You mean the weirdo with the huge backpack and the armful of white paintings?" A blonde haired girl asked.

"No that's Tom. Don't you know Tom or Jake? We've all been in the same school since junior high."

"Well we can't remember everyone in our grade."

"Anyway, Jake is the guy with the spiked hair that's got bleached tips and has a picture of a skier on his shirt." Jessica pointed outside the window, where three guys were walking to the west parking lot.

"Oh, okay. All clear now."

"Not that there's anything wrong with Tom." Jessica fidgeted with the roll on her lunch tray, distracted. "I'm just saying that Jake is the one who invited me along, is all."

"What about the other two?" Shannon didn't give up easily.

"They just met up with us before we headed to the bakery."

"Okay, enough about bread. Let's get to the bigger question … are you going to model?"

"Yeah, I told him I would."

"Awww, you'll look just like the Mona Lisa."

"I don't know about that," Jessica chuckled.

"Well either way, sounds like someone has a few potentials for the dance."

"Oh shut up. They're just being nice."

"Uh huh."

Thomas had just paid for his lunch and was about to leave. He paused for a moment to watch Jessica talking with the other girls at the table in the far corner. He couldn't hear anything they were saying with the noise of half the high school chatting about their latest dramas, but he could make out her voice amidst the din.

He grinned when she looked over and saw him. Smiling back, she brushed her hair behind her ear and gave him a little wave. Thomas managed an awkward wave without dropping his bundle of canvases, shyly dropping his gaze as he turned toward the patio doors and walked outside. Maybe school wasn't so bad after all.

On the opposite side of the circular covered patio was the entrance door to the section of the school with all the art classrooms. Thomas went into the painting classroom and sat at his desk, ready for the next class. His mind wandered, from Jessica, her smile and her voice, to his uneasy school friendships, to home.

Since his parents' divorce Thomas had been unable to borrow his dad's vehicle; he needed it for work every day. That meant he couldn't drive the guys around at lunchtime, which meant they weren't half so interested in him. And then there was home. His mother was gone; she had ended up moving out of state. He had watched for years as his parents had fought over money issues, lack of trust, and most often the old house his father had inherited when his grandparents passed away. It was an old place out in the country somewhere. Thomas' father had exhausted all their money trying to restore it, but his mother had no desire to move out to 'the middle of nowhere'. Maybe it wasn't the only reason they had broken up, but it hadn't helped.

Thomas did the best he could to not let it get him down. Still, there were days when his quiet moments alone in the painting classroom felt like sanctuary. He alternated between eating his food and sketching Jessica's hands as well as he could from memory. He wanted to capture them perfectly; afraid they might escape if he made a mistake.

6

Gentle Snow
to Soften the Embrace

Jessica took the freeway exit for Denver as the deepening gloom finally turned into full dark. As she drove down the off ramp she noticed she was low on gas; she looked out for a gas station and stopped to fill up at the first one she spotted.

She didn't know Denver at all, so she asked the gas station attendant for directions to the Wal-Mart where she had arranged to meet Shannon. It turned out her destination was on the northeastern edge of the city, and she'd gotten off one exit too early, so she gritted her teeth and prepared herself for a long drive through the city. After she'd paid for the gas, she texted Shannon to let her know she was on her way; it took her a moment to remember Shannon's new number.

That gave her something to think about as she drove through the uniform streets. Shannon had written to her during the Christmas break to suggest they spend a weekend together in January. Jessica was a little surprised, but glad she would get to see her friend and catch up. Summer was a long way off, and anyway, she was eager to hear about the new man, the one who was responsible for Shannon losing her old phone.

Shannon had written that while she was skiing in Aspen with her family, she'd bumped into a really cute guy while riding a ski lift. Her old friend wasn't the most discerning person in the world, but Shannon had made this guy sound kind of out of the ordinary. After they had skied together a couple times, they found themselves back in the chair lift, and the guy asked if Shannon would like to maybe go out with him sometime.

She was thrilled at the invitation, and had gotten her phone out so she could take his number. He told her his number twice, to make sure she got it, and she entered it on her phone as her heart raced. But when she went to put it back in her pocket, her nervous hands had betrayed her, and the phone had slipped out of her grip, flown off into a group of pine trees, and come to rest somewhere in a drift of snow.

At least it gave them an excuse to spend some more time skiing together. When the chair lift reached the summit, they had set off, exploring each thicket of pine in a vain search for the slim phone in its unfortunately white wallet. After three more runs they gave up, and headed into the lodge cafeteria for lunch. As they chatted, the guy had written his number down on a napkin, twice just to make sure, and insisted on putting it into Shannon's pocket himself. "As soon as I get a new phone," she'd written, "the first thing I'm going to do is call him and arrange a date. I'll tell you all about it when we meet."

Jessica was trying to imagine what kind of story she would hear from Shannon when her phone beeped and she got a reply to her text. *In back of Wal-Mart parking lot. Park your car, I'll drive us around. Let me know when U R close.*

The scenery on the long drive through Denver was dull, so Jessica amused herself by sending Shannon a text when she stopped at a busy intersection. *So jealous. My dad gets to see the*

Greek Slave sculpture in Florida. She smiled as she anticipated Shannon's reply: Greek what? Your dad's into slaves?

So she was surprised when the reply arrived. *Way cool. Powers' work is amazing.*

Jessica responded immediately, provoking the wrath of the driver behind her, who beeped at her to get a move on. *Wow. When did you get to know about art history?*

She made her way a few blocks northeast before the reply came. *Humanities credit.*

Jessica was impressed; imagine Shannon getting to grips with the art world! Next she'll be reading real literature. She wondered if the new guy was influencing her change of taste.

The car radio began to play 'Jealous Guy'; irritated, Jessica switched it off, and drove the rest of the way in silence; it was only a few blocks now. They would still have plenty of time to catch a movie and get dinner, and she would hear all about the mysterious stranger.

Finally she spotted the Wal-Mart sign and turned off into the parking lot. She was surprised at how big it was; you could get lost in a place like this. She compared it to the local supermarket parking lot at home, and figured you could fit four of them into this. And even in the dark, she could see a lot of vehicles parked up, as well as a line of campers and trailers off to one side.

The snow was falling harder now, and she switched on her wipers so she could see better. The snow softened everything, blurred all the edges, giving the huge parking lot the appearance of an ugly dream landscape. Picking up her phone off the passenger seat, she speed-dialed Shannon's number; lucky she'd remembered to enter the new number. She was surprised to hear an ordinary ring tone, instead of the brash pop music that usually came on when she called; obviously Shannon hadn't had time to program the phone to her liking yet, or the new guy wasn't into pop music.

She crawled along the northern end of the lot, looking out for anything that resembled Shannon's car. The ring tone had just gone to voice mail when she heard a horn honk a double tap, and a pair of headlights flashed on just to her right. The headlights were coming from a spot just next to a large ugly SUV. Jessica parked her car in the space opposite, and hung up the phone just as the robot voice was asking her to leave a message.

She grabbed her purse and coat and slid out of the car; she could come back for her bag once she'd said Hi to Shannon. She pulled up the collar of her coat to keep the snow out, and walked carefully across towards Shannon's car. She could see nothing of it beyond the headlights, but then Shannon had said she'd just bought a new car, a black one, which Jessica thought was out of character after the pink coupe she'd been driving for a couple years.

There was hardly any space to walk between the car and the big SUV, so Jessica turned sideways and slid between the two vehicles until she reached the passenger door. She opened it as wide as she could, but still had only just enough room to ease herself awkwardly into the seat. Pulling the door shut after her, she said, "Can you believe these SUV drivers? They think they can park anyway they -"

A strong hand clamped a damp smelly rag over her face. Jessica lurched instinctively back against the seat, and clawed at the hand held over her mouth. Out of the corner of her eye, she could make out a silhouette, a man, turned toward her in the driver's seat. She tried to scream, but the cloth was suffocating her, and the smell was overpowering. She felt the world go fuzzy as she breathed in the acrid fumes. Her head was suddenly heavy, and her limbs were slack, dropping away from the arm that held her. Then everything went black.

7

OF NEEDLE AND SABLE

The first thing she noticed was the low, insistent buzzing sound that seemed to emanate from inside her head. It faded only to be replaced by a dull throbbing headache. Everything was dark.

Since her eyes were no use, she concentrated on her other senses. There was a mildly sweet scent in the air, which reminded her of the stain remover her mother used on the laundry. She could hear a violin playing, softly, like it was coming from a long way off. There were two other sounds, but she couldn't identify them. A constant swish, interrupted now and then by an untidy, hollow rattling noise. And a dripping sound, rhythmic and insistent, right beside her: two dripping sounds in fact, one on either side of her.

She turned her head from side to side, trying to locate the source of the dripping tap. As she did so, she noticed a subtle glimpse of light at the edges of her vision. It occurred to her that she was blindfolded, and as the realization took hold, she felt the soft touch of gauze on her face.

She was slouched in an uncomfortable position, in a chair that felt like it was covered in leather. She tried to adjust her position, and discovered she was tied tight at the shoulders and wrists. She also realized she could feel the surface of the chair against her naked flesh; that brought her to full alertness. She tried instinctively to stand up, but her bonds were secure, and she slumped back into the chair.

There was someone else there, in the room, she was sure of it. Fear flooded her senses, but she forced herself to speak. "Who … is there someone there?"

"Yes."

The voice came from in front of her, where the swishing sound had suddenly ceased. Despite her blindfold, Jessica felt someone was looking at her. She tried to curl up, to protect her nakedness from this stranger, but other than pressing her knees a little closer together, she could do nothing; her ankles were tied securely to the cool tubular steel legs of the chair.

The swishing sound resumed. Jessica fought against the growing panic, and spoke again. "I know you're still there. I can't … why do my arms hurt?"

Swish, rattle. Swish.

"Well, Jessica." Swish. "That's because you have a couple of 15 gauge hypodermic needles in your arms."

He knows my name. He knows who I am. Jessica's heart raced and her blood pounded in her ears. It was so loud she thought he must be able to hear it too. She tried to calm herself. *He got my name from my driver's license.* Rationalizing the situation didn't make her feel any better. *What does he want? Is he going to … wait, he said needle. What's he using the needle for?*

"What do you want with me?" she felt tears sting in her eyes, and soak into the material of her blindfold. She asked the question she didn't want to hear the answer to.

"Are you going to … are you going to kill me?"

The swishing sound stopped again, and there was a long pause, which brought her further to the edge of panic. Had she provoked him into doing something terrible? Was he making up his mind? She felt every tiny hair on her body stand up, as if somehow she could pluck his intentions out of the air around her. There was another terrible second of pause, and then the swishing resumed.

"No, Jessica, not today." Swish.

Another question formed in her mind. She was naked and exposed, helpless. "Are you … are you going to …?" Her question faded into terrified stillness.

The swishing sound stopped, and her captor finished the question for her; "rape you?" she heard the sound of some object being put down briskly on a metal surface.

"You ask as if that would be a worse fate than death. Ask yourself, Jessica, which would be better or worse? Cold steel driving a new hole through your flesh, or warm firm flesh entering you where you are already open?" After a brief pause, the voice became mocking, sardonic. "I doubt you've experienced anything of either."

Footsteps, coming toward her. Jessica recoiled involuntarily, but she had nowhere to go. She felt hands on the side of her face, gentle, but even that gentleness was threatening.

A panicked "No!" had barely escaped her lips when the blindfold was lifted from her eyes. The sudden glare was intensely painful, and she blinked furiously, trying to make her eyes focus in the harsh light. Slowly she began to see the room around her, and the blurred shapes within it began to take shape. But the shape that occupied her immediate gaze was that of the man standing in front of her, a slim figure dressed in a white lab coat. Her eyes traveled upward, to see the face of her captor; instead she saw only a mask. It covered his whole face except for his eyes, and it continued around his entire head. The gauze it was made of seemed to be glazed, and its satin finish shimmered freakishly in the uneven light.

She forced herself to concentrate on his eyes. They were unnaturally dark, and Jessica couldn't figure out why at first, until she noticed the black paint on his eyelids, accentuating the darkness of his gaze. He was looking directly into her eyes, unnerving her. There was no discernible emotion in those blackened orbs.

He broke the dark spell by leaning forward and removing some tape from her arm. Placing a wad of cotton over the insertion point, he yanked the hypodermic out of her flesh, making her wince. He replaced the needle with a pad of gauze and wrapped it into place. Then he repeated the procedure on her other arm. She saw plastic tubing dangling over the arms of the chair, disappearing somewhere beside and below her.

The dripping noise subsided and then stopped. He bent down and retrieved a small glass beaker from the floor. Then he held it up close to his face and examined the contents; taking in a slow breath through the thin gauze under his nose. Jessica watched him carry the beaker over to a metal tray, where he set it down beside two other, empty beakers. There was a faint glazing of red at the base of the empty beakers. Blood: *my blood.* Fresh tears coursed down her cheeks, as if to dilute the terrible image in front of her.

"What are you … what are you going to do with it? Are you … going to drink it?"

61

The gauze-wrapped head swiveled round to face her. She could see no expression in those eyes. "Drink it? Jessica, that's disgusting."

That didn't make Jessica feel any better, but she forced herself to look at the metal tray, to try and divine the masked stranger's intentions from his equipment. There was a rag, streaked with reds and browns, and some paintbrushes lying beside it on the tray. The beaker of her blood, about four ounces of it, rested on the tray; she couldn't see any tubes of paint.

He went somewhere behind her, and Jessica heard the sound of a fridge door opening. When he came back to the tray, he had a small vial in his hand, along with a syringe. He drew some of the clear liquid from the vial and squirted it into the beaker. With the handle of a paintbrush he mixed the two liquids, humming to himself as he did so. Jessica realized that the violin music had stopped.

In numbed fascination, she watched as he poured out some of the blood into smaller specimen bottles and screwed on the lids. She heard rather than saw him take them over to the fridge and place them inside, and close the door. He came back and stood in front of her, facing a sloping easel. After looking at his work for a moment, he sat on a tall stool in front of the easel and started painting again. He dipped the brush into the beaker of her blood and the swishing sound began again. *That's what I could hear. He's painting a portrait of me using my own blood.*

Jessica's mind was struggling to accept what her senses were telling her. The masked man was working calmly, focused on the image before him, occasionally taking a glance at her before turning back to his easel, and applying a little more of her blood to the paper. He seemed entirely at ease.

She felt the salt sting of tears in her eyes again, felt the warm drops on her breast as her tears left her face. She shook her head, trying to release her hair from the ponytail it was tied into, so she could cover her breasts, hide them from his shadowy gaze. But nothing happened, except the throbbing in her head got even worse and threatened her with nausea. She looked down, as best she could, at the little pools of tears on her breasts, and the reddening bandages on her arms, the marks of the tourniquet over her biceps.

After a while he stopped working, and looked at the painting in front of him. He put down his brush on the metal tray, stepped off the stool and stood back to get a better look at his work. As he stepped back, he bumped his head on a protruding pipe. The sound reverberated through the room, as did the sound of his quiet curse as he rubbed his head through the mask.

When he had regained his composure, he went back to analyzing his painting. Apparently satisfied, he turned his gaze to Jessica, and examined her from head to foot. She turned her head away for a few seconds; afraid she might read some evil intent in his eyes. But she found herself compelled to look back at him. He was still examining her, all over, but paying particular attention to her face.

Abruptly, he turned on his heel and moved away to the far side of the room. If she twisted her neck so far it hurt, she could just make out a narrow metal door that led into a small room off the main chamber. She saw him flip a light switch; saw a light flicker on in the room, through a window above the door. He opened the door and disappeared into the room.

Unable to see her captor, Jessica did her best to examine the rest of her surroundings. On the same wall as the metal door there was a panoramic window that ran half the length of the hall. Below the window was a small metal cabinet with sliding doors; the doors were firmly closed. Through the window, she could make out a further wall, as if a corridor ran outside, roughly the same width as the small room he had disappeared into.

It seemed she was in some kind of basement. She was in the center of it, and from what she could see in front of her, it was pretty big. The ceiling was very high, and florescent tubes ran the length of it. There were also spotlights here and there, some switched on and some off.

Craning her neck to her right, she could make out a set of cupboards in the corner, with a work counter and a small sink, and a black mini-refrigerator perched on the counter. Inside the fridge, she knew, her blood was cooling in little containers; she shuddered, and resumed her survey of the room. There was another opening next to the corner units, which seemed to lead into another hallway. There were no external windows that she could see.

The walls of the basement were cinder blocks painted a harsh white. Craning her neck to the other side, she could see a few tables and chairs, none of which matched, scattered here and there. That was it. Jessica figured the hallway on her right was the only way out. She tried to work out a plan of escape, but her mind was too numbed by what she had seen and experienced.

She heard footsteps coming out of the room, and a faint shuffling noise. Then came the sound of cupboard doors opening and shutting, and the rattle of jars. The sweet scent she had noticed earlier became stronger, and the footsteps approached her from behind. She struggled against her bonds, making the chair scrape on the concrete floor, but before she could get anywhere she felt the muffled impact of a damp rag over her mouth. She jerked against his grasp for a few seconds, and then everything went black again.

He threw the chloroform-soaked rag into a sealed disposal can and grabbed a pair of scissors from a drawer. Carefully, he cut the plastic ties that bound her to the chair; he didn't want to slice her pale delicate flesh. Taking her limp arm over his shoulder, he crouched down and gathered her inert form into his arms, and carried her into the little room. Inside, there was a twin mattress on a plain wooden frame, with a single sheet and a pillow. He eased her onto the bed and propped the pillow under her head.

He went back into the main room and retrieved Jessica's belongings, stuffed untidily into a plastic trash bag, from a cupboard. Dumping the contents out onto a table, he sifted through them. There was nothing of interest in her purse. He moved on to her clothes. Her underwear was still inside the outer layers.

He went through the pockets of her jeans and found the silver ring he had taken from her hand earlier. He looked at it briefly and put it in her purse. Sliding his hand into her back pocket, he felt a crinkled photo, flattened into an odd shape from being sat on. He took out the photo and stared at the image of two teenagers, dressed up and smiling at the camera. After a moment, he crushed it in his hand, and put it in her purse along with the ring.

He stuffed her belongings back into the plastic sack and returned them to the cupboard. He took off his white lab coat, and pushed it into the cupboard after the sack. There was a metal table nearby, with a sketchbook and a few pencils lying on it. He picked them up, and strolled back into the room where Jessica lay unconscious.

8

BLUSH BEFORE BLOOM

The giant bronze grizzly bear stared down at Jessica and Shannon as they made their way to their next classes. The high school mascot receded behind them as Jessica poured out her woes to her friend.

"I feel so stupid. He'll probably just go and find another girl to model for him. I've ruined everything."

"You don't know that, Jess. Maybe he'll do the painting anyway."

"Paint what? He wanted me to model topless, for goodness' sake. And when I said absolutely not he said I could just turn my back to him, like that made a difference." Jessica was only telling Shannon half the truth; Liam had asked her to pose like Powers' Greek Slave, saying he wanted to get a sense of captivity and dignity into the portrait; he'd even quoted from the poem to try and persuade her. When Jessica had absolutely refused, he asked about a topless pose, but Jessica could tell he was already thinking of her as a failure.

"Anyway, your idea of keeping a sheet wrapped around you was a totally reasonable compromise."

"Maybe, but he didn't seem to think so. After I sat there feeling stupid in the sheet for ages, with him making countless sketches and working on a painting, he asked to take the sheet off so he could do one more final sketch." Jessica shuddered as she recalled her embarrassment. "So there I was, telling him in my silly little schoolgirl voice that I didn't feel comfortable with that. He looked at me like I was some kind of nerdy prude that he didn't even want to bother with. Then he just waved his hand like he was dismissing me from kindergarten class and went on with his big, serious grown-up painting. I might as well not have been there at all. To tell you the truth, it was kind of creepy."

"Well I guess you were compromising his artistic vision; that, or spoiling his evil plans." Shannon sniggered, but shut up quickly when she saw the look on Jessica's face. "So tell me, did he try to make any moves on you?"

"No, to be fair to him, he didn't do anything like that. He was really focused on what he was doing, making sure the pose was right and the lighting worked. He was really serious, like he's a different person altogether when he's painting, obsessed. Maybe if I'd seen him at work before I had to model I'd have felt better about the whole thing. After all, the nude form doesn't *have* to be sexual, if the artist is serious. It's just, high school guys and nude girls ... I don't know."

"So why don't you sneak into the art classroom and see how the painting looks?"

"You know, I might just do that." Jessica headed off to class and waved at Shannon as she went up the stairs. "See you at lunch."

"Later Jess."

...

68

Friday is the longest school day of the week. Freedom is so close it seems like forever away. But for Thomas, the day went in a series of nervous rushes, like his anxiety was catching up with him from around every corner. In biology class he sat a few rows behind Jessica, at an angle to her, so he could see a little more of her for his sketches. From here, he could almost catch her whole face in profile.

Mr. Wright was running through his lecture, but Thomas hardly heard a word. He was looking from Jessica to the clock, from the clock to the door, from the door back to Jessica. Class was nearly halfway over, and his anxiety was eating him up. Every so often Jessica would glance back at him, that shy smile on her face, and he'd turn his gaze elsewhere, and unconsciously cover his sketches with his hand.

The sound of the class door opening brought Thomas' head up from his sketchpad with a start. One of the senior girls came in carrying a small bunch of roses, and cleared her throat politely to interrupt Mr. Wright from his lecture on reptile anatomy. He looked at her with mock surprise on his face and said, "For me? Gee, I wasn't expecting flowers."

The senior girl shook her head, laughing along with the teacher, looked down at the note in her hand and said, "Sorry, Mr. Wright, but these aren't for you. They're for Jessica Shawsen; is she here?"

"Why no, she isn't," he joked. "I guess I'll just have to accept them on her behalf. Only kidding. She's right there."

He pointed to where a blushing Jessica was trying to shrink into her seat. Taking the flowers in his arms, he brought them to Jessica, bowed formally, and whispered something to her as he presented her with the little bouquet. Thomas watched as Jessica read the note attached to the flowers, shrugged at Mr. Wright and shook her head, smiling through her blushes.

"Well, that's exciting," said the teacher as he headed back to the front of the room to resume his lecture.

Jake turned to Jessica and stage-whispered, "Who are they from?"

Jessica shrugged her shoulders and shook her head again. Thomas suddenly found the lecture completely absorbing, and stared fixedly at the notes Mr. Wright had put up on the whiteboard, trying to ignore the romantic disruption to the class.

Jessica was reading the note again, her hands trembling as she mouthed the words of the poem on the card. *Roses are red, violets are blue. The dance would be great, if I could take you.* Under the poem there was another short note: *meet me at the bridge behind the cafeteria during lunch.* She folded the note up and smelled the roses, trying to hide her smile of pleasure and ignore the envious looks from the other girls in the class.

Time had slowed down again for Thomas, and Jessica too. It seemed an eternity until the bell rang for the end of class, and everyone got up to leave. Thomas came out of class to find Jake talking to Jessica in the corridor. Thomas approached them shyly and asked, "So do you know who sent them?"

"No, not yet, but the note that came with the flowers says to meet him at the bridge during lunch, so I guess I'll find out soon enough." She nodded in Jake's direction. "We're going to head over there now. You want to come?"

"Yeah, I .." Thomas choked on his words and rushed off to the water fountain to hide his embarrassment and cool his burning throat. When he felt a little better, he looked up to see that Jake and Jessica were already halfway down the corridor, heading for the doors. Jake was leaning over Jessica's shoulder as they took a close look at the note, searching for clues to the identity of the mysterious admirer. Thomas shouldered his ungainly pack and hurried after them manfully, and caught up just as they entered the main hall, under the gaze of the big bronze grizzly.

Jessica stopped suddenly, as if she'd just remembered something. "You guys, I have to use the restroom real quick. Why don't we meet up at the bridge?"

"What if your secret admirer is already there?" asked Jake. "Maybe we'll scare him off."

"Okay, I'll see you at the patio doors in two minutes." Jessica hustled away toward the restroom and left Jake and Thomas alone.

After a few seconds she peeked out the restroom door to see if they'd gone. They had; she breathed a sigh of relief and hurried off to the art room, pausing for one nervous moment before she went inside. The lights were off, but a dim light filtered through the half-open blinds. She looked around at the half-finished paintings on the tables and shelves until her eye stopped at a familiar face.

She stared at her image, captured in oils, her dark brown eyes looking back at her, as strong and serene as her own. She was shocked by the similarity, and the beauty, of her image; even unfinished, the painting had a strong effect on her. The fact that it looked so beautiful made her feel beautiful, and somehow worthwhile. Maybe her first modeling experience wasn't such a disaster after all. Then she snapped upright, and looked around in panic. The roses; she'd almost forgotten.

She found Jake and Thomas waiting by the patio doors. They set off together and soon came to the stone bridge in the school grounds. There was no one there; her mysterious admirer hadn't turned up yet. They sat together on the parapet wall to wait, the two boys either side of Jessica like guardian angels around a Madonna. Jessica took in the scent of her roses. Her experience with the painting began to fade as she considered the possibilities of her unexpected gift. Jake woke her out of her reverie with a question. "Only half a dozen. Where's the other half?"

"Hey, half a dozen is plenty. Otherwise I'd have my arms full for the rest of the day."

They waited for what seemed like a long time before Jake broke the silence again. "Maybe he's hiding under the bridge."

"Well maybe one of you brave bodyguards should go take a look," said Jessica with a mocking smile.

In winter, the stream that ran under the bridge was blocked off, so it was dry under the stone arch. Jake strode over to the opposite parapet like a man on a mission, and performed an exaggerated vault over the side. He landed on the soft dirt of the streambed, and called out in a melodramatic voice, "Hello? Is there anyone there? Come out and show yourself now, we've got you surrounded."

Thomas and Jessica, sitting on the parapet, could see no more than the top of Jake's head as he cavorted on the dry stream bed, doing his best impersonation of a TV cop. Meanwhile Jessica was getting a few odd looks from passing boys as she stared at them, wondering which one of them was heading for the bridge to meet her. Her face fell when she spied Jared Scott exiting the building with a determined expression on his face. *Oh no; what if the flowers are from Jared? What will I do?* Relief flooded her when she saw him cross the quad and hustle into the cafeteria.

She sighed a faint sigh, a mixture of relief and general frustration; where was this guy? Then a quiet voice beside her began to recite: "Roses are red, violets are blue." Jessica turned to face Thomas, surprise etched on her face. He stammered a little as he finished the poem: "The dance would be great, if I could take you." His voice had subsided into a whisper by the time he finished and blushed deeply, looking down at his feet.

"These are from you?"

"Yes." Thomas looked her in the eye, trying to appear braver than he felt. Jessica blushed too, but to Thomas' relief she didn't seem too offended.

"Thank you."

"So, do you want to go, you know, with me?" Eagerness overcame embarrassment.

"Yeah. Yes I'd like to." Now it was Jessica's turn to feel awkward.

Jake vaulted back onto the bridge, duty done. He wiped the dried mud off his pants and rubbed his hands together. Then he looked up at the blushing couple on the parapet wall. "Hey, what's up with you guys?"

"The flowers are ... from Tom." As Jessica spoke, Thomas gave a little shrug of acknowledgement.

"Oh, okay. Pretty tricky, Tom."

Jessica stood up and adjusted the roses in her hand. "Well, now we know. I'm going to have lunch with my friends. Thanks, Tom. See you later."

"Later Jess," Jake called out after her retreating form, and then turned to Thomas. Thomas was sitting on the bridge wall congratulating himself for finally managing to ask Jessica out. After all those months of furtive gazing and sketching he had actually plucked up the courage to do it. Now he could relax, sort of, at least until the dance.

"Dude, only half a dozen? What is that?"

"It's all I could afford, is all. I need to save some money for the date – uh, the dance. My job doesn't pay a whole lot."

"Yeah, well, that's the life of a dishwasher, man."

"I know, it sucks, but it's better than the telemarketing job I had before." Thomas stood up and stretched his tense limbs, trying to rearrange himself into a normal human being. "I'm going to the cafeteria to get some lunch. You want to come?"

"Nah, I'm meeting up with Nick and Rob." Jake had other things on his mind, and didn't really fancy sharing Thomas' romantic triumph. Before he left, he asked, "So, we're all gonna hang out later tonight. You want to come along?"

"Okay, cool, I don't have to work tonight. Sure, I'll come."

"Cool. Oh, and if you could maybe pick Nick up from the Rec Center around seven, that'd be cool too."

"Uh, okay, yeah, I guess I can do that."

"Great! Later, dude." Jake took off towards the bleachers by the football field, Thomas already half-forgotten, and Thomas headed for the cafeteria to get lunch. Being used as a chauffeur by the guys didn't seem like such a big deal right then. It was all part of belonging, and for the first time, Thomas was beginning to feel like he belonged.

In the cafeteria, Thomas glanced over to where Jessica sat with her friends; they were all looking at him, some curious, some skeptical, some downright hostile. Thomas didn't care; he managed a shy wave in Jessica's general direction, which fired the gaggle of girls around her into a frenzy of whispering and gesturing. Jessica waved back at him, tucking her hair behind her ear; a mannerism Thomas had learnt to recognize as one of Jessica's trademark tics when shyness threatened to take over.

Thomas glanced up into the mirror along the sidewall of the cafeteria, and caught a glimpse of Liam staring back at him, with that 'anything you can do, I can do better' smirk on his face. For a moment, Thomas was trapped in Liam's gaze, like an insect in amber; but today he wasn't about to let anyone or anything spoil his happiness. He ignored Liam, grabbed his lunch, gave Jessica a last cursory wave and headed for the art rooms.

Jessica's friends were still busy digesting the news. When she'd walked into the cafeteria clutching the little posy of roses, they had gathered around her like clucking hens, Shannon the busiest, loudest hen of them all, and bombarded her with all the obvious questions.

"Oh my gosh, oh my gosh, you got roses! Someone's asked you to the dance! Well, come on girl, out with it. Who gave you the roses? Who is he?"

"Yes, I got roses." Jessica was blushing again, partly reliving the moment with Tom, partly because of all the attention she was getting now.

Shannon could hardly contain herself. "So, is it Jared? No, let me guess, it was Jake. Or the wrestler guy?"

Jessica waited a moment for the hubbub to die down to the point where she could actually hear herself think. "Actually, it was Thomas. Thomas King asked me to the dance."

"Thomas? You mean ..." Shannon was in a different state of shock now. "So, did you say yes?"

"Of course I said yes. I couldn't say no right to his face, not after he'd gone to all that effort, could I? And anyway, it was such a sweet thing to do." Jessica looked around the cafeteria, and spied Tom getting his lunch. He waved awkwardly, and she gave a little wave back, tucking a stray hair behind her ear as she did so. But her friends weren't about to let her go so easily, especially not Shannon.

"So Jess, you think you'll enjoy going to the dance with him? I mean ..."

"You mean he's a loser." One of the other girls came out with it; what everyone was thinking.

"Come on, none of you even know him. He's kind of quiet, is all. And anyway, last time I looked, it was my choice who I go to the dance with."

"I don't know, Jess, I think he's a little bit, well, creepy." Shannon didn't want to push it too far, so she tried a joke. "Hey, maybe he's a vampire, that's why he's so quiet in the daytime. Maybe he's planning to take you to the dance and then spirit you away and suck your blood."

Jessica's patience was wearing thin. "Well, you're the real vampire fan here, Shannon, why don't you go with him? It'll be just like in the cheesy books you read."

"You said you liked them too."

"Not as much as you do, obviously."

"Well, okay, if that makes me a vampire expert, here's my advice." Shannon pulled an expression of exaggerated concern and said, in her best Van Helsing voice, "Just promise me that you will wear a crucifix, and take some garlic for prot-"

Shannon's explosion of laughter killed her performance, but it had worked. Everyone was laughing now, including Jessica. Shannon was relieved her friend wasn't too mad at her, but couldn't escape a feeling of genuine concern. There was something strange about Thomas King, whatever Jess said.

...

In the art room, Thomas sat eating his lunch and sketching. His head had been full of dreams when he left the cafeteria, but now he was beginning to feel that old creeping feeling of anxiety coming back. It wasn't just pre-dance nerves. It was the painting; Liam's portrait of Jessica filled his vision, it seemed to be everywhere in the room at once. It was as if Liam had grabbed Jessica right out of his grasp; he had caressed her image into oils, and the alluring picture gazed out at him, almost mocking. Liam had captured something essential about her, something Thomas was struggling to tease out of his sketches, but every time he thought he'd got it, got her, there was Liam's painting. *I got there before you, Thomas; she's mine.* He tried to shake Liam out of his head and get on with his own work, but he knew he was copying the painting, even as he tried not to. *Why can't I do my own thing? Why can't I find something original to say?*

When he heard the door opening behind him, he jumped, as if he'd been caught in the act. But it was only Cindy. She gave him a cheery smile.

"Hey, Cindy."

"Hey, mister moo." Cindy hopped into a chair beside him. Cindy was in the same art classes as Thomas, and they had developed a flirtatious friendship over the years. They didn't really see each other except in class, but he felt Cindy was a friend, and she seemed to like him for what he was; *or maybe despite what I am*, he thought grimly.

"So what are you working on?"

"I'm just finishing this drawing of … uh, of a portrait."

"So whose painting are you making a drawing of?" Cindy read the name on the back of the wooden panel. "Oh, I see, it's Liam's."

"Yeah, it looks like he got Jessica to pose for his portrait assignment." Thomas pointed off-handedly at Liam's painting.

Cindy gave him a lopsided look and grinned nervously. "I don't think Liam would be too happy if he knew you were copying his painting for the assignment."

"Oh, this isn't for the assignment. I'm just doing it for, uh, fun. Plus I was too nervous to ask her to pose for me. But I got something better than that."

"Oh really? What was that?"

"I'm taking her to the dance." Thomas blushed as he thought of his awkward triumph.

"See, I told you it was worth asking. Did the flowers do the trick?"

"Yeah, they did. Thanks. At this rate, I should have built up enough confidence in a year or two to ask her to model for me. So far the most I've been able to do is sketch the back of her head during Biology; which she probably doesn't know about." Thomas opened his sketchbook for Cindy to see.

"They look, good, pretty accurate I'd say. I sit right behind her in our History class." She moved over his other shoulder to get a better look at the drawing. Reaching around him she turned a couple pages back in his sketchbook.

"What's this?" she asked with a grin as she pointed to several strands of balled up, dark brown hair that had been taped to the page.

"Oh that's . . . nothing." He tried to turn the page, but Cindy left her hand on it and tilted her head with a knowing smirk. "Okay, so . . . she was running her fingers through her hair during class and she pulled out a few loose strands and she tossed them aside. They landed by my foot, so I picked them up and put them in my sketchbook."

"For what? Like a souvenir?" Cindy was making him feel guilty, despite the broad grin on her face.

"Yeah, kinda," he blushed. "I was thinking that I could do a tiny painting of her and maybe use the hair in the painting."

"Well, all you need now is some skin and a few fingernail clippings, and that girl is totally yours. Should I lend you a few pins?"

Thomas was too embarrassed to take the joke. "That's not what I mean. I just wanted to make it even more of a portrait of her."

Cindy realized she was making him feel bad, and changed the subject. "Now she said yes to the dance, it shouldn't be so difficult to ask her to sit for you."

"Yeah, I know. I really want to, but I don't know if I can. I'm not very good at drawing people, especially from life. I think I'd do better working from a photograph; or a painting." He gestured toward Liam's painting defeated; he just couldn't get away from it. "I wouldn't want to do a sucky drawing of her."

"You just need to practice more." Cindy took off her jacket, straightened her hair, and sat up straight on her stool. "Here, do me."

"What?"

"I'll sit still and you can practice drawing me, get some confidence."

"I don't know, I. . ."

"Oh come on. I won't be upset if it looks bad. Trust me, I've done my share of bad drawings. And besides, your drawing of her portrait looks just as good as the painting itself; might even be better once you finish painting it."

"Okay, I'll give it a try." He turned his chair toward Cindy, sat back down, propped his remaining blank canvas up with his knee, and started drawing.

"You're just going to draw straight onto the canvas?"

"Yeah, that's what I always do. Why? How do you do it?"

"I draw it on paper first. Then once it's to my liking I transfer it onto the canvas or wood panel; looks to me like that's what Liam's done too. I can show you sometime."

"Okay, thanks."

Thomas concentrated as he sketched out the basic proportions of Cindy's head. Whenever he was intently focused on something he would unintentionally nibble on the tip of his tongue with his side teeth. It made him feel like he was back in kindergarten playing with crayons. *Come on, concentrate; you're not a kid anymore.* He chatted to Cindy to stop the competing voices in his head.

"So are you going to the dance?"

"Probably not this one."

"Hasn't anyone asked you?"

"Nope, but that's okay. There's always another dance."

"Well I think it's a social status thing," Thomas changed position and carried on sketching. "Like if I were a girl then I probably wouldn't be going to the dance either."

"What do you mean, Thomasina?"

"Ugh, I hate that show." Thomas shook his head at the thought.

"Anyway, what I mean is that I got to ask someone to go, but if it were the other way around no one would have asked me."

"And why not?"

"'Cause we art nerds aren't cool or popular like the jocks, or the cheerleaders and preppies."

"Isn't Jessica a cheerleader?"

"Well no ... I mean, yeah she used to be, but not anymore. She's just on the Dance Squad now."

"That's the same thing."

"No, it's different..."

"So you want to break out of the art nerd label and into the popular group, right?" Thomas wasn't sure if Cindy was telling him off or having a joke with him.

"No, it's just ... I knew Jessica way before she was a cheerleader and she was a lot nicer then. And now that she stopped cheerleading she's back to that nicer person I remember her as."

"Oh really. Sooo, how long have you liked her for?"

"I've kinda liked her for a couple years, a lot more so recently; but last year she always had some meat-head jock hanging around her, flexing his muscles, acting like he's the king of the school."

"Well you, Thomas K, are *king* of the art nerds." Cindy was introducing a cheesy grin into her portrait.

"Yeah whatever," he grinned back, dismissing her comment while focusing on the drawing.

"Plus I really wanted to ask her to a dance last year, but the jocks would always beat me to it."

"You sure it's not the cutesy little cheerleader skirt that you wanted to ask to the dance?"

"What? No, come on, I mean yeah the outfit is kinda cute, but the personality that most of the cheerleader girls have attracts a lot of thick-skulled Frankensteins." He winced at the thought of most of the school jocks he knew.

"Well what do you expect? Those girls are basically eye candy for all the sporting events."

"Yeah, and trophies for the players."

"Maybe everyone should just date in their own social groups." Cindy glanced intently at Thomas, whose eyes were focused just as intently on his drawing. When he finally looked back up she was gazing absently at the clock.

"No, I don't mean that. I don't know. I just really want this dance to go well and hopefully after a couple more dates she might … possibly … be my girlfriend."

"Oooo look at you planning ahead. Have you decided on a date for the wedding yet?"

"What? No. What are you talking about?" It was Thomas' turn to look at the clock. "Class is gonna start soon. I need to finish my lunch." He put the drawing down and turned to his now cold food. Cindy stood next to him looking at her image on the canvas.

"Are you gonna draw my body? Or am I just a floating head?"

He swallowed his mouthful of food and shrugged. "I'll finish the rest during class."

"You want some of my hair to tape to it?" she teased.

Thomas chuckled and waved her away with a grin. Glancing out the classroom window he saw a few students walk by. Cindy always made him feel better; well almost always. Sometimes he wasn't sure if she wanted to be more than a friend, and that made him worry their friendship might come to a bad end.

"Ah crap! Liam's painting." Thomas hurried to place the unfinished oil portrait back on the wall, and his copy of it behind a larger painting belonging to another student. He had barely got it safely hidden when a few students came into the classroom.

"Need something?" Liam said to Thomas as he turned around from the row of paintings.

"Just admiring your work is all." Thomas stepped past another student, who gave him a strange look then turned to take an unfinished painting off the wall. Thomas quickly sat back down beside Cindy.

Liam looked over at his painting of Jessica, a strange mixture of triumph and contempt on his face. There was something feral about him, a predator gloating over a kill. Thomas shuddered and tried to focus on something else; he watched the other students taking their work from the wall, making admiring comments to each other, settling at their desks to continue the assignment. He felt himself slipping into the background, an anonymous detail in a crowd scene, and began to feel better.

9

THE WAITING ROOM

Jessica gradually came to. She blinked a couple of times to clear her vision, and found herself staring up at a concrete ceiling. She was lying on a mattress with a single sheet draped over her and a pillow under her head. The room was lit by a single light bulb, encased in a thick glass covering, on a metal base bolted into the ceiling. A conduit pipe led away from the light fitting and disappeared into the cinderblock wall above the door.

She tried to sit up, but changed her mind when the room began to tilt around her. The chloroform had done nothing for her headache, and she felt dizzy and nauseous. She lay back gingerly and examined her surroundings as best she could. The cinderblock walls were painted white, like the ceiling. The little room was windowless, except for the small window over the door; beyond that window there was only darkness. She had no idea what time of day it was, and she hadn't the faintest idea how long she had been in the room.

She rolled onto her side, and suddenly realized she was naked. She wrapped the sheet around her, and tried to remember. Most of her memories were vague and disconnected, but the image of the man in the gauze mask flashed constantly in front of her. She felt a wave of nausea, guilt and anger, and the creeping sensation that she had been violated. She couldn't be sure, but the feeling overwhelmed her. *What did he do to me while I was unconscious?*

She struggled onto her knees and prayed, fervently. *Pray for those who despitefully use you and persecute you.* By the time she said *Amen* she was beginning to feel a little calmer, more able to face her desperate situation. She breathed deeply, urging her racing heart to slow, and tentatively dangled her feet over the edge of the bed. So far, so good.

She sat up properly, and felt the cinderblock cool against her skin. Bracing herself, she slipped the sheet off and examined her body for signs of bruising or damage. He might have beaten her, or forced himself on her really roughly. But when she looked, she couldn't find any signs of damage or worse. The two needle marks in her arms were the only wounds. So he hadn't raped her; relief flooded her, and new hope.

Her sense of relief was mixed with confusion; she couldn't begin to understand the motives of the man who had abducted her. Wrapping the sheet around her like a bath towel, she stood up carefully and began to explore her limited environment. The floor was surprisingly warm under her. Its mild texture gave a good grip for her unsteady feet.

The room was just a little longer than the bed in both directions. She stood on tiptoe and peered out through the window in the metal door. It was hard to make out anything in the gloom on the other side, so she turned her attention back to her immediate surroundings.

In the corner opposite the bed was a sort of alcove, which contained a toilet and sink, and a shower that drained directly into the concrete floor. There was a long narrow mirror on the wall beside the shower. Jessica had the strong feeling it was a two-way mirror. The thought of him watching her while she took a shower was horrible, but the idea of being so exposed when she used the toilet disgusted her. *What kind of monster is he?*

The only other items in the room were a roll of toilet paper and a small bar of soap. She looked at the shower again, desperate to cleanse herself of his touch, but saw that there were no taps or knobs to turn the water on. She tried the sink; it did have taps, and she turned them on, grateful for the cold water that flowed out. She quenched her thirst, but it only made her realize how hungry she was; it felt like she hadn't eaten for days.

She looked at the shower vent, searching for an escape route. But she couldn't hear anything through it, so she figured it didn't lead outside. In fact, now she thought of it, she could hear no sounds from the outside world at all.

She tried again to work out what had happened. She was supposed to meet Shannon at the Wal-Mart, but Shannon hadn't been there. Instead of Shannon, Jessica had been met with a chloroform rag, and now this. *What am I thinking? Maybe she was there.* Jessica was sickened by the thought that something similar was happening to her friend. Perhaps she was being held in another room nearby.

She went to the shower vent and called out as loud as she could manage: "Shannon? Shannon, are you there? If you're there, say something. Can you hear me?" No answer came. Either Shannon wasn't there, or she was unconscious. Jessica couldn't do any more for her friend, so she went back to where she awoke and explored some more.

There was nothing much to see. The bed frame was bolted to the floor, and otherwise there was only the mattress and the pillow. She decided to look under the bed. There was nothing on the floor, but attached to the bed frame was a set of metal tie rings, at the head, middle and foot of the frame. Jessica could only imagine what he used the tie rings for. She shuddered at the thought of him torturing her, or someone else. *Why is he doing this? What have I ever done to him? I don't even know who he is.*

The needle marks in her arms throbbed, and she rubbed them protectively. As she did, she thought of him painting her, using her own blood for pigment. She tried to imagine what sort of terrible picture he had produced. The image in her mind was of a grotesque, Bosch nightmare depicted in virulent reds and clotted blacks.

Come on Jess, this isn't the way to get through this. She knew she needed to do something practical, to shake off the fear that was suffocating her, like the chloroform rag her captor had used. An idea occurred to her; perhaps she could make some use of the mattress. She got off the bed and raised the mattress off the frame.

On the wooden base of the bed, written in blood, was the name 'Rachel'; there were five bloody tally marks beside it. And below the name, she could see another: Stacey. That was accompanied by eight tally marks. *I'm not the first; he's done this before.* Her chest tightened. If there had been others, where were they now? The thought defeated her courage, and shattered her hope. She let go of the mattress, and it fell back onto the frame with a dull, sickening thud, covering the names, like earth covering a corpse. She lay back on the bed and curled into a fetal ball, clutching the pillow in her trembling hands as she cried herself back into oblivion.

10

Hanging Game

When Jessica came to again, she had the vague feeling that some sound had dragged her awake. She struggled to identify the memory, but nothing came. She lay still listening; there was a noise, from the big room, there it was again.

Wrapping the sheet around her, she walked as quietly as she could to the metal door, and peered through the small window. Someone had switched on the florescent lights; she watched them flickering into life, bathing the dark space in a sickle yellow gleam. She couldn't see much more because the door was set at an oblique angle to the room, but now she could hear sounds that indicated someone moving around in there, arranging items on a metal tray.

She pressed herself against the door, still listening, but the sound of her heart thumping and the blood rushing in her ears made it difficult to concentrate. She thought she heard footsteps, coming toward the door. She levered herself up on trembling tiptoes and risked another glance through the window. The sight of the wrapped mask on the other side made her fall back in alarm. He was here.

Jessica landed painfully on her backside and scrambled back until she felt the wall at her back. She gathered the sheet back around her and clutched it tightly against her chest, watching breathlessly as the door slowly opened. First she saw a metal tray, then he came into the room. From her low crouch, she couldn't see what was on the tray and, despite the smell of food, she was reluctant to take anything from him. He turned toward her crouching figure and leaned down, offering the tray. "Here, eat this before –"

Jessica's foot lashed out instinctively, and she scrambled further back into the room, clutching the sheet. He had held onto the tray when she kicked it, but the contents had flown around the room. There was a strong smell of chicken broth, and she could see smears and streaks of food scattered around behind him. Jessica realized she was very hungry.

He threw the tray onto the bed, an angry, jerking gesture, and reached behind his back. Jessica tensed and drew the sheet even more tightly around her. He was holding two zip ties out toward her. "Put these on."

No, I can't go through that again. Jessica attempted defiance through her terror. "No, I … I don't want to."

The metal tray smashed into the wall directly above her head. She felt the whoosh of air just before the sound made her shrink into her sheet. He threw the tray into a corner, leaned down and grabbed her by the wrist, and shouted into her face. "Put these on, now!" there was animal menace in his voice.

Jessica kicked out. Her heel caught him in the stomach, forcing the air out of his lungs, and he careered backward, mouthing a curse beneath the mask. He staggered to his feet and backed out of the room, slamming the door shut behind him. Shocked by her own actions, she lay there for a second, gathering her thoughts. She could hear him on the other side of the door, coughing and gasping, trying to get his breath back. The sounds faded; she guessed he had retreated to lick his wounds.

The sheet had slipped off when she kicked him. Jessica gathered it back around her, and stood, up, surveying the damage. Chunks of chicken and noodles were strewn about the room, sliding off the walls and coming to rest in little puddles of broth. In the corner near the drain she saw a plastic bowl, and a spoon was just visible beside the toilet. For one crazy moment she considered trying to retrieve her food, scrape it back into the bowl and relieve the pangs of hunger gnawing at her constantly.

She had gotten as far as stepping toward the various food puddles when the door burst open again. Strong hands grabbed her and threw her onto the floor. She splayed her hands out to break her fall, but he fell directly on top of her, pressing into the gritty tiles. The scent of chloroform came to her as she gasped for breath.

"You want to do this the hard way? Fine, we'll do it the hard way."

She sensed an arm reaching over her head, and then a damp rag was pressed against her face. She flailed her arms and tried to struggle, but the world slipped away into blackness. She slumped against the floor.

He stood up and stared at the tangle of limbs spread-eagled in front of him. The sheet had fallen away in places; bare skin enticed, repelled, enticed him. *Not yet.* He straightened up and looked down in triumph. *Not yet.*

Jessica lay sprawled on the platform beside the chair, limp, breathing in shallow fits. She was naked and pale in the florescent light. He looked at her for a few moments before making up his mind what to do.

Walking over to the fridge, he took out a little glass bottle, along with a small syringe. He drew out some of the clear liquid into the syringe, and walked back to Jessica's inert form. Finding a suitable vein, he injected her with the contents of the syringe.

From a shelf at the other end of the room he took a pulley and some chain, attached to which was a padded bar; another short stretch of chain dangled from the bar. He hooked the two lengths of chain together with a karabiner until they formed a regular triangle with the padded bar as its base. He fetched a ladder, and hung the pulley from a big hook in the ceiling, and threaded the chain through it. There was another hook set into the wall, and looped the free end of the chain around it.

The padded bar hung just beside the platform, hovering above Jessica. He lifted her legs onto the bar until her knees dangled over it. Taking a couple zip ties, he tied her ankles together, then used a length of light nylon rope to secure her heels against the backs of her thighs. He paused in his work, and looked down at Jessica. Her legs were raised, but the rest of her lay back on the platform, arms upside her head, her face encircled by her billowing hair. He leaned over and gently caressed her thigh.

Snapping back to attention, he reached for a hair band and tied her hair back. Then he walked over to the hook on the wall, unfastened the chain and pulled on it, raising her off the ground. Once her hands no longer touched the floor, he secured the chain again. He looked at her dangling form for a moment, and then went back to the center of the room, and rearranged a few things on the tray beside his easel. The angle was perfect; everything was under his control.

He took two needles, two lengths of plastic tubing, and a beaker, and knelt beside Jessica. He looked for a good spot, and inserted a needle into each arm, taped the tubes together and fed them down into the beaker on the floor. Something wasn't right; he took a small piece of duct tape and taped her thumbs together, to stop her arms from spreading and pulling the tubes out of the beaker.

The blood began to flow into the beaker, slow and steady, life dripping into stillness. He started to sketch the basic shape in front of him: his inverted muse. *No need to bleed and hang too long, this isn't game aging.* He smiled grimly to himself and made a conscious effort to speed up, against his better nature as an artist. He didn't want to spoil her beauty just yet; he had plans for her.

As he finished sketching, the beaker filled up. He replaced it with an empty one, took the full one to his easel, and began to paint. The serene air of a violin sonata accompanied the sibilant sound of the brush strokes.

11

MANY UNHAPPY RETURNS

Jessica woke suddenly. She had been dreaming about being on a ship, a ship rolling and pitching in a violent storm; the image that stayed in her mind was a confused version of Gericault's 'Raft of the Medusa'; Jessica, her parents, and Shannon were the crew on the raft, clinging on for dear life. The dream was gone now, suddenly interrupted, so she couldn't understand why her stomach felt as if she was still on the raft. She flung the bed-sheet aside and stood up quickly, but instantly regretted it; she felt light headed and dizzy, and immediately found herself falling to the warm concrete floor. Scrambling on her hands and knees she hurried toward the toilet. But she made it only as far as the shower before her stomach convulsed, and she vomited painful bile into the shower drain.

She must have collapsed after that. When she opened her eyes, she saw the painful evidence of her nausea lining the drain. She tried to catch her breath, but the next heave of her stomach drove toward the toilet. Her stomach was empty; she hadn't eaten for – how long? But she still retched and dry heaved for what seemed like hours before she collapsed again, her mouth reeking of bile, and the acrid fragrance of chloroform still clinging to her nostrils.

When she had recovered a little she staggered over to the sink, her skin beaded with sweat and her sore muscles shaking as she rinsed off her hands and face. She felt a dry flaky spot above her lip. Glancing over at the thin panoramic mirror beside the shower, she saw dried blood on her face; had he assaulted her? She probed with her fingertips around her nose, cheeks, and mouth. Nothing felt sore or swollen, so she guessed the nose bleed wasn't caused by any impact.

The cool water felt good on her tongue, so she gulped it down, swallow after swallow. Mistake. Her stomach started to heave again, and she doubled up over the toilet and coughed it all up. This time, when she returned to the sink, she drank only a few precious sips.

She crawled back onto the mattress and wrapped her clammy, trembling figure in the single bed sheet. Every muscle in her body was tensed from the convulsions of her stomach. She forced her brain to work, trying to remember what had happened to her the day before; what was different? Why did she suddenly feel so awful? Chicken broth; she remembered the chicken broth; it was everywhere. She looked around the room, but there was no evidence of the mess. Had she dreamed that too? No, she had kicked out at the tray in his hand and the broth had gone everywhere, she was sure it had really happened.

She unwound the sheet and looked herself over. She noticed three new injection bruises on her forearms and a thin pink line across the skin of her thighs, as well as around her ankles. But there were no other signs of injury. Her own body odor was beginning to offend her, and she worried that it might make her nauseous again. She stood up unsteadily, and headed carefully toward the sink. What she really wanted was a shower, but she made do with the miserly supply of water from the faucets, and rinsed herself off as well as she could. The bed sheet made a poor towel, but it was all she had; she dried off and laid it on the warm concrete floor to dry.

Feeling a little better, and a little braver, Jessica cautiously approached the metal door, and peered out through the small window. There was nothing out there, except a sea of darkness. She lay back down on the mattress and rested her hands over her stomach, trying to calm her hunger pangs, trying to recall when she had last eaten. For a moment, she regretted kicking the tray; but she knew she had to resist, it was her only weapon against him.

To take her mind off the incessant gnawing of hunger, she thought about her situation. Why had he brought her here? Why her? If he needed a model, surely he didn't need to go to these lengths. *The mask; maybe he's horribly disfigured, and this is the only way he can get women to pose for him. No, don't go there; you'll end up feeling sorry for him.* Jessica recalled, with a bitterly ironic smile, how she had felt when Liam had asked her to pose nude. At the time, she had thought nothing could feel worse. *Well now you know girl.*

More unsettling was the question of what he intended to do to her. When he'd finished his hideous portrait project, what then? What had he done to the other girls, to Rachel and Stacey? She refused to think about their fates, but the thought nagged at her. She couldn't help wondering how she had been chosen, how they had been chosen. Had they done something to him, something awful? *Do not suppose that ye shall be restored from sin to happiness;* the words rang in her head, as she tried to think of anything she had done to provoke someone into vengeance. Nothing came to mind, she just wasn't the sort of person to do hateful things; and yet … a vague feeling of unease accompanied her drift into fitful sleep.

12

NOTHING TO CHAUFFEUR IT

Thomas hurried to finish up his homework in time to go hang out with Jake and the others. There wasn't much space to work in the bedroom of their trailer park home, and Thomas sighed his frustration. *Trailer trash*, he thought bitterly, *that's us.* He didn't want to ask his dad about the truck until he had finished all his homework. Back when his parents were still together he could always ask the other parent if one gave him a less favorable answer. Now that it was just his father he had to play by the rules, and even then he wasn't guaranteed a positive answer.

Checking over the last questions he'd answered and content with what' he'd done, he closed his books and stuffed them back inside his backpack. He looked at his watch; there was still a little time before he had to leave. He decided to work on his Wolverine painting to fill the time.

He'd just got settled in front of the lurid, little mural when he heard the telephone ringing. His father's voice was gruff and indistinct, but Thomas could tell the call wasn't welcome. Footsteps sounded along the hallway, and there was an irritated knock at his bedroom door. The door flew open, and his father's bleary eyes fixed on him.

"Phone's for you. It's your mother. Why do you draw that crap all over the walls?" They were just crude sketches of comic book heroes, but Thomas was fond of them. He sighed and put down his brush.

Thomas went to the living room and picked up the phone.

"Hey, Tom, how ya doing?"

"Okay, mom; how are you? Dad, could you turn down the TV just a little?"

If his mother could hear the impatience in his voice, she didn't acknowledge it. His father grunted, and reached for the remote; now he could hear himself think, at least.

"So how's school? You making friends?"

"Actually yeah, I made a few friends. In fact, I'm just going to meet up with a few of them."

"That's great, Tom, I'm happy for you. I just want you to know, if you don't like it where you are, or you have any problems, you can always come and live with me. I ... I'd really like it if you did. I know the divorce was kind of hard on you, Tom. I want to do the best for you. You know that, don't you?"

"Sure, mom, I know you mean that. But I'm doing okay, and school is getting better. Plus, if I moved now, I'd have to start over, and I wouldn't have any friends."

"Well, if you ever change your mind, there's a home waiting for you right here."

Thomas glanced at the clock, hanging crookedly on the living room wall. He needed to get going. Nick would be waiting for his ride. When he spoke again, everything came out in a hurry.

"Mom, I have to go. I'm meeting up with a few of the guys —"

"I know, honey, you told me. I don't want to keep you from having fun. You have a great time, okay? Love you."

"Bye, mom; love you."

As the phone line went dead in his hand, Thomas felt a shiver of remorse, and something more. Somehow, whenever he talked to his mother, which wasn't that often, he felt like it was the last time. It was like he had forgotten to say something important, and now he would never get to say it.

He went back to his bedroom and grabbed his jacket, and cautiously approached the living room, where the television was back to playing at high volume.

Thomas' father lay reclined in a chair pointed directly at the television. In one hand he held the remote and in the other was a glass of whiskey. He was wearing dirty, worn blue jeans and a flannel shirt. His face showed the same stubble it had shown the day before, just a little longer and grayer. To his left was a small end table with an assortment of snacks lying beside a couple empty beer bottles.

"Hey dad …"

Mr. King acknowledged his son with a questioning grunt. Thomas continued, hopefully. "… I finished my homework for the weekend."

"Uh huh," Mr. King grunted back.

"Is it alright if I borrow your truck and go hang out with some friends tonight?"

"Uh, sure. But make sure you fill up the tank. Ya got it?"

"I will. Thanks." Thomas went and got the truck keys off the kitchen counter and on the way out the door he called back, "Thanks again."

"Yeah," Mr. King grunted back as he raised the remote to change the channel.

In the driveway sat a little old tan pick-up truck. It had a two-door cab but the driver's door couldn't be opened from the outside. So Thomas climbed in through the passenger door and slid over to the driver's seat. After a couple turns of the ignition he got the engine to start. Backing out of the driveway he maneuvered the steering wheel to compensate for the awkward angle the truck had been parked at. As he shifted the gears with the lever on the steering column he glanced at the fuel gage and saw that the tank was nearly empty. With a sigh he put it in drive and headed to the gas station.

Because he had to stop and fill up the truck, Thomas arrived at the Recreation Center a couple minutes after seven. He double honked the horn for Nick, who was standing inside the doors of the front entrance, leaning against the wall with his arms crossed impatiently. Nick jogged up to the truck, visibly irritated, and as he got in asked, "Dude, what took you so long?"

"Sorry. I had to get gas first."

"Whatever, just head over to fourth east real quick. I need to pick up some stuff for tonight."

"You mean the bag?"

"What? No, Rob's got that. I'm getting some drinks from this guy I know."

"Oh, cool. Sounds like we're gonna have some fun tonight."

"Yeah, most likely." Nick looked out the passenger side window. "Supposed to have some girls coming over too, maybe even your new girlfriend Jessica," he teased.

"Really? Wait, who said she was my girlfriend?"

"Nobody did. I just heard you asked her out."

"Oh, well do you think she ...?" Thomas was stopped short as Nick pointed somewhere over to the left.

"Right there. Park here." He hopped out of the truck with his gym bag in hand. Shutting the door behind him he leaned in the window and said, "Wait here; I'll be right back."

Thomas sat in the truck listening to the radio, the one piece of equipment in the vehicle that always worked, as he waited for Nick. When a commercial started to play he switched the dial over to another station. Soon there were commercials on every station so he just turned the radio off. *Oh well,* he thought, *I guess cab drivers don't always get to listen to their favorite music.* After about ten minutes Nick came back with some newly added weight to his gym bag and got back in the truck.

"Alright. Let's stop at my house real quick and then we'll head over to Jake's."

Nick's house was on the corner of the block, so he had Thomas parked the truck along the west side of the house. A small canal ran along the side of the road and many of the driveways along the street had bridges.

"Okay, just wait here and I'll be back in a few minutes." Nick hopped down into the empty canal and then climbed up on the patch of grass showing through the crusty snow. He jogged up the wooden steps of the back porch to the back door of his house and went inside.

Fifteen minutes went by so Thomas turned off the engine to save some gas. He flipped back and forth between radio stations as he continued to wait for Nick. Unable to find anything to his liking he switched it back off.

Looking at the clock he saw that it had been half an hour since Nick had gone inside. He wondered if something bad had happened, like Nick's parents had found out about the booze, so he decided to go see what was taking so long. He got out of the driver's side and stepped away then quickly spun around, reaching for the door before it closed shut behind him. Too late. Dropping his shoulders he let out an audible sigh of irritation. Now he would have to climb in through the passenger side: again. Waving away the annoying truck door he went up the back porch to the door that he had seen Nick go into, did a quick knock, opened the door and went in.

"Hey Nick, you ready to …?" Thomas started to say as he looked in the room, but stopped short when he saw Nick with his parents and siblings eating at the dinner table. Nick's father, a tall well-built man with black hair and a thick mustache, was glaring at Thomas. He set his fork down loudly in his plate, stood up, and turned toward Thomas.

"Who are *you*?"

"Oh um, I'm Nick's friend. I was just …"

"Who do you think you are? You can't just walk in while we're having dinner."

Thomas looked over at Nick, who glanced away, not wanting to get involved.

"I just …"

"You can just go wait outside until we're done eating."

"Sorry. I'm sorry." Thomas backed out the door, feeling childish and ashamed.

Thomas returned to the truck and waited, embarrassed that he'd interrupted Nick's family dinner, and a little shaken up from being yelled at by Nick's father.

After twenty more minutes or so Nick finally came out and opened the passenger door to the truck. Thomas started the engine, eager to get away as quickly as possible. Nick reached into the truck without getting in and grabbed the gym bag off the floor of the passenger side.

"Hey man … uh, looks like we're not gonna be able to go tonight."

"Really? Is it because of me?" Thomas asked.

"Nah, well kinda yeah," Nick said as he looked over his shoulder. "Forget about it. We'll hang out some other time. See ya at school." He closed the door and made his way back toward his house.

"Alright, see ya later," Thomas called out as he drove away. He felt really stupid. First, he'd bust into Nick's house like a cop; now he'd ruined the night for everyone. He hammered his hand against the steering wheel in anger and frustration, gunning the motor and hitting the brakes again as he came to the stop sign at the end of the road. *No drinks, no girls, no Jessica; nice work, Tom.*

Nick watched anxiously from the side of his house as Thomas drove away. After the truck turned the corner and was out of site he swaggered over to the front of the house, where Jake was waiting in his parents' sedan with Rob in the passenger seat. Nick climbed into the back seat with his gym bag in hand and said, "Alright, party time."

"What about Tom? I thought we were going to give him the wrong address and ditch him?" Jake asked.

"Nah, even better. My dad yelled at him for interrupting our dinner and I told him that we can't hang out tonight, so he left. And he thinks it's all his fault."

"Ha! Nice," Rob laughed.

"Well, nice work, Nick; problem solved," Jake grinned.

"Oh, I also told him that Jessica was thinking of dropping by."

"Yeah right, like she'd hang out with us," Rob said.

"Maybe not with you two," Jake laughed.

Fumbling through the contents of his gym bag, Nick thought of something else and smiled. "Rob, how much you got left?"

"Just Tom's portion of the 'clove cigarettes.'" Rob was smiling too now.

"Let's smoke it and make up some excuse to tell him on Monday," Nick suggested.

"Sounds like a plan." Jake held his hand in the air and they all high fived, laughing as they drove off.

...

A little later, in the painting classroom, Liam stood back and assessed his work. His portrait of Jessica was finished. He couldn't bring himself to paint the towel she'd insisted on wrapping around herself, so he had left out the parts she'd covered up and simply added a few mysterious swirls of paint to hint at what lay beneath.

Considering she had only modeled for him for one session, he was pretty pleased with what he had achieved. Jessica stared out from the painting, innocent and enticing; Liam picked up her portrait, careful to avoid the wet paint, and propped it up against the wall. As he did so, he inadvertently bumped into another student's work; the canvas wobbled for a moment then fell face down on the art room floor. Liam cursed to himself and gingerly picked up the painting. He was relieved to see he hadn't damaged it; it was not like him to be so clumsy.

As he turned to put the painting back in its place he noticed the white canvas, with a partly completed drawing on it. It must have been behind the one that fell, he thought. Then he looked a little closer. The figure in the drawing looked identical to the one in his painting. Liam was sure; the more he looked at it, the more it resembled his own work. *Who the hell thinks they can copy my work?* He picked the drawing up angrily; there was no signature on the front, so he turned it over roughly in his hands. *Thomas King.* Liam smirked and took the canvas into the center of the room, where the classroom chairs were stacked. He raised Tom's canvas and smashed it down on an upturned chair leg; the impact punctured the canvas, ripping through the image on it like a scar.

After putting away his equipment and materials, Liam turned off the lights and left the painting classroom, hearing the door lock behind him. He made his way to the parking lot and stopped by a dumpster. He tossed Thomas' ruined drawing in with the rest of the trash, and walked away.

13

Ties and Rags

I'm bored. Jessica lay on her side, staring at the toilet in the shower corner. The light in her room was always on, which made it difficult to sleep. She shifted her position on the mattress and wrapped the sheet around her more tightly. Although the floor was heated, the cool walls prevented the room from getting too warm; but it was the lack of food that was making her shiver.

The lock on the metal door rattled before it swung open and knocked against the wall. Startled, she tried to jump back, but she was tangled up in the tightly wrapped sheet and fell off the mattress onto the floor. She looked up from the floor and saw him standing in the doorway with the same metal tray in his hand, the unnerving mask on his face. He placed the tray at the foot of the bed and said, "Five minutes."

Closing the door behind him, he went back out into the main room. Jessica cautiously approached the tray and looked at its contents. There, in a plastic bowl with a matching plastic spoon, was a soup of noodles with vegetables and chicken chunks.

She sipped the broth tentatively and swished it around in her mouth. There was no suspicious flavor; she submitted to her hunger and began scooping the soup into her mouth. The savory salty broth was so delicious she drank every last drop and licked the bowl clean. It didn't begin to sate her hunger, but it did feel good.

As soon as she set the empty bowl on the tray she heard the latch release and the door slowly swung open. Jessica stood up and backed toward the wall, wrapping the sheet more securely around her and clutching it tightly.

He held out an object in each of his hands and said, "I'll give you a choice. Put these on," he indicated the zip ties in his left hand, "or I'll put them on for you." He nodded toward the rag with the faint smell of chloroform that he held in his right hand.

She pointed to the zip ties and held out her free hand. Before giving them to her he said, "Lose the sheet."

She glared at him in defiance; he responded by slightly raising the hand that clasped the damp rag. With a bitter grimace she unraveled the sheet and tossed it onto the mattress. Then she extended her open hand and shook it once impatiently, demanding the ties. He handed them to her and watched as she fastened them around her wrists. Stepping forward, he lifted up her hands to evaluate her effort. He looked into her eyes, then back at the ties, and fastened them each a little tighter. Stepping out the door, he turned back to Jessica, and gestured for her to go ahead.

The big room was almost in darkness, but there was one island of light. She saw a platform that rose about a foot off the ground with a couple spot lights pointed at it. Sitting on the platform was a dark brown padded storage cube with a bundle of fabric swaged around the base. Everything was pointed at the cube; she assumed that was where he wanted her to sit.

Around the room on the walls hung various paintings in brown and red monotones, all of nude women. She paused when she saw the one of herself hanging upside down.

He grasped her shoulder and said, "Have a seat," pointing toward the brown cube on the platform.

"And if I don't?" She felt stronger after the food, more ready to defy him.

"Then we'll do another *fun* pose." He pointed to the painting of her hanging upside down with the two lines bleeding out her forearms. "Like last time."

She shuffled over to the cube, a picture of resentment, and sat down with her feet up, her legs close to her chest, and her arms resting on her knees, her right hand grasping her left wrist. She glared back at him as he tied a thin line to the ties on her wrists. He circled around her with his arms folded, squinting through the mask's eyeholes, as he looked her up and down. He went and picked up his easel and repositioned it on the spot where he'd stopped circling.

She refused to let him slip out of her sight, watched him carefully while he moved around the room. As he went over to the fridge and grabbed a couple jars, she tried to see what else was in the fridge, but he shut the door and set the items on the tray beside the easel before she could get a proper look.

Jessica watched as he unscrewed the cups and poured the dark red contents into a larger glass beaker. The insolence in her voice surprised her. "What? No needles today?"

He finished emptying the cups and set them aside before he responded, his voice calm and threatening. "Who says I have to use needles to bleed you?" He squinted and extended both his hands toward Jessica, using them to frame the composition in front of him.

She felt the blood leave her face and a chill run up her back. So he did have other plans for her; she shuddered at the thought. But she wasn't ready to relinquish the courage she had found so recently. Instead she focused on her anger and glared back at him as much as she dared.

Completely ignoring her spiteful expression he said, "That pose is fine, but just relax it a little bit."

"Ha!" Jessica laughed out loud. "Relax!? Are you kidding me!? You talk to me like I'm some hired model in your art studio. Like ... like this is completely normal. You really think I'll just do whatever you want?" She wanted to go on, give him a really hard time, but she stopped herself; ruefully she realized she may have been better off keeping her mouth shut.

"Actually yes, I do. I know you'll do what I want, and here's why," he said. "Either you can do what I tell you, or you can be unconscious and I'll position you however I please."

"What, like when you throw me in that room each night?" Her voice began to fail her. "I can't stand to think of the ... the things you do when I'm unconscious."

"Then don't." He ignored her anger and hurt and finished setting up his materials.

"Relax the pose."

She didn't move, held him in her gaze.

"You seem a bit tense. Would you like something to help you relax?" He placed his fingertips on the jar of chloroform.

She imagined the smell of the anesthetic and her stomach churned. Not wanting to puke up the only meal she'd had in who knows how many days, she gave in and relaxed her leg, and her left shoulder, and sat up straighter. He nodded his approval and went over to the stereo and turned on some instrumental music.

Jessica watched for a while as he began sketching, but she soon grew uncomfortable under his gaze and started looking around the room. She found herself staring at the exterior of the tiny room where she'd been kept.

Noticing her intent gaze toward the corner room, he said, "It was once an old bomb shelter. The kind a lot of old homes had during the Cold War. I remodeled it, along with some other parts of this place."

She ignored his comment and continued looking around the room. There were a variety of chairs and tables around the place. There wasn't much else to look at; little had changed from what she had seen the first time she woke up, strapped to the chair.

What had changed were the numerous paintings hanging on the walls. She didn't remember seeing them there last time. Her eyes widened when she came to the one of her strapped in the metal and leather chair; the first painting he had done of her. What she found more horrifying than the knowledge that it was all done in her blood was how beautiful it looked. It was nothing like she had imagined it to be; horrid drips and nasty black clots. Instead it was a soft, delicate rendering of what appeared to be a lovely young woman, nude, dozing in a chair. There was something about the style of the paintings, something that stirred in her memory.

He hadn't painted any of the needles or restraints that she distinctly remembered. In contrast, the painting of her hanging upside down had all the tubes and needles, but it still managed a lightness of touch that felt unnerving. Realizing this wasn't some frantic act of insanity, but the work of an artist completely calm and in control, set her even more on edge.

Her attention moved toward the narrow hallway to her right. The one she was certain must be the only way out. Not wanting to reveal her intentions, she panned her gaze around the room, looking at the dozen or so paintings that hung on the walls. Two of them were definitely of her, but she didn't recognize the figures, all women, in the others.

He snapped his fingers and she looked back toward him.

"Hold your head still," he said.

She looked away from him again, defiant. "Like I said, pose, or I will pose you," he warned.

She brought her head forward and glared right at him. Unfazed by her bitter stare he continued sketching. After a while he put the pencil down and picked up the glass beaker, with the dark red ransom he had extracted from her sloshing from side to side, and a couple paint brushes.

"You can relax your head."

She stared down at the floor; glanced up at him when he wasn't looking. His mask, although it seemed to be evenly wrapped all over, actually had a thinner layer over the mouth and nose for breathing. She imaged it would be similar for the ears so as not to inhibit his hearing. *What is under that mask?* She listened to the music, accompanied by the sound of the paintbrush scraping across the paper. The sound brought back fragments of memory from when she first found herself in this place.

Her heart started racing and her breathing became shallower and faster. A feeling of panic rose up, and she couldn't quell it. Without conscious intent, she darted for the right side of the room. But she was instantly thrown down onto the floor of the platform, landing on her side. The thin line fastened to the zip ties on her wrists was stronger than she had anticipated. The cube on which she had posed was attached firmly to the platform too. Nothing had moved, except her.

He put his brushes down, his body language suggesting the mild irritation of a kindergarten teacher scolding a naughty toddler. "You think you're the first one to try that? Get back on the cube and into the same pose."

She hesitated, glancing at him and then over to the narrow hallway at the far right side of the room. His eyes rolled behind the frayed openings in the mask; he left his spot by the easel and approached her. She tensed as he leaned over toward her, pulling a stainless steel knife with a curved jagged blade out of his pocket, to her surprise, he cut the line that tied her wrists to the cube. She looked at him, confusion on her face.

"Go ahead, have a look," he said. Confident, indifferent; in control.

She got up and ran for the right side of the room, around the corner of the narrow hallway, and right up to a bookshelf.

"What!?" she exclaimed.

He was sitting on the cube, watching in amusement. "Grab the right side of the bookcase and shove it toward the left."

Jessica couldn't see any other option so she gripped the bookshelf and shoved it toward her left. It slid with a light grinding sound into a space in the wall beside it. Behind the bookcase was a heavy-looking metal door and above the handle were three different locks. One was a standard dead bolt, another was a magnetic card reader, and the third was a numeric keypad. She slammed her fists on the door and let out a scream of frustration. That calm ironic voice sounded behind her. "I know. It clashes with the rest of the place, but I was going more for function than form."

She beat her fists against the door.

"You can't get out. And no one can hear you. So you might as well *sit* back down and hold still."

She trudged back over to the platform, defeated. He had repositioned the cube, and tidied up the cloth. She sat back down, crossed her legs and folded her arms, staring, with as much anger as she could muster, at the man who held her there.

"Where's Shannon?" she demanded.

"I don't know what you're talking about." He sat back down in front of his painting, apparently uninterested in her question. "Go ahead and get back into the same position."

"Where is she?"

"How should I know? Now, if you don't mind?"

"You're incredible. You're talking to me like this is just a normal modeling session?"

"If you'd like I can get in your face, scream at you until you break down in tears? Or I could put you under and spare myself this time-wasting conversation."

"Tell me where Shannon is."

"I told you Jess, I don't know."

"Don't lie to me. You were in her car. You had her phone and you …"

"Let me save you some time and mental effort." He slapped his brushes down on the tray and stepped out from behind his easel. "When the security questions to your email are *'What high school did you go to?'* and *'What was your high school mascot?'* it isn't all that difficult for someone who knows just a little bit about you to break in."

"What are you saying?"

"I'm saying that for the past few months you have been emailing me. Whenever you thought it was Shannon; it was me. I went into your address book and changed the email address that you had saved under Shannon's name and replaced it with a very similar one. So the lost cell phone on the ski trip, the car, and planning to meet in Denver? That was all me. Shannon is irrelevant; for now."

Jessica was angry about the invasion of her privacy, but at the same time glad to hear that Shannon was not in the same situation as she was. He gave her an impatient glare until she finally repositioned herself on the cube, as she had been earlier.

"Why was there dried blood under my nose?"

"Probably because you waited too long to wipe it off."

"Do you enjoy slapping me around when, when you …" she couldn't bring herself to say it.

She saw him tense his shoulders, and slowly exhale, as if to calm himself down. "Your nose bled because of the anticoagulant I injected in you."

"What for?"

"The term is pretty self-explanatory. You know, to prevent coagulation of red blood cells; the kind that would cause a stroke, a pulmonary embolism, or cardiac arrest. You were hanging upside down for some time, Jess. Lucky for you I prefer fair skin over purple." He resumed painting, and silence hung between them for some time.

The silence was too much for Jessica. She had to talk, to get something out of him. "What's with the mask? Are you horrifically scarred, or is it to hide your guilt at what you're doing?"

"Think of me as the Phantom to your Christine, if you like, the beast to your beauty." He continued painting.

Jessica tried another tack. "Who's Stacey?"

"Stacey." He gave a contemplative sigh, "Stacey was here before you."

"So where is she now?" She wasn't sure she wanted to hear the answer, but she had to ask the question.

"She's gone."

"Well, then who's Rachel?"

"She was here before Stacey."

Jessica's voice betrayed her unease. "What do the tallies by their names mean?"

"What do you think they mean?"

She really didn't want to think about that; it was horribly obvious what they might mean. "And how many tallies do I get?"

"At this rate it won't be many."

He got up and began putting his things away. As he did so he pointed to a painting, hanging on the far wall, of a short-haired young woman, nude like all the others, who was crying and said, "You see that painting over there? That was Stacey's last portrait. It was difficult to do because of her constant fidgeting. I thought of putting her under at first, but this way, I feel, more accurately captured the little details toward the end."

He put away a couple items into the fridge and rinsed the brushes off in the sink.

"Then slightly behind you to your left you'll see a girl hanging upside down, suspended by her hands and feet. That was Rachel's last portrait. Both of them asked about the mask too. And I was gracious enough to let them see what was under the mask; after finishing their final portraits."

Jessica stared at the contorted posture of the young woman, suspended so painfully in the painting. It looked much worse than the inverted one of her. She tried to analyze the image, glean some meaning from it, something that would tell her about her own situation, but nothing came. She quietly asked, "Why did you do this to them? What could they have possibly done to you to deserve this?"

Hearing nothing in reply, she turned to see where he had gone. Suddenly a damp rag was clasped over her face. She threw her hands up and knocked him under his jaw, tilting the mask up enough to expose his chin; revealing the start of a scar that disappeared up and under his jaw line. But his grip held, and with his free arm he restrained her from taking another swing at him until she collapsed.

Very carefully, almost tenderly, he laid her head down before throwing away the chloroform soaked rag. With a quick adjustment he repositioned the mask so he could see properly out of the eyeholes. He went and got a white sheet and spread it out over the platform. After making a few deliberate crinkles in the material he picked Jessica up and placed her limp form on the center of the sheet, resting on her left hip, with her chest against the platform and her head resting on top of her hands.

Once he had gotten her into position he removed the mask and set it over on the table. Running his hand through his hair and taking a deep breath of undisrupted air, he began sketching her from various angles. It was easier to capture her essence this way, without her incessant questions, her defiant gaze. And she was beautiful; more beautiful than the others, more precious.

What he wanted, more than anything, was for her to cooperate with him, pose as he wanted her, while she was awake, so he could get her eyes as he wanted to get them. Alive, penetrating, serene. *Perhaps, in time.* He sighed and smiled wistfully; *Jessica, if only you knew.* Taking another jar of her blood, he went back to work.

14

A STEADY RAZOR
AND A SHARP HAND

Waking to nausea was becoming a horribly familiar routine. Jessica scrambled over to the toilet, abandoning her protective sheet and vomited and retched until her stomach finally let her relax. She staggered to her feet and began to wash herself, to rinse away the nightmare of her daily torture. Her hands met an unfamiliar smoothness, and she looked down; her public hair had been shaven off. She was immobilized by shock for a moment, then a truncated scream of rage and impotence escaped her.

She marched over to the metal door and looked through the window, wanting him to be there so she could vent her rage at him. But the big room was shrouded in darkness, and there was no noise from outside. Tight-lipped with frustration, she returned to the mirror in the shower cubicle and examined her body. She had been comprehensively shaved; her armpits, pubis, and legs were smoothly naked. He had been very careful; she couldn't see a razor burn anywhere. *He doesn't want to spoil his model's looks. Not yet, anyway.*

Jessica was struck by an awful thought: *if he could do all this when I was out, what else could he do?* She went back to her examination, but could see no signs of other abuse. Surely, she thought, she would know if he had violated her. She shuddered at the prospect of waking up knowing she had been raped by the masked monster; she was quietly, horribly sure it was going to happen, that and worse. *Poor Rachel, and Stacey too.*

She looked around her cell, and noticed a small metal tray. On it was a bowl of oatmeal, and beside that a cup of milk. She dipped a tentative finger into the milk. It wasn't quite cold, but it was cool enough to drink. She poured half of it onto the oatmeal, and slowly sipped the rest, giving her stomach a chance to take nutrition without rejecting it.

She wrapped herself in the sheet again, sat on the strangely warm concrete floor, and ate her breakfast, slowly, not knowing when she might eat again. As she ate, she contemplated the possibility of escape. Three locks, no four, between her and freedom. The more she thought about it, the more impossible it seemed. Even if she managed to get out of this room, find keys for the other door, she would still be faced with guessing the code for the last lock. And if by some miracle she cracked the code, what would she find on the other side of that door? She was stuck.

She thought of her parents, somewhere on the other side of the world, of her friends; did anyone know she was missing? She had no real idea how long she had been held captive, but surely it was longer than the holiday weekend. Someone must have raised the alarm by now. When she thought of her family, worried sick, fearing the worst, she shed bitter tears.

She didn't cry for long. It dawned on her that she was feeling one emotion much more strongly than fear, and that was hate. She hated him with every fiber of her being, for what he had done to her, and the other girls; for what he might do, would do, to her while she slept in a chloroform haze. And yet, there was no evidence that he had done anything to her; the daily torture of seeing her blood stolen for his paintings was the only thing she could hand her anger on.

She looked down at the empty breakfast bowl. At least he wasn't starving her. Under the anger, she felt the stirring of another emotion; it shocked her to realize she was actually grateful for the food. Her situation was bad, but it could be so much worse; he could have made it worse. And that mask, the possibility that he was hiding some terrible disfigurement: *wickedness never was happiness.* Jessica sat back on her bed and sighed.

15

THE ARTIST IS PRESENT

Thomas carried his portfolio and sketchbook into the painting studio and sat down on one of the small desk chairs beside a dozen other art students. He listened to their nervous, excited chatter while he sat quietly and waited for the class to begin. He was nervous too, although he had calmed down a little when he saw that his work was not among the first pieces for analysis. As Professor Foster began taking roll, everyone quieted down.

"Now, as we discussed last week, these first few critiques will be anonymous. By doing this it should be easier for everyone to comment and discuss the strengths and weaknesses of the work." Professor Foster looked over his students reassuringly. "Before we start, let me remind everyone that even though the critiques are anonymous, I still need your name included somewhere in the portfolio or box you had your work in."

The advanced class was for students to develop a body of work without assignments, to take responsibility for their own creations. But a lot of the students didn't really know how to constructively discuss their own artwork, let alone the work of others. This class was meant to help them develop critical thinking and discussion. Professor Foster knew most of them would simply say which paintings they liked or disliked, and then sit back and wait for their participation points. Still, he could always hope.

Thomas sat quietly at his little desk chair with a pen and his sketchbook out, ready to jot down any ideas that might come to him during the discussions. On the other side of the room, Liam sat leaning backward with his hands propped up behind his head. The expression on his face suggested he already knew what to say about the paintings that had just been put up. Thomas glanced over at Liam and then back toward the wall of paintings, his face hardening. Getting out of high school hadn't changed him; Liam was just as arrogant as ever.

After he finished hanging up the last couple paintings for the first round of discussion, Professor Foster spoke to the class, "So how this will work is each of you will comment on a set of paintings from a viewer's perspective; the tricky part will be offering a responding comment to a previous comment, as though the work were your own and you were trying to explain it. Make sense?"

After a few of them expressed likes or dislikes in the works on the wall without expanding upon why they felt that way, Professor Foster got involved more, to try and offer some real critique and give them some direction.

"Back when I was getting my MFA I studied with a gentleman who would quote from the Bible or close with a poetic reading at the end of each class. A little something that made you think. One day as he looked over my work he said to me, 'You draw so many lines. Why don't you just draw the right one? It would save you so much time.' Initially I felt a little offended by his remarks, since I thought my use of lines was a key definition of my style.

"But as I took his advice into consideration I found the truth in what he had said. Because of his honesty I was able to make my work better and progress to where I am today."

The critique session moved forward; input soon came from the other end of the spectrum, overly opinionated students who not only looked for faults in every piece of work, but also seemed to make it a priority to demean the intelligence of everyone else as much as possible. It was like watching cockerels competing in a hen house, Thomas thought; and Liam fit in really well with the other strutting males.

"I'm simply saying that, albeit the choice of color in that larger piece of …" Liam pointed to a brightly colored painting that hung on the corkboard wall in front of everyone, "is, shall we say free spirited," implying a child could do just as well, "yet if the application and composition were any more lethargic then it might as well hang over a matching sofa in a warehouse store." He sat back into his seat and snobbishly sipped his Frappuccino, glancing around the room to see if he could figure out whose work he had just trashed.

Sensing the negative feeling in the room, Professor Foster intervened. "Something this artist could try," he gave a quick glance toward the curly-haired young woman with the embarrassed expression on her face, "is to experiment with just some monochromatic paintings and get a better feel for the contrast of the piece. That might help to develop the application and composition without having to worry about color placement just yet. Then do a few analogous paintings, like green, yellow green, and yellow; or some other similar grouping of colors.

"Also make sure to use the color aid paper you bought for this class." He addressed this comment more broadly to the entire group. "Before placing a color beside another that's already on your painting, just hold up the color aid swatch and see how they react to one another visually. Color selection is key to a successful painting.

"Alright everyone, let's take a quick break and when we come back," Professor Foster flipped through a couple papers in his note book, "I'll have switched out a few of the paintings that have had enough discussion and added in newer ones. Meet back here in ten minutes."

...

When the class returned from their break they all went up to the front of the room and got a close look at the new set of paintings that hung on the wall. There were five sheets of thick high-quality paper with brown and red monochromatic compositions of a female nude on each of them. Some of the students stood a little further back, unsure what to make of them; others got close and sniffed at the work, trying to figure out if their suspicions were well founded.

Thomas stopped short of his seat when he saw the crowd of students in front of the paintings. His face turned pale as he stared at the painted profile of the young woman in the paintings. The pen he held just above his open sketchbook trembled in his hand. With as little movement as possible he turned his eyes as far to the left as he could to see Liam seated a few rows over, studiously ignoring the students and their mixed reactions to the paintings in front of him.

Once everyone had sat back down there was a short silence before Professor Foster got things going. "Judging by some of your expressions I can see you already have a pretty good idea as to how these new paintings have been made."

A hesitant hand rose up from the back corner.

"Yes, Susie."

"Is it ... blood?"

"It is, yes. According to the info in the portfolio it is done with a combination of cow and pig blood."

"Please excuse me." Susie leapt out of her chair and hurriedly left the room, her hand over her face.

After a brief pause one or two of the other students felt brave enough to try and offer a comment.

"I like the one with the Wassily chair. I remember seeing one of those at the Bauhaus museum in Berlin. I think it makes for a good composition," one said.

"The chair or the painting?" The next student asked.

"Uh, both I guess." The previous student responded.

Thomas shook his head and sighed; most of these people didn't have a clue. He raised his hand and indicated he wanted to make a comment. When Professor Foster acknowledged him he asked, "Where's her other leg?" pointing toward the same painting with the Wassily chair. The instant the words came out of his mouth he felt stupid. *Great work, Tom. Now they all think you're an imbecile.*

"Her right foot angles away from her left leg. It's there, it's just the foreshortening hides it." A tall dark haired student offered the obvious response.

"Very good. See, this is how it should work. Just keep the comments and responses flowing. It will help each of you to answer the questions posed by your own work as you try to answer those of others." Professor Foster was beginning to feel better about the anonymous critique. "Remember also that the actual artist of each different painting is present and should be both commenting and responding as well."

He was indeed present. He looked over the painting with the Wassily chair. He actually hadn't been able to finish it properly before Jessica woke up, and had decided to just leave it as it was.

"The contrast in the one on the left looks good," said another student.

A few more comments were offered, none of them exactly profound. Thomas scribbled in his sketchbook, waiting for the inevitable. He heard Liam clearing his throat, ready to perform. "I suppose, if an artist uses blood as a pigment, he, that is he or she, must expect that the work will deteriorate pretty quickly, and probably get a little pungent as it does so."

A girl in the front row dressed in punk clothes fumbled for a response. "It's a finite series, isn't that what you call it? The kind that only lasts for a short amount of time and then it's gone. So the artist has to record it some other way, take photos of it and such."

"No that's not it." Another chimed in. "If you look closely you can see that it's sealed with a clear coating. That probably preserves the color."

"So you're saying that sealing blood with a chemical fixative helps to preserve the red pigment of the hemoglobin and reduce coagulation, is that right?" Liam asked.

"Yup, pretty much."

Thomas raised his hand and said, "So when the um ... a painting is complete it's sprayed with a protective coating." Then he lapsed back into silence, embarrassed by his obvious remark.

"Yeah, maybe with a UV additive to reduce any fading from ultraviolet light," an intrigued student on the front row added.

Liam got up and went over to the paintings. He walked from one to the other, a crooked smile teasing his mouth; he looked like he owned the place, thought Thomas. Standing to the side of the paintings he faced the whole of the class and asked, "What is the point of using blood? Why not use some red watercolor paint?"

Finally, someone had asked the question that mattered. There was silence in the room; no one had an answer. So Liam had to answer his own question. "Perhaps it brings a higher level of meaning to the work; in using a living organic medium, so to speak, to create an image of a living thing."

Liam's response, like his question, went way beyond most of the students in the room. They watched, slightly awestruck, as he sauntered back to his seat, and sat down. But he hadn't finished his performance. "As profound as that may seem, here's the real question: why not go the whole way and use human blood instead of blood from an animal? Seems to me that the connection between what the artist is aspiring to create and the result we see here is flawed by the source of the medium."

Thomas felt he had to try and offer something; Liam was taking the whole class over. "Is there any difference in blood color between cows or pigs and humans?" Most of the class had turned to look at him. He wished his sketchbook were bigger so he could hide behind it. He lamely answered his own question. "Probably not, I imagine."

"Well, we are getting some great comments here, but let's make sure we give everyone a chance to voice their perspective on the paintings." Professor Foster gestured to the rest of the students, and watched in dismay as most of them shrank from his sight. After a few moments of silence, just to keep things moving along Professor Foster started talking.

"I have to agree there, about the source of the paint. Paint, when using the term as loosely as possible, can be any type of pigment combined with a binder." He stood up and gestured with his hands toward the blood paintings. "Paint is an antithesis of Aristotle's ideas of 'non-contradiction' – a thing is what it is and can be no other.

"But with this artist's subject matter and type of medium there definitely is a contradiction. I think that if you were to either paint the animals whose blood you use or use human blood to paint the human figure, then the power of your work would resonate more clearly. Although I have to say that these paintings have a powerful effect on me."

Several students jotted down each word Professor Foster had said. In essence, he hadn't said anything different from Liam, but he was the professor, whatever Liam thought.

"Alright. Thank you to everyone whose work we discussed today," Professor Foster concluded. "Next class we will finish up with those we didn't get to today and then after that we'll look at all the paintings again, but we'll ask the artists to reveal which works are theirs."

As he gathered up his sketchbook, Thomas glanced over at Liam. He was still in his seat, basking in his small triumph. Thomas felt like a fool when Liam was around. He thought he'd shaken him off after high school, but here he was again, making Thomas' life just that little bit more miserable.

At the front of the class, the red nudes hung, mute, staring out at their maker.

16

DOUBTING THOMAS

The Friday of the ball was the slowest school Friday of Thomas' life; the morning went so slowly it was almost going backward, like someone had doused the clock in chloroform. He waded through the morning's classes, fretful and anxious and excited all at the same time. At least they had Biology on a Friday.

Mr. Wright must have been teaching them something, but Thomas didn't remember a word of it. He was staring at the back of Jessica's head, following the curves and graces of her dark, silky brown hair. Peaches: once or twice, when they had worked on a lab assignment together, Jessica had turned her head, to look at the clock, or to check her notes, and her ponytail had brushed against his face. The scent of peaches was what stayed in his mind, the soft caress of her hair and the scent of peaches.

He daydreamed as he gazed, imagining the scent of peaches filling his world as they danced together at the ball, the touch of her hair as she leaned her head on his shoulder, the smooth glide of her cheek against his; he had drawn her profile so often, and now he would feel the texture of his dreams against his face.

Everything was ready. He had prepared meticulously, laying out all the pieces in his mind, preparatory sketches for a glorious painting, the image of Jessica, dancing with him, a vision among the anonymous figures in the background. Her corsage was waiting at home, laid out beside his suit; the pick-up truck was as clean as he could make it – if he couldn't drive a cool car, at least he could take her in a clean vehicle. He'd worked extra shifts at the restaurant, so he could take her someplace worthy of her, on their date. The dance was just for them, their destiny

His gaze returned from his dreams to Jessica; she was wearing her hair in a ponytail today; he liked it best when she did that, so he could see more of her, the details of her cheeks, her neck. His sketches were less anonymous when he could see a little more, not just the back of someone's head, but Jessica, unmistakable and true. He dreamed of drawing her portrait; face on, drinking in her gaze as he brought the lines to life. Liam's painting had only captured her, made her his slave, but Thomas would liberate her in pencil, or better in oils. After the dance, after their date, he could ask her to pose for him, and then when the next assignment came, he would produce her with a flourish. Her beauty, his masterpiece.

The sound of the bell brought him back to reality with a start. Around him, the other students were getting ready to leave class for lunch. Thomas hurried to put his stuff away and catch up with the departing crowd, and maybe get a chance to chat to Jessica before she left.

He saw her out in the hallway, and caught up just in time to see her shake her head at something Jake had said. "No, I guess I'll pass on the bakery today. I'm gonna go straight to lunch with my friends; we have a lot to talk about."

Thomas saw his chance. Since the incident with Nick's dad, he hadn't hung out with the other guys after school. So if Jake was out of the way, he could talk to Jessica in private, just how he wanted it. He sidled up to her and said, "Hey Jessie, you looking forward to the ball?"

"Yeah, I am; it's gonna be fun."

Jake reappeared. *Go away, I don't need you right now.*

"Hey, mind if I walk with you guys?"

Thomas desperately tried to think of a way to get rid of Jake. Then he had an idea. "So, you taking anyone to the dance, Jake?" He already knew the answer, and figured Jake would be embarrassed into leaving. But Jake smiled back at him.

"Nah, we're just gonna hang out at my place."

"Who all is 'we'?" asked Jessica.

"Me, Nick and Rob." Jake realized he'd made it sound like the guys who couldn't get a date were sharing a sad pizza, so he quickly added, "A couple girls are planning on showing up later too. And probably a few more people when the dance is over."

Thomas could see that Jake wasn't planning on leaving, but he still wanted to talk to Jessica, to give himself the feeling she was there for him. "So, Jessie …" He felt awkward, grasping for something to say that wouldn't make him look a fool in front of Skeptical Jake. "So, what does your dress for the dance look like?" *Great work, Tom, that sounded really lame.*

"Well, Mr. King, you're just gonna have to wait and see." Flirting. *She's flirting with me.* Jessica looked ahead and waved to a bunch of girls in the hall. Shannon was gesturing at her and mouthing some words Thomas couldn't make out.

"See you guys later." She was gone. Thomas, deflated, turned to Jake.

"You wanna get some lunch?"

"Nah, I'm gonna meet up with Nick and Rob." Thomas knew what that meant. Nick and Rob wouldn't want to see Thomas turn up with Jake.

"Okay, see you later." Jake gave him a lazy, offhand wave and disappeared, leaving Thomas alone, his hands flexing, grasping for something that seemed to be just out of reach.

Jessica was staring silently at her food, unable to touch it. She heard Shannon's voice from somewhere far away. "Sooo, are you all excited for tonight?"

"Yeah ... I guess."

"What's wrong, girl? You got a date, you're a winner."

"I don't know. I should be feeling good. But I was talking with this girl, Amie, she's in my Biology class. She told me Tom's been staring at me all through class; made me feel kind of weird."

"Hey, come on. He's asked you to the dance, so he obviously likes you. He's just dreaming, is all."

"Yeah, I'm sure you're right. It's just ..." Jessica picked distractedly at her lunch, and let her fork fall onto the plate. She started to speak, then stopped, then had another go.

"And she also told me that Tom asked her to a dance last year. She said it was kind of weird. He hardly talked to her, just stared and smiled in a strange way. And he would only dance to slow songs."

"So he's not much of a rock 'n roller. Most guys aren't. You ever see Jake dancing? Ugh!"

"Actually, there's more. A friend of one of Amie's friends told her that Tom was, well, kind of stalking her before the dance. Wherever they were, he was there too, not saying anything, just looking."

"Yeah but where's the proof? Sounds a lot like a bunch of so and so said that someone's friend's sister's cousin's roommate said… blah blah blah." Shannon had spread her fair share of gossip and knew a lot of rumors need to be taken with a grain of salt; like a juicy salted steak that is. Still she was beginning to feel bad for Jessica. "Well, tell him you're sick and you can't go. It's only a dance."

"I can't do that. I already spoke to him, just before lunch. He knows I'm okay. And besides, we've already got our dresses, it would be such a waste." She looked absently at her friends, imagining them in their party dresses, glamorous and glad.

"You can just dance with the rest of us. We can all meet up when we get pictures."

"Yeah, you're right, it's not a problem, really, I'm just worrying over nothing. Nerves, I guess."

When in doubt, Shannon always reached for the vampire joke book. "Don't worry, Jess, I'll borrow the garlic spray my mom uses for cooking. You'll be quite safe." Shannon's voice was comical, but her eyes betrayed her concern for her friend.

17

HEMOCHROMA

That excuse of a critique; he hadn't received a single piece of worthwhile feedback from the other students. If it wasn't for Professor Foster, and the things he had said himself, he might as well not have been there. Never mind; here in his secret studio he could carry on with his work, and not worry about a few fools in a classroom.

Jessica stood beside a stone post that had been anchored to the floor. Her wrists were bound together and fastened to a line attached to the top of the post. A needle with tubing was inserted into each of her arms. As she stood there she made an effort to keep her elbows straight, and leave her hands in front of the naked flesh where her pubic hair had once been.

She couldn't get over what he had done. By shaving her he'd stripped her of the last bit of concealment she had. She felt completely exposed, and she was fed up with being his plaything, his mannequin. Unable to bite her tongue any longer she spat out, "Am I so threatening to you that you feel like you need to shave me bald? Does it make you feel like you have more power over me?"

He looked up, a little surprised at her comment, and she sensed a movement beneath his mask; was he grinning? "What are you talking about?"

"Don't talk to me like I'm stupid. It's a common reoccurring theme throughout Art History, that many male artists portray women without pubic hair in their paintings in order to make them appear weaker and more fragile." She shifted her weight back and forth, uncomfortable; she was growing tired of standing. "There was even an art critic, who prior to his marriage, had only ever seen the nude female form depicted hairless in works of art, so on his honeymoon night he was so shocked by his wife's pubic hair that he divorced her."

He chuckled and shook his masked head. "Is that what they say in Art History? Really?" He turned toward his painting and looked at his work, then turned to survey her again, the master. "So tell me then, how does it feel to be the *Greek Slave?*

"Powers' sculpture holds more beauty than any of your twisted paintings. Even though you obviously see me as a slave, that's a naïve view of his sculpture; and adding some fake cultural background to this situation doesn't make it any better. Besides, despite people like you who view it as sexual and derogatory, the *Greek Slave* is also empowering."

"This," he pointed his brush at the painting and her modeling, "isn't sexual."

"Ha! Right," She scoffed. "And I suppose your little rape room is a cozy bed and breakfast."

She could see his eyes harden behind the mask as he rose out of his chair. Both his fists were clenched and he stepped menacingly toward her, but then turned suddenly to go off to the corner kitchen. From one of the top drawers he retrieved an x-acto knife. Then he turned deliberately, like he had made some kind of decision, and walked slowly back to his chair and sat down; he placed the knife on the try beside him. "So, tell me, Jessica. Do you feel empowered?"

"No." She looked down at her nakedness, "Just vulnerable, increasingly vulnerable." She eyed the knife sitting beside a paintbrush.

"Good, use that inspiration to maintain your pose." He turned his gaze away from her, ignoring what she had said. Picking up the knife, he scratched away at the painting where the zip ties obscured the line of Jessica's wrists. Once he reached the white of the paper, he gently blew away the flecks he'd scraped off and resumed painting.

"By the way," he said matter-of-factly, "the story you were referring to is about John Ruskin and its only art-house gossip to say he was so shocked by his wife's pubic hair that he left her; actually their marriage was annulled after six years." It was good to be the professor and not the student.

"As far as you're concerned," he gestured toward Jessica's absent pubic hair, "it's just easier to paint."

"I don't care what your reason is. Just stop … doing things to me when I'm unconscious." She shook her hands in frustration and felt an instant sting. She gasped at the prick of pain and looked down at her arm. He came over, took her arm in his hand and said, "Hold still."

She swung her arms away from him, but was stopped short by the tie that bound her to the stone. Gripping her arm, he looked closely at both injection points then quickly pulled out both needles.

"I told you to hold still," he said as he threw away the needles, placed the jar of blood into the mini fridge, and bandaged her arms. "You blew through the vein in your right arm. That's going to cause a nasty hematoma later."

"You mean a *bruise*," she mocked.

"Whatever you want to call it." He turned dismissively and went back to look over his painting. With a shrug that suggested he was satisfied with his work, he began cleaning up the items he'd used while painting. After everything was put away he approached Jessica with a rag in one hand and a bottle of chloroform in the other.

"No, not again!" she pleaded. "Just let me go back to the room by myself."

He held the rag over the opening of the bottle and tipped it up until it was sufficiently soaked.

"This is the only way you'll cooperate."

"No, I'll go straight into the room and you can shut the door behind me." She had backed up as far as the line bound to her wrists would allow.

"So why should I believe you? You haven't exactly co-operated up until now, have you?" He set the chloroform bottle down on a nearby table.

"Don't!" she started to struggle, shaking the line taut.

"Hold still," he said as he grabbed her forearm.

"Just … stop raping me!" Her voice broke into a sob and she sagged against the pillar.

His arm dropped to his side. Beneath the mask his face burned, and he looked down, shamefaced. He struggled to talk past the lump in his throat. "Despite what you may think I haven't taken advantage of you. I don't need to. In time I won't even have to force you, Jess. Because before the end you'll be begging me to … just like Stacey," and then he lunged at her.

Jessica quickly took a deep breath before the rag was clasped over her mouth. She struggled for a few seconds and then deliberately went limp. He removed the rag from her face and laid her down on the floor. After putting the chloroform away he undid the line that was fastened to her wrists, picked her up, and carried her into the room. Inside he placed her on the bed, propping the pillow under her head, covered her with the white bed sheet and left her there as he went back out into the open room.

Jessica kept her eyes closed, partly to keep up the pretense, but also to suppress the dizziness that threatened to overwhelm her. Holding her breath had kept her from going unconscious, but the fumes around her mouth and nose were threatening to drag her down at any moment. She raised her head and for a second thought of making a run for it, but a new wave of giddiness forced her head right back down. She shut her eyes again when she heard the sound of returning footsteps.

She heard him come back into the room and set something down on the floor beside the bed. He lingered in the room for a moment before stepping out again. She struggled to open her eyes and looked at the small bag on the floor. *What's he going to do to me? What's in the bag?* Her thoughts were cut short by the returning footsteps. She felt him brush his fingers through her hair.

"Jessie, I know you're awake."

She refused to move, hoping he would think his assumptions were wrong.

"Do you really want to know what I have in this bag?" He watched her as he nudged the bag with his foot. Leaning close to her ear he whispered, "You're going to find out … but not this time." He pressed the damp rag to her face again. It took only a second for her to flinch and go limp.

He patted her face a few times to make sure she was out. Then he removed the mask and placed it at the head of the bed. Examining Jessica's limp form, he adjusted the single sheet that covered her. *Now?* He shifted the sheet to let the skin of her left hip show. *Maybe.* He rolled her onto her side and crossed her bare left leg over her covered right one. He turned to the bag on the floor and opened it. *Not yet, but soon.*

18

HIGH CONTRAST
FIGURE DRAWING

It was just before 7:00 PM on Wednesday. He strolled up the large two-story ramp inside the front entryway of the art department. It had been useful to him on multiple occasions when he'd needed a cart to wheel his heavier projects up to the second floor. Now he just used it as a leisurely route to the drawing studio classroom, where the Art Guild was having its modeling sessions. He looked forward to having a modeling session without wearing his mask, but at the same time he knew it wouldn't be quite as satisfying with the other students around and someone else directing the model.

Inside were a small group of students straddling wooden bench easels; drawing boards were set up on the easels. Everything was arranged in a loose half circle pointing toward the platform on which the model would pose.

In the corner, flipping through some papers, stood Michael Vance. He was a stocky, blond and stern faced grad-student, who supervised the Art Guild's activities. He knew Michael from a couple undergraduate classes; now Michael had graduated and was helping himself through his post-graduate studies by running the drawing class.

"Hey Mike. Is it still five dollars?"

"Yeah," Michael replied. "Sorry about that. If more students came to these sessions we'd be able to lower the cost."

"Is there a paper to sign for attendance verification?"

"Yeah, sure." Michael flipped through a couple papers and handed one to him. "Just sign and date on that line."

His signature was difficult to read, a series of baroque flourishes.

"Actually," Michael said as he struggled to read the signature, "you might want to print your name as well."

He quickly did so and then found an empty bench easel with a drawing board on it. As he clipped his sketchbook to the board he heard Michael addressing the group.

"Alright everyone, before we get started the university requires that I read the modeling statement. 'Artists must be respectful and considerate of the model(s) at all times'." He skimmed over the rest, "Yadda, yadda. Don't touch the model. There is no photography allowed. This is a drawing and painting only modeling session." He tossed the paper back onto the others he'd been shuffling through earlier.

"Alright, tonight we have Hailey modeling for us."

The door to the model changing room opened and a light brown haired, average-height young woman came out wearing only a robe. She stepped up onto the platform as Michael continued. "We'll start with a couple short poses and then we'll end with a long pose."

"How do you want me?" Hailey asked as she looked at the two chairs and bar stool that accompanied her on the platform.

"Just go ahead and do a sitting pose in either of those chairs. Whatever's comfortable for you."

Hailey removed the robe and set it on the other chair. She had a pear-shaped figure and regularly made an effort to keep all her body hair clean-shaven. Like most of the other university models she had a smoothness about her; most noticeable on her arms and legs. He preferred a toner body on his female models. One of his favorite class models was a shorthaired blonde who studied martial arts and had a very fit figure.

Although the majority of models that they worked from in class were female, there was an occasional male model. For him the male models were more difficult to work with. Even when the guy was somewhat tone, the lack of curves and proportional variation left him bored through the whole session.

There always seemed to be something more to it though. He couldn't draw all of them equally well. He had to have some additional interest in them, some sort of attraction to a quality they had, or some other inspiration. It was something about the way they carried themselves, the way they talked so casually and comfortably to the group as they stood on the platform completely naked. It all contributed to his aspiration to recreate their image.

During his first year of college he had done some modeling for a few art classes himself. For these he'd specified himself as a clothed only model. Aside from his dread of exposing certain sensitive areas; he feared the possibility of unintentionally becoming erect in the middle of a session. He'd heard stories from fellow classmates about the odd occasion when such a thing had happened. The model was so embarrassed that he wasn't seen in the art department again.

He had both drawn and painted Hailey many times before in other classes. Though she had an attractive and well-proportioned body, she just never seemed to fully settle into a pose. He couldn't count the number of times he had drawn her arm, then moved down to work on her legs and come back up to find her arm had moved enough that he had to erase it and redraw it.

As Hailey sat down in the softer looking of the two chairs she crossed her legs and casually draped her arms over the sides.

"Is that good?" she asked. "Good?" she repeated to the other side of the group.

"Yeah, that's fine," Michael confirmed as he turned on some music. The music was preceded by a static scratching noise as he adjusted the converter from his iPod into the old beat-up classroom stereo, which looked like a relic from the 80s.

He loosely sketched in the basic geometric shapes that formed Hailey's figure. With it being only a short pose he just wanted to get the proportions and weight distribution accurately.

As a slow melody began to play, Hailey called out toward Michael, without turning her head, "Really? You're gonna play that music? If you guys want to keep doing drawings of me while I'm asleep, then fine by me."

"What should we play?" Michael asked.

"I dunno, something I could dance to."

"Right, that's just what we need is you dancing around while we're trying to draw you."

"You know what I mean; something that won't knock me out. Unless you guys wanna do a reclining pose the whole time." She winked at one of the students as she spoke.

It was that casual attitude that held enough interest for him to draw her. Hailey was always so laid back and cool about everything. If she made eye contact with any of the art students during the modeling session she would always give a friendly smile and nod before refocusing her gaze.

There was one session that he had witnessed, toward the end of the previous semester, when during a long pose, the old chair Hailey was sitting on collapsed as one of the legs broke off. She fell over backwards and landed very awkwardly. Unfazed by it she just got back up and brushed herself off, making a joke about having enjoyed her Thanksgiving holiday a little too much.

"Time," Michael called out as the alarm on his phone went off. "New pose." He handed a wooden staff to Hailey and said, "Let's do a standing one now."

With the staff in hand she set her feet, twisted her torso around and planted one end of the staff behind her.

"Like this?" she asked.

"Right there is fine."

Aside from the music playing from the stereo the room fell silent, as everyone focused intently on sketching out the basic form and pose that Hailey stood in. It resembled a mass meditation; nothing mattered except the artist and the model, the pose and its recreation on paper. Hailey's eyes glazed over a little; she was only dimly aware of the students looking and drawing, of the props around her. She felt herself tilting into the world of daydream.

...

"Hiram, I am tired." Her sensuous Italian voice made a feast of the words. "Can I rest, just a little?"

Hiram looked over at her, irritated. "Not yet. I haven't got everything yet."

Alicia sighed a long, mournful sigh. "You are cruel. I am a model, not a slave. It is the statue who will be a slave."

"But I am the master here. And I am not finished yet."

"Ah, Hiram. Last night, who was the master, hmm?"

Hiram shifted uncomfortably behind his easel. That's what he was really struggling with; to turn the sensuous beauty in front of him into the innocent creature his vision demanded. It was her fault for being so beautiful, and his for being so weak. He hadn't meant for their relationship to get quite so complicated.

"Alicia, be patient with me. When I have finished, I will have transformed you into an icon of purity. People will stare in wonder at you; they will write poems about your beauty."

"Oh, they will stare at me. They will say 'Why is she leaning on the wrong leg?' And they will stare at my hand, and what it covers. Men are all the same, Hiram, my love. You will strive for innocence, and they will perceive desire. You see the beautiful slave, and they will see Venus"

Ah, but that's where you're wrong, my wicked Alicia, he thought. *When I have finished with you, men's thoughts will be ennobled by your very nakedness.* He continued to sketch, dreaming of the finished sculpture, of a higher glory …

…

"Time," Michael's voice broke the trance. "Take a quick five minute break and then we'll set up for the long pose."

Everyone stood up to walk around and stretch their legs. Hailey put her robe back on and casually paced around the room. All the artists slowly circled around the drawing pads, propped on the bench easels, mentally evaluating one another's work.

He paused at the drawing done by a short, light brown-haired girl who was in the same drawing class as him. Her work always impressed him; sometimes to the point of mild jealously. She made it look so easy. The proportions and likeness of the model were always dead on, even in a quick fifteen-minute sketch. He only knew her by her first name, Holly, and by her artwork, which she signed *H.A.C.* Whenever her work was displayed in one of the undergraduate exhibitions; he made it a priority to attend.

"Alright, let's get going." Michael called everyone back to their places.

Hailey disrobed and climbed back onto the modeling platform. She stood beside a wooden barstool and leaned her left hip into it as she twisted her torso and planted her hands on the seat.

"Like this?" she asked Michael. They had obviously discussed the pose during the break.

"Yeah, that's good, but don't lock your knees. Unless you wanna pass out."

"Yeah that's just what we need, another session where I fall on my butt."

This casual rapport was what he felt was lacking in his secret modeling sessions. Although his attractions to his personal models were rooted in much deeper and complicated emotions than he'd ever have with a class model, he still wished there was something more. Perhaps Jessica would be the one; perhaps she had always been the one.

19

CAUSE FOR CREATIVITY
OR DEAL FOR DESIRE

Jessica's mind wandered as she waited for his instructions. She thought of her parents, and if they had interrupted their precious cruise when they had heard; she thought of Shannon, how wracked with guilt she would be when she learned that he had used her to lure Jessica into captivity; most of all, she thought about the sinister little bag, and what could possibly be inside it. He had her sit on the same cube (now draped with a white sheet) she'd modeled on before. She was a bit surprised when he didn't direct her pose but just told her to pick something comfortable.

She sat with both knees bent and her ankles crossed. One knee rested outward horizontally while the other was vertical, forming a ninety-degree angle. She held her bound hands in front of the vertical knee and rested her forehead on top of it. In this pose she felt that she had concealed as much of her body with her limbs as she could without simply curling up into a ball.

They had been silent in the open room for some time, both content to just listen to the music. Jessica listened to the sound of the brush across the paper, surprised to find she was curious about the image he was making. She was beginning to feel almost comfortable here, posing for the masked stranger. If it weren't for that bag, and the chloroform, things wouldn't be so bad. *Jessica, what are you thinking? This guy is a monster. Think what he did to the others.*

She wanted to talk, but couldn't think of anything neutral to say. Finally she said, "Last night, I was awake when … when you …" She trailed off and felt her face burn with some emotion she could not identify. She took a deep breath and continued, "I feel like I'm just some sort of toy for you to play with."

At first he showed no sign of having heard her speak. Then he looked at her for a moment before he resumed painting. "Of course I knew you were awake, Jess. I anesthetized you a second time to rectify my previously rushed attempt."

She didn't want to ask him for anything, any favors, but she couldn't help herself. "The chloroform makes me sick." She continued before she could stop herself. "So, um … please don't use it anymore." She could hear a faint echo of her voice where she rested her forehead on her knee and talked down into her chest.

He paused and looked at her for a moment, considering the potential of what she had said. When she was unconscious she was whoever he wanted her to be, but it never seemed real enough. The idea of her submissive cooperation excited him.

He took a deep breath and replied as calmly as he could. "You do as I say, and I'll consider it."

He stared at the painting without seeing it; his focus was distracted from creativity to desire. He could never simultaneously yearn for her and paint her at the same time. For him, these were conflicting emotions; one could not exist while the other was present. Out here, in his studio, she was model and muse, beauty and form, contour and line. It was only in the corner room he would let himself see her as something else.

Early in his college career he had been in an introductory figure drawing course where one of the students had to be removed from the class. Whether he realized it beforehand or not, this other student was letting his desires control his thoughts during the modeling sessions. The guy would draw furiously, putting excessive energy into every stroke. A lot of the time he was really distracting to anyone seated too close. It seemed as though he was deliberately drawing attention to himself, as if he wanted to be found out.

Standing back to watch as he worked, a few of the students noticed that he only seemed to draw breasts and thighs and then tried to include them in some sort of cursory contour. It was very clear he was not drawing the models, and it was just as clear that his interest was less than artistic. He remembered him with a shudder; that wasn't how it was meant to be. Art and sex were two different things, even if they were both to be found in the same person. He looked back at Jessica; her pose was closed, but somehow erotic. He shook his head; *two different things.*

After he finished the first painting he also drew some close up views, at different angles, of her hands and feet, on the extra space at the margins of the paper. Then he cleaned up. He went and got a rag and the bottle of chloroform and set them both on the table beside him, this time leaving the lid on the bottle. He placed his hand on the bottle and said, "Go lay down on the mattress."

She glanced at the bottle of chloroform beneath his hand and then toward the corner, and her cell. She got up hesitantly and walked over to the room. Her feet dragged on the floor as she walked, and she swayed from side to side; she had become increasingly weak the past few days. She felt so helpless that she didn't dare resist him.

Inside the corner room she knelt by the edge of the bed, listening to make sure he was busy. When she heard him getting something out of the cabinets in the other room, she quickly bowed her head and prayed, the words of scripture echoing in her head: *for behold, blood cometh from every pore.*

He stood on the modeling platform in the large open room with his arms crossed. Looking around the room he counted the number of paintings that hung on the walls. *It's still too soon. There's so much more I can do here.* He went to the counter and picked up a second bag. Placing it beside a similar one that sat on the table he deliberated between the two. *On the other hand, we could always have a little preview.*

As the sound of his footsteps approached Jessica rolled on to the mattress and lay flat on her back, with the bed sheet pulled up to her neck. Taking a few deep breaths, she prepared for what was to come next. He stood in the doorway with a small bag in each hand. Through the frayed eyeholes of the mask she could see his unblinking eyes, points of burning darkness in the harsh light of the room.

"Call it an early night." He reached for the door and closed it behind him. She lay quietly on the mattress, alone in the little room, and listened as he left for the night, turning off the lights outside of the bomb shelter.

20

SWEET HEARTS BAWL

As soon as he got home from school, Thomas rushed into the bathroom to shower and get ready for the dance. Standing in front of the small mirror above the sink he spiked his hair a couple times before he got it right, brushed his teeth twice, trimmed his nose hairs, plucked his eyebrows, shaved, and clipped his fingernails. Everything seemed to take two attempts.

Hanging from the closet door in his bedroom was the tuxedo he had rented the day before. It consisted of a pleated white dress shirt with dark red cufflinks and studs. The pants were black and boasted a silky black stripe. The jacket was also black, with silky lapels, and the vest underneath was black and red; there was a matching bow tie. Black and white shoes with stiff waxy shoelaces gleamed up at him from the floor. He left it as late as possible to put them on; he just knew they were going to be stiff and uncomfortable.

He walked through the living room, waiting for a comment; his father sat mute in the recliner, looking straight past him. In the kitchen, Thomas reached into the fridge and retrieved the red and white corsage he had bought for Jessica. He popped open the corner of the plastic case that held the delicate arrangement and sniffed the crisp, cool roses. *These can't even come close to how lovely she'll smell tonight.* Grabbing the keys off the counter he hustled to the front door, then paused and turned toward his father. "Thanks for letting me borrow your truck."

"Yep, have fun." Mr. King didn't take his eyes off the television.

The screen door clanged shut as Thomas hopped down the plywood steps and opened the truck's passenger door. Gently setting the corsage on the dashboard he put his foot on the floor mat, and was about to climb in, when he noticed the crumbs scattered across the seats. Frustrated at the sight of this new mess he hurried back into the house. With a baleful glance at his father he grabbed the vacuum cleaner and an extension cord.

"Something wrong?"

"Yeah, I washed and cleaned out the truck yesterday so I wouldn't have to do it today; now there's crumbs all over the seat."

"Well, if you've got something better to drive you go right ahead." Mr. King tilted the whiskey bottle to his mouth.

Thomas bit his tongue and went outside to clean up the mess. He made sure to clean the seats and let the rest of the truck slide. Quickly gathering up the extension cord and vacuum cleaner, he placed them right inside the front door, but before he could close it he heard his father's voice. "Hey. Don't leave that there. Put it away where it belongs."

Thomas let out an irritated sigh as he carried the cord and vacuum back to the closet saying, "Give me a break. I'm gonna be late."

"Watch your tone, boy."

Thomas quickly closed the door and whispered, "Whatever, ya drunk jerk."

He scrambled in through the passenger door, closed it behind him, and slid over to the driver's seat. Before starting the engine he took out a CD from inside his vest and placed it in the glove compartment. On the burnt CD were two little hearts drawn with a black Sharpie marker. Clicking the seatbelt into place he turned the ignition, pulled out of the driveway, and headed toward the east end of town.

...

The east side of town was the upper-class part of the city. Rich kids lived around this area. Thomas was unfamiliar with the roads. He wasn't a rich kid, and he didn't know any rich kids: until now. Driving a little over the speed limit as he passed the church, he came to the intersection with deep-set gutters, and nearly scraped the undercarriage of the truck as it jolted up and down.

As he approached the house on the corner he checked the address written on the piece of paper in his hand. He pulled the truck into the driveway and turned off the engine. Before getting out he checked himself in the mirror one more time and reached for the corsage; it had bounced onto the floor when he crossed the intersection by the church. He looked it over; there was no damage. He breathed a sigh of relief.

Getting out the driver's side he made certain not to shut the door tight, so he could get back in later without having to climb over the passenger seat. Taking a few deep breaths he stepped up the front porch and rang the doorbell. As he waited he glanced over at the porch swing to his right. All around the porch railing was a bare vine; in summer it would nearly enclose the porch space with leaves and flowers, making it more secluded. Just the way he liked it.

The door opened and a fair skinned, round-faced man, wearing glasses and a dress shirt with rolled-up sleeves greeted Thomas with a friendly smile, "You must be Tom. Come on in." Mr. Shawsen closed the door behind him and gestured toward the sofa. "Here, have a seat on the couch while you wait. Jessica should be down any minute now, but you know what young ladies are like on a date." He winked at Thomas and left him to wait.

As Mr. Shawsen went upstairs to tell Jessica that her date had arrived, a slender, dark-haired woman came out of an adjoining room.

"Hello," she said. "I'm Jessica's mother." She extended her hand towards Thomas, who quickly stood up from the couch and shook her hand. He noticed that her skin looked far too tan for the middle of February, and was glad that Jessica took after her father in that respect.

"So is that quaint little pick-up truck out there yours?" Mrs. Shawsen's voice held more than a suspicion of distaste.

"That? Oh, no. That's my dad's truck," he cleared his throat. "I don't have a car, yet."

"Oh. I see," Mrs. Shawsen favored him with a tight-lipped grin before going back into the kitchen.

Thomas sat back down, chastened. Holding the corsage in his lap, he nervously bounced his knee while he waited for

Jessica. Looking around the room he saw a shelf in the corner with several pictures of a dark-haired little girl. Next to some of them were trophies and certificates. One that caught his eye in particular was of little Jessica proudly holding up a violin and bow, displaying a huge smile fenced with silver. He had forgotten that she used to have braces when they were in junior high.

The stairs creaked, and Thomas turned toward the sound. Jessica came slowly and gracefully down the staircase, in black strappy heels, taking one step at a time. She wore a silky red dress with slim straps over the shoulder. It followed her form from her chest to her hips and then cascaded outward, billowing and floating with each step. Her hair was drawn up and back, curling strands dangling behind her head, lightly brushing her neck.

Thomas, suddenly aware that his mouth was open, clapped it shut, swallowed hard, and stood up holding the corsage in front of him. Extending the small flowers toward her, he said, "Wow. You … you look really beautiful." He felt his face redden, and cursed himself for stammering.

"Thanks," she replied, her blush matching his.

"This is for you," he said, presenting the small bundle of red and white flowers.

Jessica extended her wrist, palm down, toward him as he removed the corsage from the plastic case. Lightly holding her forearm, he gently slipped the lacy wristband over her hand and into place.

Her mother came around the corner with a small white rose in her hand and gave it to Jessica. She took the pin from the wrapped stem and stuck it through Thomas' jacket lapel.

"Alright you two, have fun," said Mr. Shawsen. "Don't stay out too late. Try to be back before eleven."

"Bye, sweetheart. Have fun at the ball." Mrs. Shawsen waved to the young couple in the driveway. *She's weird,* Thomas thought.

Thomas opened the passenger door for Jessica and held her hand as she stepped in. The weak, rusty old shocks let out a faint creak as she sat down. He went around to the driver's side and opened the door that he had left unlatched and hopped in, the shocks groaning under the weight of two people. Once both their seatbelts were on they pulled out of the driveway and made their way into town.

The first half of the drive took place in an awkward silence. Neither one of them could think of something to begin a conversation with; finally Thomas turned on the radio and asked, "What kind of music do you like?" He pushed a few preset buttons. "There's rock, pop, country, oldies, classic …"

"Oldies are good," she answered before he pressed the next button.

"So, do you know where we're going?" Thomas couldn't hide the excitement in his voice.

"Somewhere where there's food, I hope, right?" She grinned nervously back at him.

"Yep." He waited until she looked over before saying, "Carlisle's. You ever been there?"

"Nope. I haven't. Where is it?"

"It's the new steak and seafood place up at the north end of town. It's supposed to be really nice."

"Oh okay. I remember hearing about a new restaurant opening at that end of town. Too bad it's another steak and seafood place. There's already tons of 'em around the valley."

"Oh, do … don't you want to go there? We can go somewhere else if you want."

"Oh, no. No, its fine," she reassured him. "I like steak and seafood. I'm just saying that we have a lot of restaurants like that around here." She stared out the passenger window, mildly embarrassed.

Carlisle's restaurant resembled an oversized winter lodge. Given the town's location in Colorado it seemed quite fitting, if a little tacky. Thomas pulled the truck into the parking lot and killed the engine.

Thomas walked close beside Jessica, trying to casually brush hands to see if she would let him hold hers. But she kept her hands together in front of her as they walked through the cool evening air up to the entrance doors. He lightly touched her shoulder, indicating for her to stop. Stepping in front of her, he opened the door to let her in. She stepped through the first set of log doors then paused in front of the second set and looked back at Thomas with a grin. He hurried to the next door and opened it chuckling.

In the center of the foyer was a large fireplace with a warm gas-burning log aglow in the heart of it. All the waiting seats were full of other high school students, all dressed up for their dates. The girls wore a variety of dresses. The guys all seemed to just be wearing dress shirts with ties and slacks.

Though he stood out a little from the rest, Thomas didn't mind being overdressed for his date with Jessica.

The host, standing at the front desk, beside a baby grand piano, approached the newest couple to enter the restaurant and said, "Good evening. How many are in your party tonight?"

"Just the two of us," Thomas said. "And I have a reservation under 'King' for a booth near the fireplace."

"Let me see," the host scanned over the list of names that sat on the front desk. "Ah, yes. Here we are. Right this way."

They walked passed all the others who sat waiting, catching a few envious looks from couples who seemed to have been waiting for some time. The host led them around the corner into a big, spacious room with a large double-sided fireplace in the center of it. Stopping them near a booth two tables from the fireplace he gestured with his hand.

"Here we are. This is the closest booth to the fireplace. Will this be alright?"

"Yes, it's …" Thomas started.

"It's perfect. Thank you," Jessica finished.

"Very well, your server will be right with you." The host left a pair of menus and returned to the foyer.

Jessica and Thomas looked over their menus. They glanced at each other and exchanged nervous smiles. After pretending to survey the menu for the third time Thomas finally asked, "So what would you like to order?"

"I don't know. It all looks so good."

"Well, you can get whatever you want."

"Really?" she grinned. "How about the full lobster with filet mignon?"

"Where is *that?*"

"Down in the bottom corner of the menu," she flipped her menu around while pointing to the special entrée. "The one that says *'ask your server for pricing'.*" She cracked a smile across the table.

Thomas was relieved to see she was only kidding. "Well, anything but *that.*"

Through the rest of the meal they did very little talking. Among their school friends they had been able to speak more casually, but now that it was just the two of them they were having a hard time coming up with any kind of a conversation.

Jessica glanced around the room once in a while, to see if any of her friends and their dates were there as well. When she didn't spot anyone she knew, she returned her gaze to the food in front of her.

Wishing he had his sketchbook with him, Thomas glanced at Jessica whenever he thought she wasn't looking. Her shy, virtuous posture held a beauty he could find no words for; his hands ached for a pencil so he could strive to recreate the angel before him. *She's like a Vermeer portrait; cool, pale and lustrous.*

Jessica had ordered a seafood Alfredo pasta with a Caesar salad and Thomas had a tender loin steak with a baked potato and a cup of soup. The two of them shared a slice of chocolate decadence cake for dessert. After Thomas paid for the meal they made their way out through the parking lot and when they came to the truck Thomas stopped and explained, "So here's the thing. The driver's door won't open from the outside. So I have to climb in first before you can get in." he shrugged his embarrassment. "Otherwise I would totally open the door for you."

"Oh, that's okay; go ahead."

He unlocked the passenger door and slid over to the driver's seat, then held out his hand to help her in.

When they arrived at the main entrance to the school there were pink, red, and white balloons everywhere. Inside, the hall was packed with over-dressed classmates. Some were done up so much they were hardly recognizable. Amidst the chatter of excited voices they could hear the faint thud of a subwoofer down one of the hallways. To their left was the line to get pictures taken and to the right were a series of signs showing where the dance room was located.

"Do you want to get pictures first?" Thomas tried not to sound too eager.

"Sure," Jessica replied as she searched the room for Shannon or any of her other friends.

Thomas didn't like having his picture taken, but this was different. Once he and Jessica were framed in the same shot they wouldn't be two nervous individuals trapped in a school dance together; they'd be a couple. It would be a record of destiny.

Once it was their turn the photographer had Jessica and Thomas stand in front of a backdrop of grey cobblestones with a fake marble column prop.

"Okay Miss, can I get you to stand by the column right here and then you, sir, stand behind her." The photographer gestured with his hands while he spoke. "No, no. Not that far. Stand a little more to her left. Right there. Good. Now place your right hand on her right hip."

Thomas felt his hands go moist and his throat go dry as he placed his hand over her hip bone.

"Now with your left hand," the photographer continued, "Reach around and place it on her stomach. Then you Miss, put both your hands on top of his."

Thomas reached around and pressed his hand against her. She placed her hands over his and pulled it up a little higher. When he felt his thumb come to a stop on Jessica's belly button he realized he'd placed his hand a little too far south for decency.

The photographer took the picture and said, "Alright good. Okay one more. Something fun. Something spontaneous."

Thomas and Jessica paused, glanced at each other and back at the camera, shrugging their shoulders, unsure what to do. So to help move things along the photographer suggested, "Well let's see, you could jump or pretend to run away or pick her up or you could …"

Seizing the moment, Thomas slipped his arm behind her back and lifted her up off the floor. Awkwardly laughing from being caught off guard and slightly embarrassed, Jessica struggled to regain her composure for the picture.

"Alright, now *that's* what I'm talking about. One, two, three," he snapped the picture and the surrounding lights flashed.

"Very good, you two. You make a cute couple. Have fun!"

"You can put me down now." Jessica felt light headed after her brief flight.

Thomas set her down reluctantly, his face still glowing from the excitement of holding her in his arms. Her face was flushed too, but more out of awkwardness than anything else.

Following the signs, they were led down to the cafeteria, where a steady bass pounded and a sea of students jumped around in clumsy attempts at dancing. They found a place among the other couples and Jessica started dancing casually beside Thomas, who shuffled back and forth while swaying his arms. This was really not his thing.

It seemed like an hour before a slow song finally started to play. Thomas breathed a sigh of relief. Finally something he could actually do. He took Jessica's hand in his and placed the other on her back. She politely grabbed his hand and moved it a little higher up her back.

Thomas flashed her a nervous grin and said, loud enough to be heard over the music, "Sorry. I guess you're taller than I realized."

"It's the heels." She gestured towards her feet.

After an awkward period dancing to a couple slow songs and ignoring Thomas' inept shuffling to the faster pop songs, Jessica saw Shannon at the other end of the dance floor and waved. She stopped dancing and leaned closer to Thomas' ear, saying, "I'm gonna go talk to my friends for a minute. I'll be right back." She held up the edge of her dress as she scurried over to her friends.

"Okay," Thomas called out across the crowd.

...

A swish of silk and a flash of red floating by caught Liam's eye. He turned and watched as Jessica came to a stop around a small group of her friends. He stared at her slender frame, enveloped in the rich silky red fabric, with her perfectly defined bare collarbones and shoulders. *Too bad she didn't model in that.* His eyes swept over her, measuring and framing, then he turned away, apparently satisfied.

...

Thomas found a free seat, not too far away, and waited for Jessica to come back. As he listened to the pop tunes blasting out he thought how glad he was to be taking a break and not having to pretend he liked to dance. All he wanted to do was to hold her in his arms and gently move while some slow romantic music played.

Finally, after what seemed like hours of waiting, a slow song began to play. Thomas hopped up and looked around the room for Jessica. She wasn't in the corner where he had seen her earlier. He hurried around the edge of the dance floor, trying to see where she was, until he noticed that some students had opened the back doors of the cafeteria and were dancing out on the patio. As he stepped out the door he saw Jessica talking with Shannon and her date.

"... so you just let us know," Shannon reassured Jessica.

"Yeah," Jessica replied, a frown of worry on her face. "I'll make sure to ... wait, here he comes."

Thomas jogged over to the small group and said, "Hey Jessie, you up for more dancing?"

"Um, sure," she replied as Thomas took her hand. She glanced back, biting her lip, and waved bye to Shannon with her fingers.

"Hey, you guys can dance with us," Shannon suggested.

"That's alright. Thanks anyway." Thomas led Jessica away from the crowd.

"We'll be over here Jess, if you change your mind." Shannon's voice had an odd tone to it.

Near a small outcropping at the edge of the patio, Thomas stopped and switched their hands, placing his other on her back; a little higher than necessary, just to be sure. They danced slowly beside the three tan brick arches that supported the south side of the classroom above the patio.

After a couple false starts, Thomas finally spoke, "If the music was louder I'd take you over to the bridge to dance."

"No, that's okay."

"It's much nicer out here. It was a good idea coming out. It was getting too hot inside."

"Yeah," she answered absently.

He looked into her eyes and waited until she looked back before saying, "You really look very pretty tonight."

"Thanks," she smiled and looked bashfully towards the ground.

The music stopped and for an awkward moment they just stood there. Thomas still held her as they waited to hear the next song. When a thumping bass started up they let go of each other and Jessica said, "Hey, can you get me a drink?"

"Oh, yeah sure. I'll be right back."

"Thanks. I'll just be over talking with my friends."

...

Liam weaved around a few students to get a clear view of Jessica. She was leaning forward on the railing underneath three arches as she stared down at the football field. The upper part of her bare back flexed and relaxed as she adjusted her arms on the railing. *I love the definition in your back, Jessica; it would have been great to paint. Sooner or later.* Just as he was about to go back inside, she turned around and saw him. He gave her a friendly nod and a confident grin. She replied with a shy little wave as she hurried over to her friends.

...

Inside the dance room cafeteria, Thomas felt the obvious temperature difference from outside. The heat wave of adolescent bodies dancing in a confined space was enough to make him recoil.

On a linen-covered table, in front of where the fountain drinks machines were located, sat a few jugs of water with some slices of lemon floating in them. These particular jugs had lids that locked on top. No doubt the school board's response to the spiked drinks from last Homecoming.

There was a short line of people waiting for drinks. Thomas didn't mind the wait; at least it meant he didn't have to try and dance to the fast stuff. Just as he filled the two cups with water an announcement came over the microphone, "This next song will be the last one, so all you cute couples hold your sweetheart tight."

Thomas hurried back outside to find Jessica. She was still talking with her friends and had her back to the patio doors. Walking over he nudged Jessica's shoulder with her drink and asked, "May I have this dance?" bowing slightly as he spoke.

"Oh good. Thank you." Jessica took the drink from his hand. "Just let me finish my drink real quick." She turned back towards her friends as she drank the water.

The song was halfway over when she turned back and handed Thomas her empty cup. Placing his cup inside hers, he quickly set them both on the ground.

"Aren't you going to throw those away first?"

"I'll get them when the dance is over. Here ..." He reached out to her. She took his hand and they walked over to their previous spot by the three arches, and danced until the DJ announced the end of the dance. When the music stopped, Thomas pulled her closer and squeezed her, an awkward hug. He let go with a smile and went over to the cups he had set down and took them to the trash.

When he got back to Jessica she was in a huddle with her friends again. He stood quietly beside her until there was a break in the conversation, and then asked, "You ready to go Jess?"

"Yeah, sure." She started walking with Thomas toward the bridge and turned back to her friends and said, "See you guys."

"Bye, Jessie. See ya later." Her friends waved and smiled.

"Call me when you get home, okay?" Shannon called out.

Thomas deliberately slowed his pace as they walked past the bridge where he had first asked her out, hoping it was as symbolic for her as it was for him. He picked up the pace as they headed toward the parking lot on the west side of the school where the truck was parked. When they got to the truck, Thomas put his hand on her shoulder and said, "Hold on a second." Climbing in the passenger door he slid over to the driver's side, opened the door then got back out of the truck and came around to the passenger side, where he held the door open for her.

She shook her head with an awkward grin and said, "Thanks."

...

They listened to the music that played on the radio during the drive back towards Jessica's house; there was an air of contentment between them, things had passed off okay. As they got onto the road that would lead up to the foothills where she lived, Thomas turned the radio volume down and asked, "Did you have a good time?"

"Uh yeah, yeah tonight was fun."

"Well, it's not over yet," Thomas said with an excited smile as he flipped the signal lever and turned left just before the road that would have curved up to the foothills.

"What, what do you mean? Where are we going?"

"It's a surprise."

"I should really head home. I don't want to get in trouble for being late."

"No, don't worry about it. It'll just take a few minutes."

"Well, what is it?"

"You'll have to wait and see," he said. His eyes sparkled with an expression Jessica hadn't seen before.

Thomas had turned the radio off and they drove in silence for a few minutes. He was thinking about the surprise he had planned. Jessica sat wondering where they were going and worrying that she might get home later than her parents had said. If she was honest, that wasn't all she was worrying about.

Going around a sharp turn, Jessica felt something hard tap her foot down on the floor. She reached down to feel what it was. Leaning forward to see in the low light she realized it was an empty whiskey bottle. She pushed it back under the seat and quickly sat back up.

"Something wrong?" he asked.

"No, ah it's just … the strap on my shoe was loose, is all," Jessica replied as she glanced out the windows to try to get an idea where they were going. She noticed that they were heading toward the canyon entrance. With a little concern in her voice she asked, "Can I have a hint what the surprise is?"

"A hint … well," he held out from responding until they had gotten a little bit closer, and then said, "It's right here."

He turned the steering wheel to the right and brought the truck to a stop. They were in a small parking area near a little park, beside a large pond, just before the canyon entrance. He turned off the engine and switched the ignition over so that only the radio was on. When Thomas reached over to the glove box, Jessica flinched and closed her knees together. As the compartment door dropped open, he said, "Excuse me. This truck's a little cramped."

He put the disc with the two hearts drawn on it into the CD player and turned up the volume a little, too loud for anyone sitting inside the cab. Then he stepped out of the truck, making sure the door didn't latch, and coming around to the passenger side, he opened Jessica's door. Extending his hand to her he asked, "May I have this dance?"

Jessica didn't say anything. She slowly got out of the truck and, with a nervous look on her face, took Thomas' hand.

They slowly danced in the little area beside the empty park, to the romantic music playing from the stereo inside the cab. There was nobody else around. The only light came from the full moon, high in the night sky. It flickered over the rippling water in the pond and Thomas noticed it subtly shimmering off Jessica's hair, cheeks, and shoulders.

When the second song started to play he let go of her hand, wrapped his arms around her and pulled her closer, still keeping rhythm with the music. She leaned her face down on to his shoulder. Noticing that she was shaking and hearing her sniffle a couple times, he whispered into her ear, "What's wrong?"

She took a shallow breath and said, "I'm … I'm just a little cold … is all."

Thomas took off his jacket and wrapped it over her shoulders. He pulled her close to him and they started to dance again.

She continued to shake a little, so he rubbed her arms up and down to kill the goose bumps. She sniffled, and a sound like a gentle sob escaped her. In a shaking voice she asked, "Can we go now?"

Thomas stopped dancing and lifted her head. With a trembling hand he lightly touched her face and kissed her on the forehead. She closed her eyes as he touched her cheek and a couple tears trickled down her face. When he stepped back he looked in her eyes and said, "Happy Valentine's Day, Jessica." His voice nearly failed him, and he felt a lump in his throat.

Jessica replied in a whisper. "Thanks."

She walked slowly back over to the truck and got in. Thomas came around the other side, climbed in and started the engine back up.

...

As they drove, the CD Thomas had made continued to play the slow romantic songs he'd burned for him and Jessica to dance to. He turned the heater up for Jessica, who was huddled on the other side of the cab, still wearing his jacket. She leaned against her door and sniffled a few more times.

When they passed the church just before her house, Jessica sat up, wiping her eyes and nose. She folded down the passenger visor and checked her makeup. Quickly taking off the jacket, she handed it to Thomas as they pulled into the driveway. When her hand found the lever and she pulled the door open, Thomas said, "Goodnight Jessie."

"Goodnight." Her voice was hardly more than a whisper.

She shut the truck door and hurried up to the front porch of her home and went inside.

Thomas drove home the long way. He looked out at the world around him, bathed in moonlight. He felt like he would never be able to get to sleep; his heart was still pounding.

Although it didn't go exactly as he had imagined he was still very happy. Their dance in the moonlit park replayed in his mind over and over again. He wished he had kissed her lips instead of her forehead; that was the only thing he wanted to be different. The fact that she seemed to be so moved by the romantic gesture that she cried a little bit made Thomas feel that he'd done something really special for her; something that no meat-head jock would ever think of. He couldn't wait to see her again; next week couldn't come soon enough.

21

A Light in the Hall

Thomas stood silently in the art department hallway, staring at the paintings that had recently been hung up in the glass display cases. The anonymous critique hadn't been especially enjoyable for Thomas, but he felt better knowing that the attention was only being put on the artwork and not so much on the artist, not directly anyhow. Along with a few of his own paintings there were a couple students from his class as well as other classes. A few panels down from his own work he was looking over the paintings he was certain were done by Liam.

He had rarely seen Liam's work since high school and was certain that if he did look at them for too long in Liam's presence he'd be sure to provoke a mind-numbing speech about the greatness of each piece. Actually Thomas had always admired the way Liam handled paint and what he was able to do with it. But Liam's new paintings caused Thomas to rethink his initial admiration, one way and another.

As he moved down to the next student's work he heard light footsteps padding down the hall, and out of the corner of his eyes he noticed someone stop in front of the red-tinted paintings. He angled his back toward the person but kept his ear tilted that way, waiting for the inevitable sound of disgust that most people made when they read what the blood works were made from.

Instead he heard a familiar voice call out. "Mister moo, Tom is that you?"

He turned around and saw Cindy Miller staring back at him with a huge grin on her face. They walked toward each other. Cindy flung her arms out wide and wrapped them around Thomas in a big hug.

"How have you been? I haven't seen you since … well, in a long time." She avoided mentioning their high-school days; she carried her own personal pains from those days, and she was sure Thomas felt the same. But it was good to see him, after all that time; Cindy realized with a start that her heart was beating fast. Maybe. Maybe this time.

"I've been alright. Just painting, going to school and working. You?"

"I just transferred here this semester. I had no idea you were here too." She took hold of his arm and pulled him over toward the paintings in the display case. "Look all the awesome talent in this place. Which ones are yours?"

"I'm not allowed to say just yet. The Advanced class is keeping the works anonymous for the first few weeks."

"*Advanced* huh? Sounds pretty spiffy." She hopped back over to the display case. "Check these out. Says here that these are done with pig's blood." Cindy paused as she looked more closely at the earthy red paintings.

"Oh my gosh. Tom, is that Jessica?"

An uncomfortable look came over his face and he glanced away.

"That *is* her. I saw the other two models and didn't recognize them and I figured this wasn't anyone I knew either but ... Wow! You okay with it? I mean I know how upset you were when that other guy did oil portraits of her."

"Um yeah, no that's just ..." he shook his head and dismissed the question. "She's a good model. It's fitting that she gets painted, don't you think?"

"Really? Huh, I never thought someone like her would model nude. I mean, her being so *molly* and all. And it's not like her family is short of money. Very strange."

Thomas didn't know what to say, so he said nothing.

"Well I guess if she felt okay about doing it, then I feel okay about it too." Cindy smiled and shrugged.

"Yeah," Thomas replied quietly, looking at the floor.

An excited expression lit up Cindy's face as she said, "Can you imagine how cool it would be if Jessica donated some of her own blood for the paintings? Talk about making a portrait of someone. It would be like the one of Dorian Grey. You know?"

"Yeah, well I know what you mean, but it would actually be the opposite; in the story his portrait aged in his place. But yeah, still a cool concept."

"You should ask her to model for you," Cindy regretted saying it the moment it came out.

"Nah, I don't know ... after ... after what happened ... I ..."

"Maybe she's gotten over it. No harm in asking, right?"

"Depends on what you're asking for."

"Well, if you are ever stuck for a model" Cindy shyly glanced down at the floor. "I guess I could model for you."

"What, like nude?" Thomas nodded toward the paintings in the display case. "Or covered or something." He looked as foolish as he felt.

"Uh, I don't know, we'll see." Cindy glanced up at the clock on the wall. In need of something to break the silence she said, "Well, cool, cool. If you decide you need a new model to paint, let me know." She began walking away toward the stairs. Thomas called out after her, "How about next week? Maybe in the evening sometime?"

"Okay, yeah. Just let me know. I gotta get to class. See ya later."

"See ya."

22

TWITTERPATED

Thomas floated through Monday; he was still in a dream; everything had gone so well. He couldn't wait for Biology class; he wanted to ask Jessica how she felt, about the dance, about their private moonlit dance afterwards, about him.

But when all the students in Mr. Wright's class were finally seated, Jessica was nowhere to be seen.

When class got out Thomas asked Jake, "Have you seen Jessica at all today?"

"Nope," Jake replied. "Oh hey, how'd the dance go? Did you get some?"

"No, we mostly just danced, but I did kiss her forehead and I ..."

"That's it?" Jake interrupted. "Ha! Whatever, I gotta go. See ya later."

"Oh, hey wait," Thomas stopped Jake. "Check this out." He reached into his back pack and pulled out a ceramic sphere with a little cup at the top, and three short cylinders that stuck out the sides.

"What is it?" Jake asked.

In a low whisper Thomas replied, "It's a bong. I made it in Ceramics. They were fired over the weekend and I just picked it up this morning."

"Does it work?"

"It should. You see the bowl on top? Well the hole in it extends down a hollow cylinder almost to the bottom. You fill the sphere half way full with water. Then see these three parts that stick out near the top? You put a straw or small tube over them to smoke it through."

Thomas had researched the terms *bong* and *water pipe* to get an understanding as to how one was meant to work. He knew now that it was normally used to smoke marijuana with; but he wanted to give his friends the benefit of the doubt and believe that they really were only smoking that herbal clove stuff Rob had mentioned.

"Awesome!" Jake said as he took the ceramic sphere out of Thomas' hand. "We'll let you know if it works. Later."

"Um, okay, later."

Thomas watched as Jake walked away with the bong he'd made, feeling a little confused. He'd just done something good for his friends, hadn't he? He knew their pipes weren't very good and wouldn't last very long. He wondered when they would share that portion of the clove stuff, or whatever it was, that he'd helped pay for. He sighed; maybe he just didn't fit in, anywhere.

He cheered himself up by thinking of Jessica in her beautiful red silk dress, her hair teasing her neck, the scent of peaches. He couldn't wait to get the pictures from the dance and see how the two of them looked together; especially the one where he had picked her up. His heart had wings; he just wanted to know, had to know, if she felt the same.

...

During his painting class, Thomas sat beside Cindy and told her all about the dance.

"Oh, you sound so cute, together." Cindy smiled dreamily at him.

"Yeah? You think?" Thomas asked. Could he tell Cindy? Why not? "I even wrote a poem about it, over the weekend.

"Oh can I read it? Pleeeeze!"

He hesitated at first and then gave in.

"I guess."

Reaching into his backpack he pulled out a small notebook and turned to the back pages where the poem was written. Before handing it to her he added, "I'm not very good at writing. So it's nothing like super awesome or anything. And the language is kind of, kind of old-fashioned"

He handed it to Cindy. She fell silent as she read the poem.

Upon that night, a moment not too soon;
The end of an evening beyond compare;
Where thou and I danced underneath the moon;
To thee I say the feeling 'tis still there.
A sweet melody doth make the mood strong.
To season the moment canyon wind blows;
Embracing thee; the feeling can't be wrong.
Destine to be with thee? God only knows.
While held in mine arms I feel thee quiver;
A chilling wind blows, I wish this to lack;
Mine jacket to thee, yet still thou shiver.
By affections hand I comfort thy back.
Thou beginst to cry, worry not mine ears,
For she weeps not sorrows; she weeps love's tears.

Cindy looked up at him, eyes blurred with tears. "Aw, you are so sweet. That's so romantic."

"Thanks. I used the iambic pentameter rhythm that I learned about in my Shakespeare class."

"Are you going to give this to her?"

"Yeah, I wanted to give it to her today, but I haven't seen her at school."

"Well, you could write another one while you wait," she said with a tearful grin.

"I actually have started another one."

"Oh can I read it?" Cindy held her hand out to have the notebook back.

"No, no it's not finished yet. But maybe tomorrow I'll let you read it."

"Deal."

They both went to work on their drawing assignments. They were both thinking about the poem, and Thomas and Jessica's love story. Thomas thought about the possibilities that lay ahead. Cindy did her best to enjoy the vicarious romance, the obvious joy of her close friend. Maybe, one day; just maybe.

23

POWER REASSURING WOLVES

That Friday evening as Jessica was lying on the mattress resting, she heard a loud slam in the outer room, followed by a series of things being moved around in a deliberate attempt to make noise. The door opened and he came inside with the usual zip ties in his hands.

"Come here." She walked up to him, still holding onto the sheet. He snapped his fingers and pointed for her to leave it on the mattress. She grudgingly did so before he said, "Turn around." Something had set him in a foul mood and she thought it best to just do as he said without questioning him.

He held her wrists together as he bound them behind her back. Grabbing her arm, he directed her forward out the metal door and into the open room. "Just go sit down on the platform."

Jessica sat down on the white drapery that had been laid out on the platform, with her knees bent and feet pointed to the sides. She used her hands behind her back to support herself. After some time of watching him aggressively sketch out a drawing on a piece of paper, only to tear it off, throw it aside, and start on another one; she dryly asked, "Is something wrong with the pose?"

In his same angry tone he replied, "No."

"Did I do something?"

"Not yet."

After tearing off a few more pieces of paper he finally calmed down enough to start an acceptable sketch.

"Raise your right knee up, and hold it there."

"You got a good enough view there?" She was surprised how catty she sounded.

"It's not about the view." He took a deep breath to re-focus. "It's about the composition."

"Sure it is," she said in a hushed voice, but still loud enough for him to hear. She sighed. To think, back in high school, she'd thought posing would make her into the Mona Lisa. Now, she felt more like the figures in Egon Schiele's paintings, or Lucian Freud's: victims, painted the color of cadavers.

Over the few previous days Jessica's anxiety had been gnawing at her increasingly. Of course she was worried about what he might be doing to her or what she imagined he was doing to her, but what really bugged her was the thought that she was becoming accustomed to it. This whole mad situation was beginning to feel routine.

"I want you to stop using me," she said timidly.

He stopped painting and leaned against the easel to look at her more directly, "What, as a model? As a paint supply? Or what?" He shrugged.

"For sex. I want you to stop."

"Ha!" he blurted out. "So we're back to this little fantasy again." He stepped away from the painting and looked down at her. "You always were quick to jump to conclusions."

She was taken aback by the bluntness of his comment, but more so at the germ of truth she felt resonated within it.

"I just … I want you to stop raping me, please."

"Really?" His shoulders tensed and his face turned toward her. "Is that what you think?"

He stood up and kicked his chair over onto its side. "You have no idea what rape is." He stepped onto the platform; glowering down at her he continued, "Rachel … she knew once or twice, and Stacey, well, she was a fast learner, but you? I have never touched you."

She struggled to swallow before saying, "But, you … each night when I was unconscious … and the bags…"

"You really are a stupid, naïve little girl, aren't you, Jess? A dumb little Mormon bunny; you think you wouldn't know?" His voice rose with each word. "And you're an ungrateful bitch. I am the only thing keeping you alive."

"Yes, and I appreciate that, but it's still …"

"Do you have any shred of comprehension of what it means to be *beaten* to the point you couldn't even crawl away if you wanted to? To actually be forced into sex?"

"But …"

"You have never even been touched. Not just by me, you have no idea."

Fed up with being interrupted she shouted in a quacking voice, "Without my consent, it's rape!" She shuddered as he towered over her. His eyes were livid; they threatened to erupt out of the wrapped mask. Suddenly he grabbed her behind the neck and stood her up onto her feet.

"You think so, huh?" he hissed. "Fine. I'll show you, right now."

He shoved her over onto the nearby metal cart and bent her over the top of it. Reaching for a bungee cord that hung on the wall he laid it behind her neck and fastened it to the base of the cart. Then kicking her feet apart he fastened her ankles to opposite sides of the cart.

Stepping in front of her, he slammed his hands down on both sides of the cart's surface, making her jolt and scream at the sudden nearby force. She desperately tried to cover her backside with her bound hands.

He hurried over to the drawers then came back and slammed a couple different objects onto the cart beside her. Darting from one corner of the room to the other he came back with some other objects and slammed them down on the cart.

"How about this? Think it'll fit?" he grabbed a few items off a shelf and threw them on the floor around her. "How many of these do you think I can cram in there!? Why not get a few more guys down here and form a line."

Jessica desperately tried to wriggle the cart away from the growing terror behind her. She was certain he was going to violate her with any object he could find. In her attempt to get away the cart tipped over and her face landed with a smack against the concrete floor. With her face against the floor and her backside vulnerably raised in the air, she sobbed uncontrollably for fear of what she was sure would follow.

He stormed toward her, turned away, and then indecisively turned back and away again. Finally he stomped over to the other side of the room, grabbed something, and marched toward the bomb shelter. She didn't see where he was and she couldn't hear anything over the sound of her own sobs. Exhausted from weeping for what felt like an hour, Jessica slowly subsided to a quiet animal whimper.

Just when she had felt like she could breathe again, he came out of the corner room and walked over to her. She let out a shriek as he grabbed hold of her hips. From somewhere far away she heard her own voice pleading, "No please, oh please don't … don't please!"

Gripping her hips he lifted her and tipped the cart back upright. A sudden smack of paper against her face made her wince and turn her head away.

"Look at it!"

Jessica slowly opened her eyes to see pen and pencil sketches of a partially draped reclining figure.

"Last night," he flipped the pages back. "The night before," he flipped back the pages again, "and the night before that." Each page showed a different view of Jessica reclined on the mattress unconscious, appearing to be sleeping.

"But … the bag?"

"This bag?" he said as he unzipped and threw the canvas bag onto the floor. Inside she saw various pencils and pens with a few other drawing supplies.

"I do have another bag," he said menacingly, "and that bag has something completely different in it."

Then he removed the bungee cord from the back of her neck and cut the ties that bound her ankles and wrists. She collapsed onto her knees and wrapped her arms around herself in a futile attempt to stem the shivering that wracked her body.

"Get on the platform," he said in a flat stern voice.

She quickly scrambled across the floor on her hands and knees until she was on the platform.

"Now lie down," he said as he gathered some of the scattered objects off the floor and placed them back atop the upright cart.

She dropped onto her side and curled up into a fetal position.

He stood over her for a moment, looking down at her; her disheveled figure quaking on the floor below him. He went to his easel, repositioned it and the chair he'd knocked over, and sat down. Jessica cautiously glanced up to see what was happening when he snapped at her.

"Don't move!"

She quickly put her head back down and stayed there, holding herself in a fetal position. He painted for some time, going slower than he normally did. Then finally, when he had finished, he stood up and in a calmer voice said, "Get up and get in there," pointing to the corner room.

Jessica stood up to go, but fell back on to the floor, weak and light headed. She crawled over to the corner room, through the metal door, and up onto the bed. She pulled the sheet over her and lay flat on her back.

He stood in the doorway with the drawing bag in one hand and the other bag in the other and looked down at her. She met his gaze for a second and quickly closed her eyes and turned her head away. The metal door slammed shut. She opened her eyes and saw that he had placed a small fold out stool at the side of the bed. Sitting down he leaned closer to her and in a whisper said, "Let me show you what I have in the other bag."

He grabbed her wrist; instinctively she tried to break free of his grip, but it was no use. Her strength was spent and her whole body shook from its prior exhaustion. From the bag he pulled out a set of Velcro restraints; he used them to bind her hands together and attached the Velcro tie to the ring under the head of the bed. With the other restraints he tied her legs to opposite sides at the foot of the bed.

He took the bed sheet and spread it out over her quaking form. Very intricately, he tucked the drapery around her, molding it to every curve and crevasse, except for her bound, bare limbs.

Jessica felt numb. She knew she was crying only because she could feel the wet course of tears down her cheeks. She stared up at the ceiling, only watching him through her peripheral line of sight.

"You see Jessie," he began as he reached into his pocket and pulled out a stainless steel Spyderco Harpy knife with a blade like a hawk bill. He ran the dull backside of the blade across her cheek. The touch of the cold steel on her skin seemed to freeze the salt in her tears. "When you cry wolf too often and no wolves turn up ..." He placed the tip of the blade to the mouth of his mask and cut a small slit in it. Then he delicately cut away a square of the material, exposing his bare mouth, twisted into a predatory smile. His voice was little more than a sibilant hiss. "Guess what, Jess? Here come the wolves."

24

From one Storm to Another

"Well, I never want to see another tropical storm, least-ways not from a boat. Who'd have thought you could get such terrible weather in such a beautiful place? I thought we were going to end up on a raft, like the wreck of the Medusa. Hey, come on, it wasn't such a bad joke. Carol? What's up?"

Blaine looked at his wife, slumped in front of the PC, her shoulders heaving. She didn't answer, and he could hear her quiet sobbing. "Carol, honey, what's wrong?"

"I got an email from Jessie."

"Great, what does she say? How's it going with the musician guy? She hasn't answered any of my emails."

"She says she's …" Carol tried to stifle her sobs, and failed. "She says she's dropping out of college and going to live with him in some kind of commune. She's going to work as an artist's model. Nude modeling. And she says," Carol's sobs rose to a pained crescendo. "She says she doesn't ever want to see me again."

Blaine crossed the room and laid his hands on his wife's shoulders while he read the email. His heart lurched as he confirmed what Carol had said. How could his baby do this to them? He reached into his pocket for his phone and dialed Jessica's number. *Hi, this is Jessie Shawsen. Leave me a message and I'll call you right back.*

"Jessie, it's dad. I need for you to call me, sweetheart. I'm real worried, and I want to hear that you're okay. Call me as soon as you get this. I love you. Bye." He redialed as soon as he'd finished, got the same voicemail.

Blaine paced around the den. He couldn't make sense of it at all. Carol had gotten a couple emails from Jessie, cheerful messages about the new guy. Nothing to indicate she was about to drop out. A sinister intuition nagged at him. *This isn't right. This isn't Jessie.* But he couldn't figure out what to do. Maybe he should head up to her college and make a few enquiries? But first he needed to help Carol. He gently brought her to her feet, wrapped her in his arms, and waited for the sobbing to subside a little.

"Honey, there's nothing we can do right this minute. Why don't you go lie down and rest for a while? I'll get on the phone and see what I can find out. You need to rest, honey, you look all worn out."

He led her to the stairs, and pushed her gently away. "Go on honey. You know it'll make you feel better."

"Okay, you're right. I ..." Carol didn't trust herself to say any more. She trudged wearily up the stairs. At the turn of the stairs she looked at her bedroom door, turned instead to Jessie's. She pushed the door open, looked at the photos and mementoes of her daughter's life. "Oh, Jessie." She sat on her daughter's bed, and then lay down on it, pressing her face against the pillow, burying her tears in the comforting scent of

Jessica. 'Oh, Jessie. Don't do this to me. I don't want to lose my baby girl. What have I done?"

25

MOIST CLAY IN THE KILN

The next day in Biology, Thomas was elated to see that Jessica was there; now he could finally get to talk with her. He sat behind her, watching her intently all through class; he was too nervous to sketch her. His stomach churned; butterflies danced in the approaching hunger of lunch time. When the bell finally rang, Jessica had already packed up; she was obviously in a hurry someplace. She quickly got up, left the classroom, and headed down the hall. Thomas had to jog to catch up. "Hey Jessie, wait up."

She slowed her pace but kept walking.

"Hey I noticed you weren't in class yesterday."

"Oh, um yeah," she said with a sniffle, her voice groggy. "I was sick over the weekend and yesterday."

"That sucks. You feeling better now?"

"Sorta," she sniffled and coughed.

Thomas took his bag off his shoulder and awkwardly fumbled through it as he tried to keep up with Jessica's quick pace. When his hand found the notebook with the poem on it he said, "So anyway, I wanted to give ..."

"I gotta go," she said abruptly and jogged toward her friends over by the lunchroom entrance. When she joined the group they all glared at Thomas for a second then traipsed off into the cafeteria.

Puzzled over what had just happened, Thomas stuffed the notebook back into his bag. He decided to go ask Jessica if something was wrong. Walking into the lunchroom he found her standing in line with all her friends. They all looked his way as he walked towards them and then quickly looked straight forward, as if to ignore him. He came to a stop beside Jessica and asked, "Hey Jessie, can I talk to you for a second?"

"Uh, yeah, just give me a minute."

Her friends circled around her and started talking in hushed voices; Thomas couldn't make out what they were saying. He waited for them to finish talking, patient and a little apprehensive. They got out of the line and started walking away. Thomas walked along with them, slightly separate from their group. When they left the lunchroom Thomas tried again. "Hey Jessie, I -"

He was stopped short by Shannon. Jessica's red-haired friend turned around abruptly and with both hands shoved Thomas back as hard as she could. "Just leave Jessica alone!"

They all hurried into the nearby girls' restroom and slammed the door shut.

Thomas stood there stunned; he had no idea what was going on. He felt a lump form in his throat and a knot in his stomach. Glancing around, he noticed several people staring at him. He left the area and went to the painting classroom; he needed to be alone, to get away from the shock and embarrassment.

He sat at a table in the empty painting classroom with the lights still turned off. He tried to figure out what could be wrong; he couldn't think of anything, but he had the horrible feeling that it was his entire fault. He struggled to calm his breathing and relax. He trudged over to the light switch, and the room flashed into view. Thomas' eyes opened wide and his heartbeat quickened. There, drying on the wall, was a second painting of Jessica; she was wearing the same red dress she had worn to the dance. He picked it up gingerly and looked on the back. *Liam Hobbs*. How did he manage to do that? How could he?

His stomach churned; he put the painting back on the wall and looked for the portrait he had started. He moved the other student's painting he had left it behind: nothing. He checked around the room and behind all the other paintings: nothing. It was gone. He looked again at Liam's paintings. *Does she like him more than me? Is he trying to steal her away from me? What do I have to do? What have I done?*

The door opened and Cindy walked quietly into the room. She looked at him, and past him to the new painting, and then sat down beside him. He just stared down at his notebook, lying mute on the desk in front of him.

"You okay?" Cindy asked.

He didn't say anything, stared blankly into space.

"Is that the new poem?"

He nodded mutely, slid the notebook over for her to read.

Holding thee fair maid, I held everything;
Feeling emotions beyond mans' measure;
If a heart had a tongue, then mine wouldst sing.
Thou art the finest gift in God's treasure.
No longer to hold for long to embrace,
We danced amongst the stars by the moon's light;
Within will of mine to kiss thy sweet face.
A conflict inside where heart and mind fight;
With something this deep I do not dare chance,
For thy sweet heart I can't afford to lose;
Conflict in thee whether to live this dance;
I know mine own heart, 'tis thee that must choose.
If thou say this false then please tell me why,
For when I didst embrace thee, thou didst cry?

"It's really good," she said quietly, and handed the notebook back to Thomas.

"Thanks," he whispered.

"Are you okay?"

"No," he swallowed hard. "And to make things worse …" he pointed to the new painting of Jessica in the red dress.

"Is that yours?"

"No, it's another of Liam's. She probably thinks he's a better artist than me and likes him better and …"

"I don't know why she would think that." She made as if to say something, hesitated and asked, "What happened?"

"Well, I tried to talk to her today, but she kept running

202

away from me, walking over to her friends. So I waited politely for them to finish so I could talk to her. Then one of her friends shoved me away and yelled at me to leave Jessica alone and then they all went into the girls' bathroom."

"I'm sorry Tom, that's really, really mean of them. When I heard I didn't for a moment think they would take it seriously."

"Think what? What did you hear?"

"Well, I didn't talk to her, myself. I just overheard her talking with her friend in History."

"Well what did she say?"

Cindy's face went pale as she tried to summon up the words. "She told her friend that, well … after the dance … she thought …"

"What?" Thomas turned and looked at her, pain and anticipation fighting in his gaze.

"She thought … you were going to rape her."

203

26

STILL LIFE

A blanket of silence enveloped the room; a blanket of muffled horror. Jessica lay motionless on the bed, spread-eagled, her arms and legs still tied by the restraints. She stared blankly at the ceiling. No tears came; she'd used them all up, wasted them. He had draped the bed sheet over her again, mocking her with modesty.

He sat beside the bed on a fold-out stool, fastening the last button on his shirt. The masked head turned toward her, the dark eyes appraising, questioning. "So Jessica," he leaned over and stroked her hair, tenderly, "Was it as horrible as you imagined it would be?"

"No." her voice was tiny, a little pin-point of shame in her numbness. The truth was, along with the terror, the guilt, she knew there had been something else. Pleasure. She registered this blankly now, but at the time, it was almost the worst feeling of all.

"You're welcome, by the way. You know, neither Rachel nor Stacey ever received all that extra attention beforehand. That was just for you, Jess. Just for you."

He opened his bag of drawing materials and took out a sketchbook. Propping it on his crossed knee, he began to draw her in profile. He was humming something, something classical that Jessica didn't recognize, as he worked.

Jessica listened to the sound of the pencil scraping over the paper, of his voice humming contentedly. The cold numbness was lifting; she could feel the impression of his lips on her neck, all over her body, the guilty pleasure they had brought. He hadn't kissed her face or mouth at all. She remembered how she shuddered at the first touch, how her sobs had given way to other sounds. A door had been opened; a shameful door to a shameful world.

No one will rescue me. She heard a sigh escape from her mouth. *No one. How could anyone rescue me from this?*

27

ECSTASY AND AGONY

A faint, rhythmic tapping sound roused Jessica from her sleep. Tap, tap, then a grinding sound, then the tapping again. When the sound stopped she listened intently; nothing. She heard the metal door open and wrapped herself instinctively in the sheet. She felt shaky and weak; hunger was gnawing at her, she hadn't eaten since the previous morning.

There was a light nudge at the foot of the bed and then the door closed. She peeked out from under the covers and saw a tray with breakfast food on it, sitting at the foot of the bed. Beside the tray were a towel and a couple tiny bottles of soap.

The tray held a small plate of scrambled eggs, a bowl of hot oatmeal, a couple slices of bacon and a glass of orange juice. She attacked the small feast desperately, wolfing it down. In her haste, she let a slice of bacon fall between the mattress and the wooden bed frame. *Damn; I want that bacon.* Setting the half-empty glass of orange juice aside, she lifted up the mattress to retrieve the savory crispy bacon strip. Something caught her eye; something new. She looked at the names scrawled in blood and recoiled in shock. On the base of the bed frame, below the name Stacey, she could see her own name written in blood, with seven tally marks beside it. She finished her meal distractedly, barely registering as the orange juice slipped down that it had a gritty, slightly unpleasant taste.

She stood up and made her way to the bathroom. Her head felt light, and she walked unsteadily; it was as if she hadn't eaten at all. Stumbling, she braced herself along the wall and made her way to the toilet to sit down.

Afterwards, when she was washing her hands, she heard a clanking noise from the plumbing, and then water came flowing out the shower head. She knew this meant that he was watching her through the two-way mirror and had turned on the water from the other side of the wall. Normally she made an effort to keep her back to him as she washed, but this time she just sat down by the drain to ease her dizziness. She scrubbed the soap over her body again and again, savoring the flowing water, but still feeling unclean.

The water shut off and she slowly got up, grabbed the towel and dried herself off. She began to pull her hair back to tie it; the metal door opened and he said, "Don't. Just leave it down."

Her dazed eyes struggled to focus on the blurring mask in front of her. She had a sudden urge to take a swing at him; she raised her arm but it simply floated through the air. The momentum threw her off balance and she toppled over, but felt the pressure of his hands as he caught her.

He carried her into the open room, the world flowing by her in a haze of soft edges. On the platform were a couple tables with several cushions stacked on them; the whole arrangement was covered with a white sheet.

Laying her down on the cushions atop the platform, he said, "Just recline here." He positioned her floppy limbs on the pile of cushions. "And don't fall off." Settling into the cushion pile, she let her legs dangle over the edge, and he leaned her backwards, draping her left hand over her waist.

He seemed to float by as he retrieved a needle and began feeling her arm for an insertion point. She watched him from a long way away, vaguely following the slow ballet in front of her. Once he found what he was looking for he wrapped the elastic tourniquet around her bicep and stuck the needle in about halfway down her forearm. He draped the tube that ran from the needle across her waist and down to the beaker beside her. Her blood began to pool in the glass jar as he positioned the easel.

There was no chair beside the easel this time. He planned on standing while he painted this pose. Before starting he replaced the jar beside her with an empty one, and then he began to paint. The music was slow and quiet. Jessica felt like she could fall asleep, but she wasn't sure what would happen if she did. Lethargically she said, "It's nice not having my hands tied." After waiting a few seconds for a response she added in a slow slur, "I feel a little … little bit less like Powers' sculpture and more like a Bernini. You know, the Saint Theresa thingy."

His silence didn't really trouble her today; she wasn't sure she would have understood any answer he gave; everything was so far away, out of reach. She laid her head back and stared up at the ceiling, trying to think clearly, but she couldn't concentrate for more than a few seconds.

"Do you want me to be in ecstasy for this pose?" She chuckled, drunkenly. "Or is pretending to be … be asleep alright?"

"That's fine how you are."

"I'm fine?" She snickered.

"How was your breakfast?" he asked. "To your liking I hope?"

"Sooo good!" She slurred, "Except the juice was orange. Oops, the orange juice was a little gritty, like … like the ones with added calcium." She had the impression her head was rolling form side to side, but she couldn't do anything to stop it.

"Sorry," he said, "the tranquilizers were difficult to grind into a fine powder."

Through half shut eyelids she saw the mortar and pestle sitting on the counter. Her head rolled back and she succumbed to sleep.

…

She awoke to find her body shivering uncontrollably; her skin had become moist and clammy. *I'm cold.* She raised her head up to speak to him and as she did she glanced down at the beaker beside her. The twenty-four-ounce glass jar had over-filled with her blood and was pooling on the platform.

She made a clumsy attempt to get his attention; her voice didn't seem to be working. As he saw her reaction he pointed a remote toward the stereo. A familiar melody began to play.

"Do you recognize this song, Jessica?" he asked, looking away from her and focusing on the painting. She couldn't be sure, but she got the feeling his hands were shaking as he hurried to finish the last parts.

Fumbling for the tube, she pulled the needle out from her radial artery and sat up, wavering as she looked around the room with glazed eyes. Struggling to swallow, she said, "I don't feel … good. I don't …"

She slipped off the cushions and landed hard on the platform, knocking the jar and its contents over. The sight of so much of her own blood strewn across the floor brought her to her senses. She crawled toward him, trying to escape from the pool of her own blood. Her movements were erratic, and her breath came in uneven gasps. A sudden thump on the floor beside her caught her attention. Next to her face she saw the empty wrapped mask lying on the ground. Looking up to where the mask had been, she tried to focus; she had been dreading this moment, wanting this moment. His face swam into focus.

"Tom?"

Thomas stared coldly down at her. Here she was, the pathetic creature, the one who had caused him so much pain. Well not any longer; he was in control now, and he could erase the pain at a stroke. And soon he would do just that. Erase it all: all of it.

She rose like a ruined mermaid from the pool of blood and reached out to Thomas with a sticky red hand, begging, "Something's wrong, Tom, I … please help. Help me ,Tom. Please."

She collapsed back into the pool of blood. Everything sounded like it was under water. The faint song playing from the stereo echoed in her ears. She knew it now. It was the song she had danced to with Thomas, a lifetime ago, beside a park, underneath a full moon.

Thomas stood above her, his arms folded, watching the faint movements of her mouth.

"Please …"

28

Dogs are Better than People

It was late Sunday evening at the veterinary clinic; most of the doctors and staff had gone home. It was a week since he'd snatched Jessica. Thomas crouched beside a cage containing a grey pit-bull cross with a cast on its leg. He stuck his fingers in between the bars and scratched the dog's shoulder. "Who's a good boy, Bruce? Huh? That's right, you are."

The door from the front waiting room popped opened and a young man with strawberry blond hair and bushy eyebrows stepped through. He looked a little older than Thomas, but not much. When he noticed Thomas crouched beside the dog cage he snapped, "Yo, mop bitch. Quit screwing around and get back to work."

Thomas didn't say anything, but stood back up and continued mopping the floor. Although his primary duties were cleaning and housekeeping in the animal clinic, Dr. Hooper frequently had Thomas assist him during operations. It mostly consisted of handing items to the doctor when he requested them and monitoring the vital signs of the animals. Most recently he had helped with the recovery of a dog that had been hit by a car and lost life-threatening amounts of blood. Ever since then, Thomas had kept a close eye on Bruce's recovery. He knew what blood loss could do.

The rude young man continued, "You finished filling out the inventory report yet?"

"A mopped floor or inventory report you were supposed to do?" Thomas snapped. "Pick one, Roger."

"Finish the inventory first so I can get out of here. Then do the rest of your scrubbing." Roger picked up a clip board with the inventory sheet attached to it and tossed it on the table beside Thomas. He stormed back out into the front waiting room, sat back behind the reception desk and resumed watching a video on the computer. Whenever Dr. Hooper was around, Roger made sure to treat Thomas a lot better, but since the clinic had closed for the day, he was free to be as cruel as he wished. And he liked to be cruel.

Thomas leaned the mop against the wall and knelt back down beside Bruce.

"You know, if this building caught fire, I'd get you out of here first. Then I'd come back for the other animals, but that douche bag," he gestured his head toward the front waiting room where Roger sat. "He'd be toast."

Thomas kept scratching Bruce's neck for a moment longer, then went over and picked up the inventory sheet. Walking over to the waiting room door he cracked it open just a hair and saw Roger sitting at the desk, laughing at a video on the computer screen. He closed the door quietly, picked up his backpack, and got started on the inventory.

Complaining to Roger was a cover; Thomas was pretty glad to take the inventory. It was an easy alibi and got him what he wanted. For every ten items he counted, he wrote eight onto the inventory and slipped two into his backpack. He continued through the list, adding to the supplies in his pack: anticoagulant, chloroform, gauze, and a few other supplies.

If it weren't for the free supplies at the veterinary clinic Thomas wouldn't have wasted his time working there as a janitor. As much as he despised the douche bag out front, the ironic fact was that Roger made things that much easier for him.

After finishing the inventory, Thomas took the form up front to Roger, who gave it half a glance before signing it off.

"Took you long enough," Roger grunted.

"If you want it done faster then perhaps you should do it next time."

"No, next time you can do it faster." Roger looked at him arrogantly, and smiled a crooked smile. "Also don't forget to clean up the mess in the front waiting room."

"What mess? There isn't any …"

Roger causally tipped his extra-large soda off the reception counter; it splattered all over the floor.

"Mop to it," Roger said as he put his coat on, clocked out, and left.

Thomas resumed mopping the back rooms after seeing to the new mess in the front waiting area. He found rare moments of peace whenever he was alone at the animal clinic. No, not really alone. The company of the animals was some of the best he could hope for. There was no judgment in their eyes, no ulterior motives. *Maybe I should try drawing a few of the animals. Bruce might like to see his portrait in oils; definitely oils, not blood.*

Once he had finished cleaning up he locked the clinic and headed for his apartment near campus. He spent hardly any time there, but it was a useful storage space. Mostly he just stopped by in time to alternate the light switches, so it would appear that someone was actually living there. As far as his neighbors knew, a shy introvert insomniac tenanted the place; Thomas was happy to keep it that way, after all, people had thought a whole lot worse things about him. These days he spent nearly all of his time at the old house out in the country-side, where he was keeping Jessica; where he'd kept Rachel and Stacey.

He picked up a few drawing supplies and a couple other items out of the kitchen. Then he loaded them into his car, took a quick look around, and started driving to the west end of the valley.

29

JELLYFISH IN THE CLOUDS

Clouds. Clouds, and a strange floating jellyfish. Jessica shook her head, and quickly thought better of it, the world pitched and rolled, threatening her with nausea, before it settled back into a vague equilibrium. None of her senses seemed to be quite right. Sounds were muffled and distorted, and her vision was a collage of soft patches of color and light. She felt overwhelmingly numb, a numbness only interrupted by the occasional stinging sensation. Was that the jellyfish?

It occurred to her that her eyes were only half open; she made an effort to open them fully. At first, they didn't want to obey her at all; it was cozy here in the half-light, among the clouds. She was happy, sort of. An odd thought made its way through the haze, like a drunk crashing her little party. *Am I dead?* Jessica dismissed the question; *who cares?*

It was another few minutes before she could remember what it was she was trying to do. *Oh yeah, my eyes. Ouch!* Now she'd finally gotten her eyes properly open, the harsh light came as a nasty surprise, spoiling her fluffy white world with its insistence on hard edges and real shapes. She lifted her head, carefully, so as not to wake the sea monster, and looked down along the length of her arm.

It was resting on one of the clouds. Out of her hand a silken thread of white led away upward to some point above and behind her. She arched slightly backward, and saw that it ended up in the jellyfish, a weird umbilical cord connecting them to each other.

Jessica clenched her eyes shut and opened them again. This time, the world really was in focus. *Shame*. The jellyfish was a clear bag of some kind of liquid, and the silken umbilical cord was a length of plastic tubing, carrying the clear liquid into her arm. She wondered if she was in a hospital, but she couldn't remember being in an ambulance, and there were no doctors or nurses around.

She tried focusing on the cloud she floated on. It slowly resolved into a silky cotton comforter. The touch of the lush material against her skin was heavenly, a reassuring caress. She gathered the folds of the comforter around her, reveling in its warmth and softness, and floated back into dreamless sleep.

30

LANDSLIDE

School was finished for the day; most of the students had already left. Their idle, happy chattering faded into the distance. Thomas sat alone on the small stone bridge. He cupped his cheeks in his hands and stared down at the stone floor, watching his breath billow out of his mouth in the crisp air.

Two weeks ago, this bridge had been the top of the world, and he was on it, Jessica beside him, the roses in her hand. Now all he could feel was the cold stone, sucking the warmth right out of him. His world had fallen apart in such a short time; he'd been raised up, only to be cast down, left alone on a cold bridge to nowhere.

Near the parking lot at the west side of the school grounds, the lid of one of the school dumpsters flipped open. A small puff of smoke rose up as Nick and Rob crawled out, giggling and laughing, holding at an item they had found in their hiding place.

"Dude, let me see your Sharpie," Rob said to Nick.

Nick rummaged through his pockets before he found a couple markers.

"You want the red one or the black one?" Nick asked.

"Both! Yeah, both." Squinting through his blood shot eyes, Rob strained to focus and steady his hand. "Done!"

"Sweet, Dude, you're a real Da Vinci." Nick exploded with laughter that quickly turned into a rasping cough. Hey look." He pointed toward the small bridge. "There's Tom. Let's show him our artwork."

Thomas lifted his head as he heard the approaching chuckles. Rob and Nick strode up to the bridge, holding something behind their backs like a surprise gift.

"Check out our masterpiece, Tom." Nick and Rob spun around gracelessly to reveal the object they held behind them. Thomas' eyes filled with bitter tears as he stared at the torn painting. In addition to the large tear that ripped through her face, the stoned artists had added two sloppily drawn large black circles with two tiny red dots inside them.

"Quite a rack on that one, huh?" Rob snickered.

Thomas snatched it from them, violence smoldering in his face. "Where did you find this?"

"We made it." Nick chuckled.

Flipping it around, Thomas pointed to the name written on the back. "My name is on the back. It's my work. Where was it?" His voice wavered between a shout and a sob.

"Take it easy, man. Don't start a war over it. It was there in the dumpster."

Thomas stared at the destroyed and vandalized painting. He threw it flat on the ground beside his backpack and then turned away to stare down at his feet. His silence blanketed the bridge, stifling the fun out of Nick and Rob.

"Man, what a buzz kill." Nick said.

"Yeah, this is bumming me out. Let's go." Rob turned on his heels and weaved unsteadily off the bridge.

Thomas was glad they had gone, but his solitude didn't last. Before too long Jake walked up, his hands in his pants pockets, and said, "Hey dude. That artsy pipe worked real good. It's a pain to empty the water out though."

Thomas replied without lifting his head, "That's good. I guess."

Jake did his best to sound concerned. "Something wrong, man?"

Thomas sighed and said, "It's Jessie. I just …"

"Ah, she dumped ya, didn't she?"

"No." Thomas suppressed a sob. "She thought … she thought I was going to … take advantage of her … after the dance, before I took her home."

"Whoa, that sucks man." Jake noticed the ruined painting of Jessica on the ground. Thomas was staring at the opposite end of the bridge, wrapped up in his own thoughts; Jake picked up the painting and snuck it between his back and backpack out of sight.

Thomas was still muttering. "Yeah, I know. I just don't …"

"Hey I need to catch my ride. See ya later. Take it easy." Jake hurried off.

"Later." Thomas remained sitting on the parapet, oblivious to everything. Maybe if he waited long enough, someone or something would turn up and lift him out of this mess. *Yeah, maybe..*

On his way to the parking lot, Jake spotted Shannon coming out of the building ahead of him. He jogged up to her and said, "Hey, you're Jessie's friend, right?"

"Uh yeah, and you're the skier guy, Jake, that Jessie walks to the bakery with." Shannon looked at him suspiciously; he was one of Tom's friends, she was sure of it.

"Yeah, so anyway, I haven't had a chance to talk with Jessie and I wanted to make sure she's alright."

"Well she's ..."

"Only, when Tom said something about taking advantage of Jessie, I thought he was just joking."

"What? You mean ...?"

"Yeah, he said something about it back before he even asked her to the dance." Jake licked the edge of his lip and glanced over his shoulder. "Plus when I found this," he removed the painting from behind his back and showed it to Shannon, "I thought something bad had happened."

"I knew it. I told her he was a creep." Shannon practically spat at the painting. "What a perv. Wait, aren't you friends with him?"

"What? Tom? No, he just follows us around most the time. It's kind of annoying actually." He slid the painting back behind his back.

"What are you going to do with that?"

"The painting?" He paused as he tried to think of another lie to feed her. "I'm going to throw it into the trash where it belongs."

"Good! I'd hate for Jessie to see that." Shannon's face was livid. "Oh my gosh! I have to talk to Jessie." Shannon started to leave, then turned back, "Thanks Jake. Thanks for telling me."

"Yeah, no problem. Tell Jessie I asked how she's doing."

"Okay, I will." Shannon ran off to find Jessica.

Jake performed a little hop with a heel click as he strolled through the parking lot, his hands in his pockets and a smug look on his face. Around the corner he saw Nick and Rob waiting by his parents' sedan.

When they saw him approaching Nick asked, "What are you so happy about?"

"Nothing, just a good day." Reaching into his bag and pulling out the ceramic bong he said, "I've still got the artsy pipe; plus some new artwork for my room."

"Dude, that's ours." Rob replied.

"According to the back it *was* Tom's"

"Well the two improvements on it are ours." Rob struck an artistic pose.

Jake chuckled, "You guys can't draw for shit."

...

In the painting classroom, Liam lightly brushed a few finishing glazes over the red dress in his recent painting of Jessica. Looking out the window he saw two guys presenting the ruined counterfeit painting of Jessica to Thomas, who sat miserably on the bridge. A smile flickered across Liam's face as he watched Thomas rip the ruined painting out of the hands of the two other guys and throw it on the ground. *Way to go, Tom.* He went back to his work, a mocking smile playing about his lips. A winning smile.

31

GIRLS BEHIND THE CURTAINS

On the second floor of the USU art department building, Susie paused in the middle of taking her paintings off the wall and turned to Professor Foster. "Is it alright if I leave early?"

"How come? Is it because of your critique? I know some comments can be a bit harsh, but just remember to only take those that can help you better your work and ignore all ..."

"Actually," Susie interrupted, "It's just that, well, those blood paintings are next and I just ..." She cringed as she mentioned the blood works.

"Oh, that's right. How about you take a longer break and come back when we're finished with his critique? Say about 40 minutes from now?"

"Okay, thanks Steve," Susie said as she finished gathering her paintings off the wall; she carried them back to her small studio space in the corner of the large painting studio classroom. She hurriedly gathered up her things and hustled out of the room, giving Thomas a sideways look as he came in. He ignored her, and started to put up his paintings

The previous week, when Thomas had first displayed his new technique anonymously, Susie had nearly passed out after the realization that the medium he was using to paint with was blood. At the beginning of this day's class Professor Foster had revealed whose paintings were whose, and Thomas had reassured her - and everyone else - that it was simply animals' blood. But Susie still felt uncontrollably nauseous and had to leave the room.

Aside from the minor incident with Susie, Thomas felt his first critique had gone rather well; it probably helped him, and everyone else, that Liam could only make broadly speculative remarks, and not target individuals with his withering scorn.

A flush of nervousness swelled up inside Thomas. In his other classes, where his work held no connection to his dark secret, he still felt uncomfortable during critiques around so many people at once. But here he was bracing himself for an interrogation. He had to make sure he didn't give anything away.

A middle-aged woman in the group of students started things off. "I remember, several years ago, hearing about a woman artist who painted with her menstrual blood. Have you ever heard of that?"

Wincing at the question Thomas replied, "Yeah, I've heard of it, but I don't care for it."

"Why don't you care for it? Seems like it would be right up your alley," the woman replied. She looked disappointed with his reply.

"Because to me, her collection of smears and splats, which she calls art, are finger paintings at best. Plus I just think that working with menstrual blood would be nasty."

"How is it nasty? It's basically the same thing you're doing?"

"No it's very different. It's more than just blood in those menstrual paintings. It's also mucus, secretions, and tissue that are being cast out by the body. It's darker and much dirtier than the blood I use, which is clean; circulating through the body, providing life to each part. Her work is about rejection; mine is about acceptance."

"Plus it's not like you wanna gather pig or cow periods, right Tom?" A tall young man sitting in the back corner of the group joked.

"I'm just saying that it's like the difference between paint and mud. You can make a painting with both, but one will be much better than the other," Thomas replied, ignoring the joke.

Tired of arguing her point, the woman shifted back in her chair and stared forward. Thomas pinched the bridge of his nose between his fingers in an attempt to alleviate the growing headache he now felt. He took several slow deep breaths to calm his anxiety. Then he jotted down a couple notes in his sketchbook.

Realizing the conversation was in need of a shift; Professor Foster stepped in and asked, "Where do you find your models? I don't recognize any of them."

Thomas felt a slight tingle of panic crawl up his back. He'd never talked about who the individuals in his paintings were. He answered as politely and neutrally as he could, "Most are people I know. Plus some of them model at different universities."

"So you go to another university for their modeling sessions?"

"Occasionally, yes. I like having some fresh faces to work with. Most every painting on display in the hallways here is of the same three or four models."

"Well, good. Good for you. It is a wise idea for an artist to work with his or her own models. It helps with continuity, shows the developing relationship; plus it helps the work stand out. Not that your work needs any further help standing out." Professor Foster finished with a friendly grin. "Are there any more comments?"

Thomas was surprised that through the whole time his work was up nothing had been said by Liam. Then, as though the thought of him had woken him from his unusual silence, Liam confidently cleared his throat before asking in a snide tone, "Where do you acquire your 'medium'?" Liam made a gesture with his fingers to mimic quote marks.

"From the local butchers, and occasionally from the slaughterhouse out in the county area," Thomas cautiously answered. "Plus I work in a veterinary practice, so I have access to blood there."

"So they just have jars of blood for sale next to the steaks and bacon?"

"No, I know a couple people who work there who help me out," Thomas lied.

"Uh huh," Liam picked an eyelash out of the corner of his eye then flicked it off his finger before continuing to say, "It seems to me that you're just looking for shock factor. If you really wanted to bring a higher meaning to your work then you should just bleed yourself and use your own blood to paint your models, or even self-portraits. It would certainly bring a new meaning to 'pouring yourself into your work'."

"Sure," Thomas replied, eager to dismiss Liam and finish the critique. "I'll keep that in mind."

There was an awkward stillness in the room. Some of the students gave Thomas a peculiar look.

"Okay." Professor Foster stepped in; sensing a bit of growing tension. "The anonymous critiques seemed to really leave a lasting impression on a few of you. I'll have to make it a regular assignment for future courses.

"Alright, next up will be Stuart Cook. Stuart, you can go ahead and start setting up while Thomas takes his work down."

Susie Shepherd came around the corner and stopped suddenly at the sight of Thomas' work still hanging on the wall. She darted back out of the room, hand over her mouth. Thomas sighed to himself and shook his head as he placed his paintings back into his portfolio.

...

Out in the hallway, Thomas waited by the display case containing his and other students' work from the previous week. Soon he heard the sound of someone skipping around the corner.

"Hey you." Cindy greeted him cheerfully. Exaggerating her movements, she folded her arms and turned toward the paintings and asked, "So are you going to tell me which ones are yours?"

"I'll give you three guesses."

"Well, as I recall you had a hard time drawing people, but then again you were insistent on improving at it. Is this your work?" She pointed to a group of paintings, in rich oil paints, of figures draped in brightly-colored fabrics.

"Nope. Try again."

Cindy caught a slight movement in his eyes and followed the direction they had moved in. With an excited gasp she asked, "The blood paintings? Did you do the blood paintings?" Her mouth hung open at the realization.

"This is soo awesome," she gushed. "I remember when you were terrible at drawing people back in high school, but now ..." He blushed over the exuberant praise as she continued. "Not only are you a master figure painter now, but you're goin' all extreme, doing it in blood. That's just so wow. Quite a big step from adding hair to your work. How'd you ...?" She paused and looked closely at the two paintings of Jessica.

"Wait a minute. So you did get Jessica to model for you. That's so great! So things have been cleared up between you two?"

"Well not exactly ..." Thomas searched his mind for an excuse. He should have been expecting this, but he hadn't prepared for it. "She uh, actually models for the ... the um art guild at her school. I just sit in with the group."

"That's still pretty good."

"Yeah, good enough I suppose."

Cindy's brow creased as she struggled to recall something. "Hold on. I heard that Jessica's going to CSU in Fort Collins."

"Uh yeah, well …" He swallowed hard. This wasn't going right at all; he needed to think, and think fast.

"That's like what, double the time it takes to drive from here to Mountain Valley?" She squinted as she did the math in her head. "That's like five, six hours." She stopped and tilted her head suspiciously, still grinning.

"You still like her? Don't you?"

"What are you talking about? I …"

Her voice became less playful as she said, "It's pretty obvious, Mister. Aside from driving an entire day to sketch her during a modeling group at a college many, many miles away … the biggest giveaway is your paintings themselves."

"What do you mean?"

"The way you paint her; it's just so clear. The others have a more deliberate brush stroke and a kind of awkwardness to their poses, but with her it's more delicate, more natural. You must have spent a lot more time painting her than you did the other two."

"No, it's not like that. She's just another model. And besides, the other paintings were earlier models. I still hadn't quite figured out the materials at that point."

"Does she know you use blood to paint her?"

"Yeah, she knows."

"What do the other students at the figure group think when you're painting around them?"

"Oh, I don't paint the finished piece at the figure group. I just uh, draw while I'm there. I reference the um, drawings back in my studio."

"Oh! Do you have a space upstairs in one of the classrooms?"

"Um, no. No, I paint at home, at my home studio. I like the privacy."

"Exactly! Right? Too much distraction makes it hard to paint." Cindy composed herself before continuing. "So … I can model tonight if you aren't busy."

"Right now?" Thomas mulled over which model to work with: a willing one here or a forced one in his secret studio. "Yeah, okay. Let's go," he replied. The opportunity of a fresh face to work with was appealing.

…

Cindy flipped on the lights of her apartment in the Garden Courts complex, just across the street from the university's football stadium.

"Are any of your roommates home?" Thomas asked.

"I guess not; but even when they are I hardly ever see them. They're either out or shut in their rooms." Cindy tossed her backpack into her own room. "Where do you want me to pose?"

"Wherever is fine; somewhere we won't be interrupted would be preferable."

"We'll just do it in my room then."

Thomas carried one of the dining table chairs into Cindy's room. Inside was a single-sized bed with bright green sheets. Above it was a couple of comic superhero posters and there were similar posters around the room.

"Still keeping up with the comics?"

"Of course," she replied.

He positioned the chair facing the bed and propped his sketch pad on his lap.

"You can go ahead and have a seat just there," he said, pointing to the mattress.

"Hold on just a sec." She stepped into the small private bathroom in her room. "I wanna change first."

After she closed the door, Thomas got up and looked around the room at the various items on the walls and shelves. He stopped to examine the variety of glass bottles, filled with brightly-colored water, which sat in the windowsill.

"There's an easel in the closet if you'd rather use that." Cindy's voice was muffled through the bathroom door.

"Thanks, yeah I think I will."

Opening the closest, he found the easel off to one side and to the other he paused at the sight of Cindy's wardrobe. A few of the outfits she had regularly worn during high school hung beside her newer clothes. He found something comforting in the familiarity of his longtime friend.

The bathroom door clicked open. "Now I know it's not the same as your other models. I'm just not quite ready to show my *girls* to the whole art department."

She stepped over to the opposite side of the easel. She was wearing a green and gold pashmina draped over the top of her head; it hung down both sides of her face, covering most of her breasts and stopping just past her hips; otherwise, she only wore simple black panties. Thomas stared blankly at the beautiful combination of fine fabric with fair skin. Her neck, clavicles, sternum, and stomach were all nicely framed in the extended 'V' shape of the green and gold fabric.

"Is this okay?" She asked.

"Uh, yeah. No, it's good. I didn't expect … well, this." He cleared his throat. "I guess if you're okay standing, then right there is good."

He stepped over to a desk at his left, turned on a desk lamp and angled it toward Cindy.

"Can you rotate just a little this way?" He directed her with his hands. "So you're facing more at an angle rather than straight on? Right there, that's great."

Thomas stepped behind the easel and began to sketch out the basic shapes of her figure. "Before I start on your face, hold your hands up by your neck and open the fabric around your face a bit more. There, that's perfect."

For some time they both stood there silently. He had finished most of her face and hands; there was only the pashmina and her torso left.

Cindy broke the silence as she reminisced, "Remember back in high school, when you and I snuck out of art class to go play strip poker in the back of your car?"

A smile formed across Thomas' face. "Yeah, we both got down to our underwear and then neither of us was able deal the next hand."

Cindy chuckled. "We just sat there for a while blushing, and finally put our clothes back on and went back to class. No one even noticed we were gone for the whole ... what? Twenty minutes?"

"Yeah." Thomas grinned awkwardly as he struggled to focus on drawing. As he attempted to render her torso, his mind kept wandering and wondering what was beneath the pashmina. He'd drawn and painted so many nudes before; so he wasn't sure why it should matter. The more he stressed over it the more he realized how much more sexualized this pose was, because of the fact that he was only being teased with a slight hint of her figure. His desire to see the rest of her began to outweigh his focus on drawing.

Sensing the awkwardness in the room, Cindy asked, "Wanna see a trick?"

As Thomas looked up she bounced two of her teeth out and then back into place in her mouth.

"What?"

"They're connected to my retainer. I can make 'em dance." She grinned. "I have to say though, it makes me a sorta weird kisser."

"How did that happen?"

"Oh, it…" Cindy instantly regretted bringing them to his attention; they were leading the conversation in an awkward direction. "It's from that day on the bridge, when the football players… yeah." She swallowed uncomfortably. "When I tried to stop Jared he, well…" She bounced the two prosthetic teeth again around a lopsided grin.

Thomas looked away, and rubbed the back of his neck. Cindy relaxed her stance, feeling stupid for bringing up such a bad day; the pashmina slid off the back of her head.

"Oops, let me fix that real quick." She shook out the pashmina to reposition it. As she did so he got a brief glimpse of her full breasts. Thomas felt his face blush and his head spin. He fumbled around hurriedly, trying to gather his things, and in a strangled voice said, "Sorry, I … I need to go. I've got work to do."

Cindy put on the robe that hung on the side of her bed and followed him out into the main room of the apartment. "Tom, are you alright? I didn't mean to upset you."

"No, don't worry about it. I just need to go." He rushed toward the door. "I'll talk to you later."

"Okay." She watched him go, the beginnings of a tear forming in her eyes.

...

Back at the painting display case in the art department, Thomas stood there for some time staring at the paintings he'd made of Jessica. Paying no mind to the janitor pushing the motorized floor scrubber behind him, Thomas crossed his arms and nibbled absently at his thumbnail as he compared the technique between the other girls and Jessica. He could see it now; Cindy was right. He was a different artist when he painted Jessica, more original, more alive. He frowned and dragged his thumb out of his mouth; what else had Cindy seen?

32

CUTTING LIPS

Jessica's strength came back slowly as the weeks went by. Thomas tended to her constantly. He kept her on the IV drip for the first few days; then he fed her, and washed her, and watched over her, anxious and attentive. She was too weak to leave the room, so he drew her where she lay, passive and unmoving on the bed.

She hadn't said a word to him since he had shown her who was behind the mask. She was in a private world, a world of soft, sinister confusion. She barely noticed when he sketched her, or rearranged her to suit his view. She felt as if she was watching the world from a long way off, and she was in no rush to get back to reality; not that she was sure what reality meant anymore.

The day came when she was able to get up and walk around the room without feeling like she was going to collapse at any moment. She sat back on the bed, leaning against the cinderblock wall, staring down at her hands. Her voice startled Thomas; he looked up from his sketch, and she repeated her words.

"So what is the point of wearing the mask any more, Thomas? I've seen your face. I know who you are. What are you hiding from now?"

He didn't answer, just went back to his sketch and his own thoughts. She was right, in a way. But the mask made him feel more in control. And it had an effect on his work, like it was a catalyst for inspiration; he couldn't explain it, to her or to himself, but he could see it in the quality of his drawings. He sat on the fold-out stool, his back against the metal door. He wanted to make it clear to her that she wasn't going anywhere, not yet.

Jessica hadn't really expected him to answer. What could he say? She drifted back into her own thoughts. What was she now? In a single moment, he had stripped her of everything she thought was unique and valuable, had spoiled her. At the same time, he'd awakened a set of feelings she didn't know what to do with; and those feelings connected with the Thomas she'd known at high school, but she couldn't figure out how.

She ought to be angry with him, and she was angry. But that wasn't the only thing she felt. Every time she thought she was certain, that she hated him, he performed some little act of kindness, some tender gesture that undermined her at the same time it comforted her. He was making it difficult to hate him, and she hated him for that, too.

Thomas heard a small sound, a suppressed sob. He turned his masked face toward her, and the quiet rustle of the gauze gaze alerted her to his attention. She was angry at herself for betraying her tears to him.

"What have you done to me, Tom?" her voice gained strength as the torrent of words poured out. "What you took from me, that was meant for my husband, it was precious. You've made me into some … I don't know, some worthless thing, an object. I'm not a life model, I'm a still life, a hollow vessel, an empty husk. I …" she trailed off, defeated and confused.

238

Thomas put down his sketchbook, and got ready to answer her, but she found her voice again, interrupted him before he could begin.

"I can't even look at you. I don't want to see your eyes, knowing that you're just staring at me, thinking up things to do to me. I'm exposed, totally, and you're hiding behind that mask, waiting for …"

Thomas tried again, "I'm not thinking of anything; I'm just trying to draw you."

"Sure, Tom. I'm just the model, right? You're not thinking of raping me again, sure. You've ruined me, Tom. Ruined my future; who's going to want me now?"

"Don't give me that pious bullshit. You enjoyed it. You're no different than the others. At least they didn't come out with all this religious crap. I look after you, Jessica, I've saved you. And all I get is this …"

"Saved me? You kidnapped me. You took me away from everything, from everyone. You raped me. You expect me to be grateful?" She stood up, naked, defiant, and took a step toward him.

"Sit down."

She ignored him, took another step forward. "You think your crime is justified because you've given me some food? What happens when people find out, Tom? You really believe they're going to think you're the good guy?"

"I said sit down."

"Or what? You gonna have another tantrum? Throw your toys around some more?" she was right in front of him now, hands on hips, superior. He sprang off his stool and grabbed her by the wrists, pinned her against the wall.

"Shut up! Shut up or so help me I'll –"

"You'll what? Rape me? For the *whopping* two minutes you'll last. It's not much of a threat anymore, is it? The goods are already soiled. You'll hit me, maybe? Come on then, hit me."

He tightened his grasp on her wrists, and leaned into her, wanting to cut off her voice, stop her accusations. Suddenly she thrust her face at him, and kissed him, hard, spitefully. He let go of her wrists, and her arms fell to her sides. She pulled back, a look of triumph in her eyes. He smiled momentarily, then his mouth twisted into a sneer. His palm whipped across her face and her head snapped to one side. Hot tears sprang onto her cheeks.

Thomas stormed out of the room, slamming the door shut behind him. Jessica slumped onto the bed, reaching for anything that would cover her naked body. Her hand went to her face, feeling the hot red print of his hand. She was more confused than ever. She'd thought that she would be able to hate him more easily if he hit her, abused her. But it had taken so much to get him angry enough to slap her; she felt like she'd bullied him into it.

Her anger melted in a welter of confusion; confusion and curiosity. She was spoiled, but maybe she wasn't worthless after all; maybe, to one person at least, she mattered.

33

Two Books

Sometimes when Cindy walked, she gave Thomas the impression she was dancing. Her steps were light, and her body swung to a rhythm only she could hear. But he could see it. He imagined her as a Matisse dancer, a sinuous block of color.

"Hey Tom, wait up!"

He paused at the door leading out to the art department courtyard. Glancing down at his hands, suddenly sheepish, he said, "Look, about the other night. I …"

Cindy interrupted him. She wanted to get her apology in first. "I know, it's all my fault, Tom. I should never have brought up that day; that was really stupid."

"No, I was okay about that. It's just I have a certain way of working, and I … I probably just overreacted. I'm sorry." He passed his hand over his face, trying to erase the image of Cindy posing in the same circumstances as Jessica.

"Are you sure you're okay about the other stuff?"

"Sure. Don't worry about it."

"Well, that's alright then." Her usual smile came back, and Thomas relaxed. "So, you wanna walk me to the shuttle bus? My next class is way over at the other end of campus."

"Sure. I'm done for the day here, and I have some time before I start work at the vet clinic."

They ambled through the courtyard, passing under the polished limbs of a chrome sculpture that turned and swiveled in the wind. A crowd of tiny Toms and Cindys shone out from the faceted spindles.

"So, are you gonna paint me in blood now? Do I get to choose if it's pig or cow?"

Thomas answered seriously, a frown of concentration on his face. "I'm not sure."

"Not sure? How come?"

"Well, it doesn't really fit with the process of the others, the ones in that, uh, series. But I definitely want to make some kind of painting. Maybe just some boring old oils." It was his turn to grin impishly.

"So, can I see how the sketch turned out? Am I an okay model?"

"Sure, why not? And yes, you're a great model, the best." Thomas fished around in his bag. He drew out a sketchbook and flipped the pages until he got to the sketch of Cindy. She took it onto the shuttle bus, and he had no choice but to follow. As they settled into their seats, he asked, "So, what do you think?"

Cindy stared at the drawing of a beautiful young woman, looking serenely into the distance, her lush curves half hidden in the folds of ornate drapery. "Tom, it's … it's just … Wow! You've come a long way from that floating head you drew of me in high school."

"Thanks, I really appreciate that, especially coming from you."

"I look, well, sexy. You know, not like some trashy celeb, but really sexy. I never felt sexy before. It's quite a feeling."

The shuttle bus came to a stop. Cindy looked up, startled, and grabbed her things, handing the sketchbook back to Thomas. "Gotta go."

She stopped in mid-stride, and turned back to him, leant down and gave him a kiss on the cheek. "Thanks, Tom, you really made my day."

Thomas watched her go through the window of the bus, as it turned around to head back to his end of the campus. The imprint of her kiss was a cool ghost on his cheek. He was glad Cindy was around; she was a real friend, whatever happened. He put back the sketchbook and took out another, turned the pages, staring at the drawings of the dark-haired girl, now draped, now nude, always mysterious, always beautiful. His finger traced the line of her hair, caressing the paper.

…

Jessica sat on the bed, the comforter wrapped around her, her knees drawn up into her chest. She had too much to think about, wanted to think about nothing at all. But it wouldn't go away. She knew she had to take some control of the situation. And there were things she could control. Her room, for instance.

Tom had come to refer to it as her room too. She rehearsed the words in her head as she looked around. *My room, my bed, my pillow, my shower. I'm relaxing in the hot water of my shower, it feels good.* In the last few days, he had turned on the shower faucet more regularly, and the hot water really did feel good.

She thought about praying. Whenever she was alone, she took time to pray, and it always helped. She didn't pray for release, not always; she tended to ask for things related to that particular day, that particular moment. Despite her confinement, the routine of posing, every day felt a little different. Things were changing; she didn't know how exactly, but things were changing, coming around to her advantage. *Old things are done away, and all things have become new.*

34

The Five Sirens

Later that same day, feeling refreshed and a little stronger, Jessica came out in the open room to pose for Thomas.

"Are you going to bleed me again?"

"I have an ample supply in the fridge… for now."

She hadn't struggled or fought him, but her lack of resistance hadn't made him feel more in control; if anything he felt less in control of her now than when he had first taken her. He only had her do reclining or seated poses, so as not to tire her before his painting was finished.

"When did you grow your hair out?"

"What?" Thomas was startled by the question.

"Your hair?"

"A couple years, maybe. Why?"

"Nothing."

"If it really is nothing, then why ask??"

"It looked better short."

Thomas sighed turned back to his painting. The next question gave him more to think about.

"So why do you paint with blood?"

It took him a moment to answer. "You know, I don't think I've ever been able to answer that question exactly the same way twice."

"So who else has asked you? Stacey? Rachel?" When Thomas didn't answer, a shocking realization hit her.

"So, you've shown these paintings to people?"

"Yes. Well, not all of them," he glanced at a couple paintings that included the tubing and restraints, "but I show some of them at the critiques for my advanced painting class at the university. If anyone asks, I tell them it's animal blood from a butcher shop. Which means I never really answer the question at all."

"Do they think your paintings are bizarre?"

"Not as much as you'd think. There are plenty of weird paintings around in college. And the other figure painters just relate to the subject.

"The nude is a common theme throughout art; no one really questions it anymore, apart from maybe a few feminists. But for me it's more about the process and the meaning, and the blood is central to that. I don't really know what people think of the medium, because I haven't really been honest about it; and some of them freak out at the thought of animal blood, so I'd hate to think what' they'd do if they knew the truth. I'd like to talk to someone about it; it's a difficult medium to work in."

Jessica wondered if he was really oblivious to the risk he was taking. "What if someone recognized the models, and started asking awkward questions?"

"It hasn't happened yet." *Actually, it has.* He remembered Cindy's identification of Jessica with a shudder, but quickly dismissed it; there was nothing to worry about. "Besides, it's not like anyone is looking for the women in my paintings."

His words hit her like bullets. How could no one know that she was missing? By now someone must have noticed she was gone. Surely her parents must have found out, or at least her roommates.

"Family or friends would file a missing persons report." Jessica tried to sound more confident than she felt.

"If they believed them to be missing, then perhaps they would." Seeing the confusion in her face, he went on. "Your parents have been on a cruise for the past two weeks. They sent you an e-mail when they were back in Florida. Oh, I forgot to mention, your father was able to visit The Greek Slave sculpture before the cruise departure. He told you how impressed he was that Powers was able to capture the emotions of the slave on her face.

"I found it only fitting to have you recreate the pose, seeing as you spoke so highly of it with your father."

"What else did they say?"

"They just rambled on and on about the cruise and sent some pictures." He frowned as he fixed a small blemish in the painting. "The reply they got from you told them about a guy who's trying to make it as a singer/song writer, how you met him and how in love with him you are."

Jessica's face was a study in shock. "But, I never …"

"Exactly. I sent them that false story; and when they wrote back and began lecturing you about how you need to stay focused on your classes, or find a proper boyfriend with real potential in life, I told them, as you, that you'd decided to drop out of college and move to California with your musician boyfriend."

Jessica's face was a mask, but her mind raced. For the first time, she allowed herself to acknowledge what had happened to Rachel and Stacey. They hadn't just disappeared into thin air. She couldn't quite bring herself to say it, even to herself; but she knew.

And her parents weren't even looking for her. Or if they were, they were looking in the wrong place. She felt worse about that than she did about the fates of Rachel and Stacey. And that, in turn, made her feel selfish and worthless.

She was alone, and she had to fight alone. After the way he had looked after her, brought her back from the brink of death, she didn't think he would kill her, not yet anyhow. And that gave her time, and time gave her hope.

She brought the stilted conversation back to Tom and his work. "You were trying to explain why you paint with blood." She watched him flinch, then regain his composure.

"Well, where shall I start? Throughout history the painting of portraits was meant as a way of immortalizing an individual through art, capturing their image."

"Like a photograph."

"No! Nothing like a photograph. Photographs are … they don't tell the whole truth."

"Okay." Jessica thought of the pictures on her bedroom wall, and was forced to agree.

"Artists have concentrated on the human figure, on the portrait, for centuries. I want to do more than just follow in that tradition; I want to bring something else to it, to make it new. I don't want to be just another painter, making just another portrait."

"You could say that all those artists have tried to capture the essence of the individual; but they've done it using oils, or watercolors, materials that only reflect the reality of the person they're portraying. I've taken it a step further; I actually use the essence of the individual as the medium in which I portray her. It's not just an image of you on the canvas, it *is* you; the painting of you is made of you. What could be more essential than your blood?"

"Why do you need a part of me in the painting? Like you said, all those artists over the centuries really did immortalize people in their works. And you were pretty good with oils, weren't you? This stuff with blood, isn't it a little like voodoo?"

"You can call it voodoo if you like. But as I see it, this way I have a part of you, right here in the painting. It's not just an image; I have so much more here."

Jessica felt the heat in her cheeks. *That's for sure, Tom; you've had so much more.* Was it pain or pleasure brought the blood to her face? She didn't want to think about that just now.

"Have you ever done a self-portrait? Ever wanted to immortalize yourself?"

He didn't seem to notice the sting in the question. "It's something I'm considering, once I finish this series."

"This series?"

"Yes, I'm calling it *The Five Sirens*."

"Why five? I thought there were only three."

"It depends on which myth you choose. Anyway, I've already gotten the first three. I'll do the other two before summer."

Jessica shuddered. If he had plans for other models, then his use for her had an end to it. She felt bad for the others too; the ones who would have to endure this after her. She wondered why there were to be five victims, what they had done to deserve this, or what he thought they had done. Maybe he had given her a clue; it was worth a try.

"Why sirens? Do you imagine us as part human and part … something else?"

"No, I'm not thinking of siren as the mythical half bird, but the other famous image, the charming, beautiful women who beguile men and lure them to destruction with their seductive singing. Like in homer, you know; Odysseus tied to the mast. Do you know Draper's painting of it?"

"So all these sirens sang to you?"

"That's right."

"And me?"

He paused to look at her for a moment. *You sing to me even now.*

The mask wasn't doing much of a job of hiding his feelings. She could feel his desire; see it, naked in his eyes, like the naked reflection of her. And she was afraid that same desire was obvious in her own face; how she wished she were the one in the mask. She blundered on, not sure where her questions were leading.

"Jane Harrison says the siren's song starts at midday, and when it ends, it portends death."

"Then the trick is to kill the siren before their song ends."

"That's just escaping from the song; you can't escape the silence that follows it." As she spoke, Jessica heard a sinister voice in her head: *neither can you, Jessica; neither can you.*

She asked him the question that burned the most in her confused mind. "Why did you let me live? I was on the edge of death that night. You put me on the edge of death and then you pulled me back; why?"

He fixed her in his dark gaze. "You still have another verse to sing."

They fell into troubled silence. But Jessica knew she was getting to him, and didn't want to let up. "So who are the other two, the last two sirens?"

"I'd rather not say. I'm not entirely sure I'll be able to get both of them. But the next one should be easier than you were."

"Do your models really have to be captives? Couldn't you just find volunteers to model and donate their blood willingly?"

"Oh there are plenty of people who would model for me, and even donate their blood; however, in this series, the identity of the models is crucial to the body of work. And you know there is much more to this than just modeling." She felt that heat in her cheeks again. "It's only once they are all captured in these paintings that I can be at peace with this body of work and move on."

"Who is the next one, Tom?" she pressed. An image of Shannon came into her mind.

"That's enough. Switch to another pose."

Jessica rotated onto her side and lay down on the hard platform. She waited for a comment or an instruction, but none came, so she relaxed into the pose.

"What do you mean by peace? Why aren't you at peace now?" she asked. Thomas glared at her as if she was intruding. She sensed the answer was there, but knew she would get nothing but this silent stare. "On one level or another I'm sure we all want some form of peace, even if most of the time it feels out of our reach. I try to find it in the little things, like reading books, playing music, or driving on the freeway knowing I don't have anywhere in particular to go."

"I remember seeing a picture of you holding a violin in your hand. Do you still play?"

"I do, but it's mostly for fun. I picked it up at my parents' house before I headed to Denver so I could ..." Her words died in her mouth.

"Too bad your car's still in Denver."

Jessica didn't answer. Suddenly there didn't seem any point in talking to him.

Damn it, my leg's gone to sleep. She sat up and stretched her legs to get the blood flowing again. This time it was Thomas who broke the silence. "I've seen you praying in your room."

"So?"

"What are you praying for? That I'll let you go?"

"It depends on the day."

"So what did you pray for this morning before you got up to shower?"

"That you wouldn't …" What was she supposed to say? "That you wouldn't use me today. It's been working so far." Jessica allowed herself a small smile. "But most of the time, I pray for you."

"What makes you think I need your prayers?"

"Do you believe in Heaven and Hell?"

"I've heard of it. But I have better things to do with my Sundays."

His casual dismissal of her beliefs provoked something like spite in Jessica. "I know that whatever happens here, there'll be something better, when all this is over." She looked up, beyond him, for a moment. "But what have you got to look forward to, Tom?"

Thomas reacted like he'd been stung. He threw down his brush, marched over to her and grabbed her by the wrist. He yanked her off the floor and frog-marched her to the little room.

"Here, Jessica; why don't you go and find someone else to pray for? Someone who gives a shit?" he slammed the door shut behind her and hustled over to the hi-fi, where he turned up the volume of the music until it filled the room, and his head.

When the music finally faded, Thomas sat in a trance. He stared into his latest painting, through the painting. *What do I do with her?* He looked up at all the paintings of Jessica that were hung around his studio walls. As the paintings progressed, he could see her changing, gaining confidence and poise, gaining some kind of control. She had already outlasted Rachel and Stacey combined, and he knew he hadn't finished with her yet. *I want to keep her. I want to keep her forever.*

35

THE BRIDGE

The week passed in hours of lead. Thomas was completely miserable; he wanted to talk to Jessica, to clear up any misunderstanding, but she avoided him like the plague. He spent even more time alone and spoke to even fewer people than before. The odd time he was able to get a glimpse of Jessica, she was immediately surrounded by a posse of her friends, who dragged her away. *Away to safety*, he thought bitterly, *away from the monster*. He'd seen the looks in their eyes. He felt like Actaeon, stumbling across Diana bathing with her nymphs in the forest; an intruder, a mortal in the lap of the gods. And he knew what had happened to Actaeon.

Biology class was the only time he could see her without the intervention. He sat a few rows behind her, as always, and looked at the back of her head, as always. Occasionally she would glance back at him and every time she did he turned his gaze away from her. He couldn't believe she thought he was going to do something bad to her, when he had only wanted to give her a romantic surprise. Confusion beset him; he was in love with her, but he was too angry at her to think straight.

The rumors had continued to spread throughout the school. Students that he didn't even know were glaring at him as he walked down the halls. The only comfort he found was from his friend Cindy, when they had lunch together in the painting classroom.

"It just keeps getting worse," Thomas said. "More and more people keep staring me down in the hallways."

"Don't worry so much about what they think," Cindy reassured him. "You and I both know that you wouldn't do anything like that."

"It's not as much about what everyone else thinks, but mostly what she thinks. You know how it is; they talk to her, and she starts to believe what they say, and then it gets worse."

"Well, maybe if you talked with her you could explain everything."

"Don't you think I've tried?" Thomas interrupted. "Every time I try to go near her, her friends just huddle around her and lead her away from me."

"What about in your Biology class? You could try talking to her then, or maybe pass her a note or something."

"I don't dare; I'm afraid she might scream at me in the middle of class." He stared down at his lunch and tried to calm the anxious butterflies in the pit of his stomach. "Plus, I don't think any of the teachers have heard the rumors, not yet anyhow, and I'd like to keep it that way."

"Well, the dance pictures will be ready to be picked up tomorrow. You could talk to her when you give them to her."

"I doubt she'll even want them."

Cindy bit her lip and turned back toward her sketch-book. Struggling to find a solution for Thomas, she doodled absently until an idea came to her.

"What if I talk to her in our History class and tell her I have a friend that thinks she's really cute and wants to meet her? Then when she comes with me to meet this mystery man I'll take her to you and you guys can talk."

"Really? You'd do that?"

"Yeah, of course."

"You think it'll work?"

"Sure it will. She doesn't know you and I are friends and I've talked to her off and on during class. So I'm not a complete stranger."

"Okay," Thomas said, a gleam of hope breaking through his worries. "Can we meet at the bridge outside the cafeteria?"

"You mean the one just outside that window?"

"Yeah, would that work?"

"Will do. I'll try and meet her after your Biology class and then she and I can walk to the bridge before lunch."

"That sounds good. Thanks Cindy."

...

The next morning Thomas arrived at school a little earlier than usual. He had left home at first light, deciding to walk to school instead of taking the bus. He went to the commons area to pick up the dance photos from the ball. He waited impatiently behind the crowd of students for a few minutes, and then darted for the first gap that appeared in front of the boxes of photos. Thomas hurried up to the J-M box before the other students, eager for their own pictures, crowded back in.

Once he found the packet with his name on it he walked over to a quiet corner and sat down to look over the photos. He took them out of the paper sleeve, like he was handling holy relics, or ancient artifacts. It felt like a step back in time to that wonderful night. He remembered how he had felt with his arms around her; the warm glow of excitement came back, just for a moment.

The first picture was the standard school dance photo; every couple who'd ever danced together had this one. It was of them standing beside one another with his arms around her waist. Glancing at where his hands were placed in the photo he winced at the realization that they were hovering toward indecently low.

Looking at the second picture, Thomas felt a smile form on his face and a warmth blossom in his chest. In the image of him lifting her up and into his arms, they had more genuine smiles on both of their faces than in the previous photo. He was so glad he had summoned the courage to pick her up at that moment. *So what, Tom? She's never going to look at this picture. She's never going to talk to you again.* His head sank onto his chest. He heaved a small sigh, and put the photos back in the paper sleeve, carefully, like he was handling evidence from a crime scene.

By the time he got to Biology he was nervous and on edge. He could hardly bear to look at Jessica; he sat as far away from her as possible. Once the class ended, he sat still as the other students gathered up their belongings and left. He watched Jessica as she went out into the hall and saw her 'accidentally' meeting up with Cindy. When the two of them disappeared from view, Thomas sprang out of his chair and jogged down the opposite hall, through the doors, and around the building, to get to the bridge before Cindy and Jessica.

...

Jessica and Cindy walked down the hallway and up the stairs towards the lunch room. Jessica was relieved to find herself talking to the only person in the whole school who didn't want to talk about what had happened after the dance. Everyone seemed to know more about it than she did. As they walked, Cindy told Jessica about a friend of hers, a guy she referred to as Clark.

"So, Cindy, I'm just curious, but, tell me," Jessica asked hesitantly, "if this Clark friend of yours is so great why don't you date him?"

"Well, I would, but it's just, you know, he really likes you." Cindy smiled and shrugged. "He says you two have been in the same schools for years and that he's had a crush on you for forever." She found it tough to lie, even for Tom's sake, so she stared straight ahead and tried to think of the good she was doing. And anyway, Jessica had touched a sore spot. Cindy had never understood why Tom was happy to flirt with her, but never to go beyond that; what does a girl have to do?

"Well he really takes his time to express himself," Jessica beamed. The idea of meeting Clark seemed like the perfect light relief, a distraction that would help take her mind off of Thomas. "You sure you don't want me to act like I'm not interested, then maybe you two could hook up?"

"No, I wouldn't wanna do that to him. And besides, Clark's really great and all, but I'm still waiting for my Superman." Cindy giggled at her little joke.

Jessica grinned as she pushed open the doors to go outside and said, "You know maybe after we meet up with Clark we can all go have lunch with some of my friends in the cafeteria."

"Yeah, that would be uber fun," Cindy said with a nervous gin as she looked toward the bridge.

"So are we just meeting him here at the -" Jessica stopped short as she saw Thomas standing on the bridge, looking toward her and Cindy. He had a paper envelope in his hand and a heartbroken expression on his face. Jessica turned toward Cindy with a look of confusion.

"Please, just talk to him Jessie," Cindy urged. "It's all a misunderstanding, let him explain."

Reluctantly, Jessica made her way onto the bridge where Thomas was standing and stopped a little over an arm's length away. She didn't say anything, but just stood there and waited for him to speak. Thomas looked down at the envelope that held Jessica's copies of the dance pictures and said, "I wanted to give you the pictures from the Sweetheart's Dance." He remained standing where he was, unable to keep eye contact with her for more than a second. At the full extent of his arm he handed the photos to Jessica. She took them from him hesitantly, removed her backpack, and placed them inside. Once she had the photos put away and her bag back on her shoulders Thomas continued, "Jessie, I ... I never meant to do anything that ..."

Their heads turned at the same instant, as they heard the door of the cafeteria being flung open. Out of it rushed Shannon with a couple of Jessica's friends, along with Jared Scott and two other football players.

Jared came charging up in front of the rest, shouting, "Hey, you piece of shit! Get away from her!" Jared stepped up in between Thomas and Jessica, with his shoulders back and his chest out. The other two guys soon stood beside him. With both hands, Jared shoved Thomas in the chest, sending him falling backwards onto his bag.

"You think you can rape Jessie and get away with it?!"

"Jared, stop it!" Jessica shouted. "It's not like that. He didn't ..." But her voice was lost in the uproar.

Angered by the sudden assault, Thomas got back up quickly, and forced himself to stay calm. He moved toward Jessica with his palms slightly raised, looking at Jared saying, "I didn't do anything to her! I'm just trying to talk to her. So can you ..."

Thomas' words were silenced by the crash of Jared's first against his face. There was a sudden cracking sound, followed by the thud of Thomas landing on the ground. Jared and the two other guys immediately rushed him and began kicking him repeatedly. While the other two focused on his stomach,

Jared drove his hardest kicks into Thomas' buttocks as he shouted,

"How do you like it, you worthless prick?" Jared's face became beet red and the veins of his forehead stuck out. "Huh?! How do you like it?"

Cindy clawed at Jared's shirt. "Stop it! Stop it! Get off him!" She pulled at his arm, struggling to get him away from Thomas. Jared threw his elbow at the nuisance behind him, cracking Cindy in the mouth and knocking her backwards.

A crowd of students had formed around the scene on the bridge. Through the cluster of pant legs and shoes, Thomas could see people staring in shock; all except for one. Standing beside the painting classroom door was Liam, with his arms folded and a contented sneer on his face. Thomas' vision blurred at the force of another impact. When his eyes refocused he saw Jessica clasping her hands over her mouth; tears streamed down her face. He couldn't make out the expression on her face; was it guilt, or regret? Their eyes met for a moment, and she turned her face away.

The gym coach and a couple other teachers came sprinting up to the bridge to break up the assault. Jared continued to fume and curse as the coach pulled him back. Thomas lay gasping for air, curled up in a ball, blood running out his nose. Cindy knelt beside him, crying as she rubbed his shoulders. A tiny trail of blood ran down the corner of her mouth. "Shhh, it'll be okay Tom. It's okay."

Jessica stood back with Shannon and the others, sobbing uncontrollably as she watched the teachers restrain the three football players, and the broken form of Thomas, coughing painfully as he lay on the bridge.

...

The school authorities acted quickly; this was a major incident, after all. The parents of every student involved were contacted and brought in to the school immediately. Each student involved met, separately from the others, with Principal Scott, the teachers that broke up the fight; their parents were part of the meeting. Once everyone had been talked to they were all suspended and told that they would hear back on a decision on their futures after Principal Scott had discussed the situation with the superintendent and the rest of the school board.

...

Thomas sat silently in the passenger side of the old pickup truck; each time the tires hit a pot hole, he winced and squirmed in his seat. A blood-soaked bandage was wrapped around his nose, and bruises had started to form under his eyes. His breathing was still uneven and he ached all over. All the school nurse was able to do for him was clean the blood off his face, bandage his nose with some soft gauze, and tell him that he should go see a doctor to find out if anything had been broken.

Mr. King stared straight forward as he drove; accelerating and braking in sudden lurches that sent shock waves of pain through Thomas' body. The truck screeched to a halt in the driveway beside their trailer house; without looking at his son, Mr. King growled, "Get in the house. I'll deal with you later."

Thomas got out slowly and carefully, clutching his aching side and walking like an old man. His father drove off before he could even shut the door. Thomas watched as halfway down the street the truck stopped, the passenger door opened a little, then quickly slammed shut. The truck careened off down the road and disappeared.

Thomas shuffled into his bedroom and very carefully lay down on his bed, flat on his back, trying to calm the pain just enough to relax. On the ceiling of his room were glow-in-the-dark stars. Although it was only late afternoon and not yet dark enough for them to glow, Thomas found something calming about them. He tried not to think about what had just happened; he knew it would come back to haunt him soon enough. Instead he traced, with his eyes, over the constellations he had tried to replicate in his room.

...

It wasn't long until he heard his dad's truck pull into the driveway and the driver's side door slam shut. Loud footsteps came pounding up the stairs of the porch. The front door opened and just as quickly slammed shut. Thomas tensed, sending every cut and bruise into overdrive, as he heard the stomping footsteps approach his bedroom door. When they continued past and went further down the hall, he let out a sigh of relief and felt a fraction calmer.

The telephone rang. His father answered the phone, the tone of his voice making it clear he was well on his way to drunk. "Yeah?!"

There was a sound like a bottle being slammed down on a wooden table. Thomas couldn't hear much of what was being said until his father started shouting again. "What da ya mean transfer him? What about that QB shithead that started the whole - Community Service?! What kind of bullshit is that? Just 'cause his daddy's the principal and the football team doesn't wanna lose their ... Oh, but I am so exactly right!"

There was a pause as the person on the other end of the telephone spoke. Mr. King gave the caller about five seconds and resumed his high-volume tirade. "Well of course they aren't gonna press charges. You got no kind of evidence to ... Oh, yeah? Well maybe I might ... What the hell is that supposed to mean? Try to have a better day? I'm having a swell day, asshole. Well you can just shove it up your ..."

Mr. King's voice got slightly quieter. "Hang up on me? Dumb some bitch."

Thomas heard the telephone slam against the wall. He sat up on the edge of his bed listening to the footsteps rushing toward his bedroom. The door swung open and knocked a hole in the wall about the size and shape of the doorknob. Thomas stood up and ventured a question. "What did they say?"

His dad waved a half-empty bottle around for emphasis. He spent a second or two trying to get Thomas in focus, and then let rip. "It's bad enough I have to pay your stinkin' mother all that alimony bullshit, but you had to stay here and give me a headache too. She gets the money, and I get the crap. Well, now the shit's hit the fan, and it's all 'cause of you, lover boy. Now we've gotta try and find another school, that ain't easy for a rap-ist."

"What are you so mad at me for? I didn't do anything. You know ..."

Mr. King caught him right across the jaw with the bottle of booze. The glass shattered and Thomas' head hit the wall before he fell to the floor.

36

The Scars in Our Eyes

Jessica wondered if this was how animals felt in a zoo. Once the shock of captivity had worn off, did they come to see their cage as normal? She had slipped so easily into the endless routine of posing, followed by solitary confinement. She didn't even mind that she was naked in front of him; that felt normal too. Their conversations were usually started by her; it helped to pass the time posing, and she had to admit that she was more and more curious about him.

"So tell me about college. I'd ask you which one you're going to, but I guess you're not going to tell me."

"It doesn't really matter which one I'm going to. Wherever you go, you end up with a piece of paper that says 'Thank you for paying us all this money, and congratulations on leaving with no guarantee you'll ever have a career'."

"What do you mean?" Jessica had never heard anyone talk like this. "Surely a degree will help you to get a career in the arts?"

"Well, yeah, if I want to work for some lousy design company, or teach in a dumb school. But if I go and wave my degree paper in front of an art gallery, or someone who works in the real world, they're going to laugh at me, and then ask me what my work is like. The degree will be irrelevant, probably worse than useless."

"So why bother?"

"Because, if I'm lucky, I'll gain some valuable experience, and get to exchange ideas with like-minded people. Plus if the teachers are okay, I might get to improve my technique and refine my skills. The paper will be meaningless, but the time is well spent."

Thomas turned back to his work; Jessica pondered what he had said. She'd always assumed that having a degree was the most important thing for her career. The idea of having to show the fruits of one's labor, rather than quoting a qualification, was scary. She began to see that being an artist was maybe not such an easy option. *But it still doesn't have to be like this.*

Thomas had obviously finished the painting; she changed pose, without being asked. After a few minutes of silence, she asked the question that had been gnawing at her for a few days.

"Where did you go, when you left Mountain high?"

He put down his brush, and sighed, a hollow, hopeless sound. He looked over at her, following the curves of her body from toe to head, and his gaze came to rest on her face, a haunted gaze. Reluctantly, he started to speak.

"After that day on the bridge, it was about two weeks before I was transferred to the South Campus High School, where all the trouble makers get to go."

"Why did it take two weeks?"

This time his sigh was impatient. "Because it was nearly two weeks before I was released from the hospital."

Jessica was going to ask another question, thought better of it. He took a deep breath and continued.

"After your football goons had finished with me, I was pretty beaten up. And that was before my father got to take his revenge on me for spoiling his day. Bones get broken; people do too. He was angry with me for costing him a day's pay. He'd been drinking. The school principle called, and that made him even angrier. Then he got to thinking about the hospital bills. I guess he snapped.

"I woke up the next day in the hospital. The doctor told me that in addition to my busted nose, two fractured ribs and broken tail bone, I had a fractured jaw. He asked me if all that had happened in school, in the fight. I looked out the window of the recovery room and saw him standing there, already drunk, and told the doctor yes, it had all happened in school. But it hadn't. After the phone call from the school, he came into my room and smashed a whisky bottle across my face."

"But how could he do that to you, your own father?"

"How could he do that to me? How could you do what you did to me?"

"I didn't …"

"You didn't what, Jessica? Everything that happened, happened because of you. Everything." He gestured at the paintings on the walls around the room. "All of this is … is because of you."

"I didn't ask Jared to do that! He just heard some rumors, and blew it all out of proportion. He thought you'd actually raped me, instead of just planning to."

"Planning to rape you? What are you talking about?"

"That's what I was told."

"Who told you?"

"I heard it from Sh ... from one of my friends, and she heard it from Jake."

"Jake!" Thomas stood up so quickly the chair fell from under him. He stood there, holding the beaker of her blood, glaring.

"I didn't plan to rape you. I planned to do something romantic, to make you happy. If you hadn't disappeared into a crowd of your friends every time I tried to talk to you, I could have explained. But rape; no, Jessie, nothing was further from my mind."

The words slipped out before she could stop them. "Well, look how far you've come since then." She froze, but it was too late. His eyes burned with anger. He turned away from her, and hurled the beaker against the wall. Blood spattered over the wall and the floor, and shards of glass embedded themselves in paintings.

Jessica stood up, terrified. "I ... I think I'll just go to my room."

"Get back here!" he whipped around to face her. "New pose. Now!"

He grabbed a large black pedestal and threw it onto the platform. Tossing a folded sheet of white drapery onto the pedestal, he snapped his fingers and pointed to the prop. Jessica stepped timidly onto the platform and arranged herself against the pedestal. Her fear had given way to guilt. Guilt and pain. She had tried to suppress the wound of that terrible day, and now she'd opened it right up again.

At least she'd had her dad to help her through. He'd taken time off from seeing his patients to help her work through the trauma. She'd been so terrified, standing there, watching Jared and his friends tear into Tom. Her dad had helped her to find the courage to face the ordeal that came after that horrible day. So she was able to tell the school board that she hadn't been raped, that actually nothing had happened. But her courage had still failed her. With all her friends saying he was planning to do something to her, that he deserved what he got, she found herself unable to disagree when the principle had asked her if Thomas had tried to do anything to her. By then, she was so confused she wasn't sure what had happened. Facts had slipped into the miasma of rumor and innuendo around her.

She'd lived with that lie for so long, it had become part of her, part of her story. Now she was surrounded with the consequences of that lie, and the guilt she'd buried came rumbling up to the surface like magma. Tears burned her face, burned tracks of guilt down her cheeks. *All this, because of me.*

. . .

It was a while before she trusted herself to speak. She looked around the room, at the now familiar paintings, and she thought about the other two sirens.

"Who are Rachel and Stacey?"

"I already told you. Stacey was here before you, and Rachel was here before Stacey." His eyes didn't move from the painting in front of him.

"Yes, but who are they?"

"You mean who were they?" Now it was Thomas' turn to look around. The paintings of Rachel and Stacey showed the same trajectory. At first, the poses were stiff and obstinate. It was only after he had bled them, forced them to his will, that he'd finally achieved his objective; the fragile, broken beauty of the last portraits. He had created them anew, out of their destruction at his hands.

"When I started at South Campus I didn't know anyone; since I was kind of a loner to begin with, that worked for me. I kept to myself and got on with my work, drawing and painting in my spare time.

"Then this one girl, Rachel, took an interest in what I was doing. She liked some pieces I'd made of skeletons, in couples. The one she liked best was of a male skeleton holding up a female one. I'd modeled it on the photo of you and me at the ball, the one where I picked you up."

"Yes, I remember." Jessica's voice was flat.

"Anyway, I told her it was about me and a girl I really liked, who didn't like me. The drawing was my way of saying that the girl and I were dead to one another."

But that wasn't true, was it Tom? Jessica kept the thought to herself, waited for him to go on.

"So anyway, she started to spend more time with me during classes and we seemed to be getting along. But she had this friend, Stacey, who was always around. At first I didn't mind her, but as Rachel and I grew friendlier, the third wheel became really annoying.

"Rachel and I would go out and do stuff after class. Not like a real date or anything, it was all kind of casual, mostly because Stacey was always around. But over the next couple of months we got closer; we'd go and make out behind the trees during lunch or after school. And Stacey would always come and find us, and then we'd have to do something else, to include her."

Thomas paused, and fixed some little detail on the painting. When he went on, his voice was rigid and quieter.

"Then one day, a Friday afternoon, I was waiting for her behind out favorite make-out tree. She came storming up with an angry look on her face. I went to hug her, but she pushed me away, and told me she'd heard why I'd been transferred from Mountain High, what I had supposedly done to one of the cheerleaders. She started to call me all kinds of terrible names.

"I tried to explain what really happened but she wouldn't listen. When she turned to go I grabbed her arm; I just wanted to make her listen. But she started shouting 'Rape!' at the top of her voice.

"So then I got arrested; they took me and booked me into the county jail for the night. Some idiot cop misread the age on my driver's license and booked me in as an adult when I was still technically a minor. And of course it was the weekend, so I wasn't able to see a judge until Monday."

It took a moment before Jessica realized that Thomas had stopped talking. He was looking at the floor, as if something terribly important down there needed his attention.

...

The memory was raw; time could not soften the pain and humiliation. His hand strayed to the scar across his abdomen. He heard their voices, felt their rough hands grabbing and slapping; saw himself, bent over the sharp edge of the metal cart, his hands gripped by one of the men as the others took their pleasure. It was like he was a ghost hovering over the scene; a ghost that could feel every blow, every stab of cruelty.

The ringleader, the one with the Mona Lisa tattoo, was readjusting his orange jumpsuit. "There, boys, just like I told you; our little trout here feels just as pretty as he looks."

Arno, the main sidekick, the one who had fooled Thomas into coming into the deserted medical room, handed his boss a lit cigarette. "Here, Jay-Dee. Hey, you think we can keep him?"

Jay-Dee grunted a brutal laugh. "Who knows, Arno? Maybe he'll get to like it here. Just in case, I guess I should mark my property; don't want the other guys getting jealous."

He stubbed the cigarette into Thomas' backside; alongside the other two burns he had called his little persuaders.

Thomas whimpered, the tiny, pathetic sound all his injured body and wounded psyche would allow. He sensed Jay-Dee leaning over him, heard the grating voice in his ear.

"You take care now, little trout. I'll be sure to come and see you later."

. . .

Thomas heard another voice, out of place somehow. It took him a moment to realize it was Jessica's.

"So what happened?"

"Well, let's just say you were lucky that the metal tray *you* got bent over had rounded edges." He laughed grimly. "So anyway, Monday came and they finally worked out I was a minor, and they took me in front of the judge, and the charges were dropped for insufficient evidence. I was free, for what it was worth.

"After that, I took my high school graduation exam a couple months early, got my diploma, and moved to – moved out of state. It wasn't until a long time after that I heard how Stacey had gotten a job working in a mall, and one of her co-workers told her the story about me and Mountain High. Someone who obviously knew the story real well; your friend Shannon." He said the name like a curse, like he needed to spit it out before it poisoned him. The rape story had dogged his life from the moment she had first made it up, and every time he heard it again, it was her voice behind the story.

Jessica was feeling like every time she started a conversation it came back on her, made her feel guiltier than ever. Now she felt like she had to protect Shannon too. She looked for a more positive subject.

"Tom, have you dated anyone else since then?"

"No. You?"

"Well, yeah, but …"

"But what?"

"Well, I dated a couple guys in my senior year, but it was mostly just going to school dances and a movie now and then."

"And what about the end of your junior year, after I left?" *Great work, Jessica; you've done it again.*

"Well, I did date one other guy."

"Oh yeah, who was that?" He was gripping the paintbrush so tight, it was beginning to creak in his hand. *If she says Liam, I swear I'm gonna …*

"Jake." Jessica braced herself for the expected storm. But Thomas just shook his head and said "Yeah, figures. He lies to your friends about me to make me look bad, and then he moves in. What was that like?"

"It was okay at first. We went to a school dance. He dressed real casual, and I felt kind of dressy next to him. Then we went out for a couple months, but it didn't work out, and we broke up."

"He dumped you?"

"Actually no, I dumped him."

"Why? Not that I feel bad about you dumping him, but what happened?"

"Well," she fidgeted with the drapery, twisting a knot of it around her finger, "he kept pushing me for a more … you know, sexual relationship."

"So he touched your butt and you dumped him."

"Yeah, well no; actually he used to try and touch my breasts when we made out. And then once he slid his hand down into my pants and, uh, went a little too far. I slapped him and told him never to do it again. And then a couple days later he went and did it again, so I dumped him on the spot. I didn't need guys who couldn't respect me."

"Guys?" Thomas made the *s* into a long, sensuous sound.

"Well, yeah, actually." She was already embarrassed from telling the first story, so what the heck? Back in my sophomore year, when I was a cheerleader, I was dating Jared."

"Obviously; the cheerleader has to date the quarter-back." Thomas' teeth grazed his knuckles.

She ignored the comment and went on. "He used to help me out in the gym, when I was doing my stretches. I'd lie down and keep one leg straight, and he'd push the other back toward my head, so I could improve my high kicks.

"He used to rub my thigh as the muscles stretched, and gradually he'd work his way down my thigh until he could sneak a few rubs, down there. At first I tried to ignore him; I didn't want to cause a scene, and jeopardize my reputation as a cheerleader. Then one day, I made the mistake of wearing running shorts during gym class. As we were stretching, he pulled my shorts and underwear to one side and stuck his thumb inside me. I shoved him away immediately and ran off into the girls' locker room, and put some knee-length tights on under my shorts.

"I was afraid to tell anyone. I thought it was my fault for wearing such revealing clothes, like I'd led him on, and anyway I was too embarrassed to tell anyone. We stopped dating; well, what really happened is he lost interest in me and started getting interested in a flirty blonde instead.

"But he never let me forget it. Whenever I saw him he'd sniff his thumb and wink at me. So between him and all the other jocks hitting on me because I was skinny and pretty, I quit the cheerleaders and went to the dance squad instead. There were a few pushy guys there too, but it wasn't as bad as the cheerleader team."

Thomas was looking at her intently. "What, you think it's funny? You think I'm a prude, right?" she snapped.

He stepped away from his work. "Let me show you something." She went to follow him, but he said, "No, stay there."

He went to the bookshelf and took down the R volume from a set of encyclopedias. He came back toward her, thumbing through the pages.

"Here it is. Jessica, let me broaden your education a little. According to the World Health Organization, 'Rape' is defined as 'the physically forced, without consent, or otherwise coerced penetration – even if slight – of the vulva or the anus, using a penis, other body parts, or an object."

Jessica didn't see his look of crooked triumph. A scene from her adolescence was playing out in her mind.

...

She lay curled up on the bathroom floor, crying. Her mother was chiding her through the closed door. "It's done now, Jessie. You can stop crying."

"You only counted to one. You said I could do it on the count of three."

"If I hadn't done it for you then you'd still be stuck with those maxi pads, and they wouldn't let you on the swim team. It was the same trying to get you out of diapers. I told you then that if you wanted to stay a baby, it was your choice. Well, you chose to be on the swimming team; you knew you'd have to start using tampons if you went on the team."

"Yeah, I know," Jessica's voice was muffled by tears, "But it hurts."

"It only hurts for a little while. If you weren't so tense and anxious about it, it would hardly have hurt at all."

Jessica came out of the bathroom, still crying. Her mother gave her a casual hug and said, "No need to keep crying about it, sweetie. You did well, and you've just taken a big step toward becoming a woman."

"It still hurts though."

"You think that was painful? Wait until you have to pass a baby through the same space."

...

She was brought back to reality by the sound of Thomas letting the heavy volume fall onto a table. He was looking at her quizzically. "You still don't get it, do you? Based on that overly broad definition, you *were* raped in high school, possibly twice. But you fingered the one guy who didn't do anything."

37

Through His Eyes

Brahms was playing in the background; Jessica didn't recognize the piece, but the familiar tonalities were comforting. She sat on a rectangular brown padded cube, larger than the one she'd posed on before. She sat at the edge; her legs crossed, and leaned back, using her arms to support herself. She listened to the music in the room and the thoughts in her head.

As she looked, for the hundredth time, at the paintings on the wall, she thought about some of the art history lectures she'd attended.

"Just out of curiosity, is it only nude women that you paint?"

"Mostly, but I've studied male nudes, still life, landscapes, and all that at school. Why?"

"It just seems typical."

"Typical of what?"

"The male artist. The male gaze."

"There are plenty of girls in my classes that also prefer the female nude as their subject matter. And no, they aren't lesbians. They and I both agree that the female form is more visually interesting than the male."

"Oh really?" she replied skeptically.

"Women have a greater proportional contrast and variety of form; that makes the female form a more interesting subject."

"Yeah, but I bet their work is perceived a lot differently than their male made counterparts."

"What makes you say that?"

"I'm saying, when a male artist paints a beautiful woman, that's a neutral subject, but when women artists use women's bodies and faces they are seen as making a political statement."

"I think you've taken a few too many feminist art history courses. Sure some of those social stereotypes exist, here and there. But it's not as simple as that. Not everyone, male or female, thinks the same way."

"You wouldn't understand. Being male, you don't see how women are shaped by the preferences of men."

"Oh really?" Thomas made a good job of imitating her skeptical tone.

"Yeah, really. We're raised to be constantly aware of our faces and the shape of our bodies and how these will affect our opportunities in life. We have to mold these parts of ourselves," she waved her hand around her breasts and toward the rest of her body, "Regardless of how insecure we may feel about them, so as to please a male audience, a dominant audience."

"These are tired concepts from the 1970s."

"Oh! Really? Let's see, the pretty girl gets asked to the dance. The pretty girl gets on the cheer squad. The pretty girl gets all the attention. Then the prettiness fades into the mature woman. She's tossed aside for the next pretty little thing."

Thomas responded. "That's why no matter how beautiful or plain a woman may be; her defining trait should be her personality. It is the smart, cultured, and intellectual woman who retains her interest. Not just some pretty face on a hollow head." He glanced at the paintings of Rachel and Stacey. "It's a rare thing to find a young woman who encapsulates both." He looked intently at her, his eyes questioning her from behind the mask.

Jessica was only too aware of the effect his compliment was having on her, but she soldiered on with her argument. "Let's be honest, if a man was looking to hire a female secretary and he had two equally qualified applicants; both with the same level of experience and education, practically identical skills, but one was more attractive than the other, he would hire the prettier one; nine times out of ten that would be the result."

"Okay, let's say I have two equally beautiful models; both aesthetically pleasing in every way an artist could look for, but one is a smart, educated, and a cultured girl while the other is a complete bubbly ditz; I would always chose the smarter of the two. But that's just me."

"Why?"

"Because we would be able to have discussions, like this one."

She settled back into the pose and listened to the music. His compliment had unsettled her, and taken the force out of her argument.

Thomas wasn't getting anywhere with his painting. He was thinking about his encounter with Cindy. *Go away Cindy; this isn't the time*. His question punctured the companionable silence.

"When I, uh, when you first got here you had a small ring on your right hand. Did your boyfriend give that to you? Is it some kind of a promise ring?"

"What? Oh, um no. No nothing like that. I don't have a boyfriend," she replied absently.

"Why not? Wouldn't be hard for you to find one."

"I just wanted to stay focused on my degree. Plus, you know, moving away from home for college made the idea of having a long-distance relationship too complicated."

"And there's no one at your new school?"

"Not really. I went on a few dates, but there wasn't anything serious. They probably lost interest." She thought about Eric Matthews. They had dated for a few months, and it was fun, but knowing that he would eventually have to move away for his residency had made them both cautious, and it had come to nothing.

"So, why the ring?"

"It helps to remind me."

"Of what?"

"To make the right choices."

There was a charged pause. "Well, it's too bad you didn't have that with you back in high school."

She opened her mouth to speak, but thought better of it. *He's right.* She decided to just swallow her thoughts and look forward.

Her father had given her the ring just after her sixteenth birthday, when she was about to start dating. He'd asked her to wear it as a reminder to make the right choices, not just with dating but with everything in her life. He'd told her how important her choices in life were at that age and how they might shape the young woman she would become.

At the time she hadn't taken any of it seriously and had stuffed the ring away in a drawer. It wasn't until after the incident with Thomas and the slimy advances from Jake that she felt the need to wear it.

Now he'd brought it to her attention, she realized how naked her hand felt without it. She brushed the thought aside.

"So tell me, how did you come by this place? It must have cost a pretty penny, with the bomb shelter and all."

Thomas put down his brush. For a moment, he looked angry, and Jessica wondered what she'd said to upset him. But his face relaxed into a blank expression, and there was a faraway look in his eyes, almost sad.

"Actually, it depends on how you look at it. It didn't cost any money; the price was, just, one life."

A shiver of fear and revulsion slithered down her spine. Had he just admitted to another crime? She tried to keep her voice level. "A life?"

"Yeah, a life. This place belonged to my mother. She was killed in a car accident a couple years ago. She left it to me in her will."

Jessica waited for him to say more, but he was already turning back to his canvas. She wanted to say sorry, to ask him something, anything, about his mother, but she didn't know where to start. In the end, she settled back into her pose, resigned to the silence.

Thomas returned his attention to the painting. He scratched around for a while, but the motivation just wasn't there. After several minutes of forcing himself to paint, he gave in and said, "That's good for tonight."

She nodded and quietly shuffled into her room, shutting the door behind her. She let out a small sigh of relief when Thomas locked the door, and turned off all the lights except a single bulb near the hallway to her room, before he left.

38

She could hear the muffled sound of two male voices coming from downstairs. Carol was curled up on Jessica's bed; this had become her automatic response whenever she felt overwhelmed by the whole situation. The two voices faded out and she heard the front door close. Soon footsteps sounded on the stairs, coming toward the bedroom.

Blaine stepped through the open door and sat down on the bed beside his wife. "I told Detective Marshall everything we know. He assured me that they'll do all they can to find out what's going on. He seems very efficient; I'm sure he can help us."

"Uh huh," she sniffled; she just wanted to hear some good news.

"I also heard back from Shannon's parents. They got a hold of Shannon and asked her a few questions. They told me that Shannon stayed at her school in Colorado Springs all through the January break. She hasn't heard from Jessica since December."

Carol sat up, bewildered by the news. "That doesn't make sense. Did you learn anything else?"

"Shannon is going to forward me the last couple emails she received from Jessica. I figured I'd go check in a minute; hopefully she's had time to send them between classes."

"Okay." Carol returned her tear-soaked cheeks to the pillow.

"Can I get you something to eat? It's getting late. I'm going to head downstairs and make something for dinner."

"No. Thanks."

Downstairs in the kitchen Blaine made himself a simple ham and cheese sandwich before heading into his den. He sat down at his desk and signed in to his email account. The sight of a new message from Shannon brought a glint of hope; he took a deep breath and opened the email. He read over the email twice to make sure he hadn't misunderstood anything.

Carol came downstairs and found her husband staring intently at the monitor, with a half-eaten sandwich clutched in his left hand. "Anything?"

"Yes, I got a few forwards from Shannon."

"What do they say?"

"According to the dates, Jessie sent the emails to Shannon just after Christmas. In them it says how we and Jessie had gone on some sort of skiing trip in Aspen and that Jessie had met a 'cute guy' on the ski lift, and when she went to enter his number into her phone she dropped it and lost it." He skimmed through the email before continuing,

"So the email gave a different phone number for Jessie, but Shannon has only been able to text Jessie at this new number. Whenever she calls she always gets a text message reply saying that she can't talk for one reason or another.

"I've also contacted CSU and none of her professors have seen her in their classes since before the break. None of her roommates have seen her either."

"Okay, let me know what else you find. I need to go eat something. I'm feeling weak." Carol shuffled out of the den toward the kitchen.

Blaine got up and quietly closed the doors of the den so he could have some privacy. He pulled up the forwarded email from Shannon, the one about the ski trip. In the email was the phone number that Shannon had been told was Jessica's new number. Dialing the number into his phone he pressed the send button and listened intently as it rang.

39

DETOUR

The pale glow of the dashboard illuminated the underside of Thomas' face. He slipped along the dark night roads in his black car, feeling gloriously invisible. Driving at night always gave him a feeling of calm. Every couple weeks he'd go for a late night drive, in no particular direction, just for the hidden pleasure of it.

He would put on an album with the score from a recent movie that had impressed him and just drive until the music was over. Depending on where he had to be the next day he would either stay at a cheap hotel or pop in another disc and drive back.

His calm interlude was interrupted by the sound of an irregular ringtone. He reached deep inside one of the inner pockets of his dusty black coat and pulled out a cheap-looking cell phone. He stared at the unfamiliar number as it continued to ring. After a while it stopped. Thomas placed the phone down on the empty ashtray and turned down the volume of the music.

His eyes flickered from the phone, to the road, and back to the phone as he waited to see if it would ring again. Nothing. He let out a short sigh of relief. His pulse started to calm down to a steady pace; then a short jingle sounded.

Reaching for the phone, he picked it up and looked at the screen. He had – Jessica had – a new message. He pressed send and waited. Through the earpiece he heard: *You have one new message. First message.*

Thomas held his breath and waited, assuming it was Shannon just calling to chat with Jessica. But a man's voice came on – *Jessie, its dad. Your mother and I are very worried about you. I got this number from Shannon and she said that you two were never planning to meet in Denver.*

I understand if you're a little frustrated with things. But please call me and let me know what is wrong. Whatever it is we can talk about it. Call me any time; I'll have my phone with me. I love you sweetheart.

Thomas looked for a moment at the little plastic object connecting him to Jessica's past. Then he rolled down the window and threw the phone straight down onto the asphalt rushing by below him, dashing it to pieces. Turning the music back up and staring out through the windshield into the night, he focused his mind on the task at hand.

40

WARMER THAN THE SHOWER

Jessica woke to the sound of water cascading against the tile and concrete floor as the shower came to life. The light in her room flicked on and the door cracked open. Thomas' head appeared in the doorway; he looked weary. "Wash up."

He left the door ajar and stepped out of sight. Jessica took a few seconds to emerge from her white feather comforter cocoon, dropping her layers on the mattress, and stepped into the shower. It was so much easier to sleep with the warm comforter and the light off at night.

As she massaged the shampoo into her hair, she heard Thomas come into the room. With her eyes closed to keep the soap out she wasn't able to see what he was doing, so she backed further into the corner until she heard him say, stifling a yawn, "Your breakfast is on the bed," he let out another yawn, "and here's a towel."

He left the room and closed the door behind him; and she heard the sound of the lock latching into place.

She stood under the shower soaking in the hot water as she waited for it to shut off. Normally, Thomas would turn it off as soon as he saw she had finished rinsing off all the soap, but today it kept running. Bemused, she tapped on the two-way mirror and yelled out, "I'm done now."

She remained under the stream of soothing water until it finally turned off. Leaning to one side, she rang out her hair and wiped away most of the water from her body before walking over to the bed for the towel. But as she reached for it, she stopped short; her hand went involuntarily to her mouth. Her eyes began to well up until sobs broke through, despite her smile.

There beside the bed lay her violin, neatly propped up in its case, alongside a small stack of her books. Atop the books was a scuffed-up thin silver ring with a small shield on it. There were a few flecks of blue color left around the shield, but most of it had been worn away. She fell to her knees and slipped her ring on to her finger, and rested her head on the edge of the bed as the tears of joy flowed.

41

THE SIREN'S SONG

RESTORED

Thomas awoke to the sound of a violin playing. He pulled himself up off the pile of cushions on top of the platform; he must have fallen asleep. At first he thought that he had left the stereo on again, but when he realized the stereo was off he walked over to the metal door of the bomb shelter and peered in.

Jessica sat on the edge of the bed, with the sheet wrapped around her like a strapless dress, cradling her cheek against the violin as she played.

Thomas waited for her to finish before he opened the door and stepped inside. He stood there without his mask; his hair was messed up and his eyelids still bore smeared traces of black paint. She looked at him with a smile, set her violin down, and walked over and gave him a hug. She didn't say anything, just smiled as she sat back down beside her violin.

"Bring that with you while you pose," Thomas said, nodding toward the precious instrument.

Jessica happily picked it up and made for the door, but Thomas still stood in the way.

"Leave the sheet."

Her smile faded a little and she removed the bed sheet from her body, reluctantly, tossing it onto the bed before he stepped aside.

For the next couple hours Jessica played anything that she could remember. She sat on an ornate-looking ottoman with wooden claw-footed legs at each corner. Most of what she could play from memory consisted of church hymns, but Thomas didn't mind what she played. Most of the time he just sat and watched her; barely doing any painting at all.

A couple hours later, Thomas realized he had only painted a few patches of color; the rest of the canvas was still occupied by the rough pencil drawing. Jessica placed her violin into her lap and said, with as much sincerity as she could summon,

"Thank you. Thank you, for letting me have some of my things." Her eyes began to show the signs of coming tears. "I, really appreciate it. That, and the fact you drove overnight to Denver and back; it means a lot to me."

"Yeah, well don't think that it changes anything."

Her gratitude faded into sadness and she reluctantly made her way to her room, but before she stepped inside she turned back to Thomas.

"I really do appreciate your kindness and you have my gratitude, but you do not have my consent." Then she stepped into the corner room and closed the metal door behind her.

42

CODE 5: 10-29v

Detective Marshall and his partner Detective Ramses perched politely on the couch, avoiding the chintzy cushions. They were treading a delicate line, and spoiling the Shawsen's prize cushions wouldn't help. The job had been a whole lot easier when it seemed clear that the daughter was simply rebelling against her parents; but with the new information they had, things had gotten a lot more complicated.

Mrs. Shawsen sat as close as she could to her husband, clutching his arm and concentrating on holding back her tears so as not to ruin her make-up. Not wanting to cause any alarm until more concrete facts became available, Detective Marshall kept his comments deliberately vague.

"Based on what we know so far, your daughter may have been planning to do this for some time; she may have made up her story about meeting her friend in Denver. It's not unusual for a young woman to rebel against her home circumstances."

"But that just doesn't sound like our Jessica," Mrs. Shawsen said, looking toward her husband. Mr. Shawsen was thinking of Jessica's photo collage on her bedroom wall. He'd been staring at it a lot the past few days. In nearly every picture of Jessica, Shannon was standing beside her.

"What I don't understand is why would she lie to Shannon about the whole family ski trip? Those two have been the closest friends for over ten years. If she was going to share a secret with anyone, it would be Shannon."

Detective Marshall swallowed, looked at his partner. *Here goes.* "We received word earlier this morning that the Denver police were able to locate your daughter's car."

"Where was it?" Mr. and Mrs. Shawsen asked in unison.

"It was found in the parking lot of a Wal-Mart at the north end of Denver. The only reason they found it so quickly was because a few parking tickets had been written out for it and it was in their system. Apparently it has been sitting there for some time."

"Did they find anything inside her car that might tell us where she went?" Mr. Shawsen asked.

"Well, yes and no," Detective Ramses replied.

"They checked the Wal-Mart security cameras footage from January 13th, when you said she was supposedly meeting her friend, and the video shows your daughter parking her Mustang, getting out, and then climbing into the passenger side of a black car, which then drove off," Detective Marshall added. Ramses, his partner, gave him a questioning look, to which he very subtly shook his head. *No.* "Thing is, she didn't take any luggage with her."

"So she left all her things in her car? All her clothes?"

"From what we can see in the security video, the only things she took with her were a jacket and her purse."

"But what about the black car? Were you able to get the license number for it?" Mr. Shawsen hunched forward in his seat, sensing that things were moving, and not in a good direction.

"At the time the video was shot it was late into the evening and snowing heavily. The plate had snow built up around it so only parts of the first three digits were visible. From the color and design it appears to be either an Idaho or Utah issued plate."

Mr. Shawsen racked his brain for any connection he could think of in either state that might have made Jessica run off, but nothing came to mind.

"I don't know of anyone that Jessie has ever talked about from either state. Plus the email said she was moving to California."

"There's no reason to assume they were going to California; the email may not have been truthful," Detective Ramses replied, "In fact, it may not have been Jessica who wrote it."

"Yes, well a lot is still speculation at this point," Detective Marshall hurriedly added, giving his partner a look.

"And the phone number?" Mr. Shawsen urged, "The alternate one listed in the email?"

"That number is for a prepaid phone which was purchased a few months ago from a mall in Salt Lake City. We checked for any credit card information that might have been used in the purchase, but the vendor's records indicated it was purchased with cash.

"We've notified the Salt Lake police and we'll let you know if we hear anything from them." Detective Marshall stood, indicating it was time for them to be leaving. Detective Ramses followed and added, "If you find out anything new, let us know as soon as you do."

Mr. and Mrs. Shawsen both nodded.

"Thank you, detective. Thank you both." Mr. Shawsen opened the front door and the two officers left.

...

Inside the undercover police car Detective Ramses asked, "Why didn't you tell them about the struggle inside the black car on the security video? I know the image was blurry, but you could tell their daughter was trying to get away from the driver."

Detective Marshall sighed. "It's not enough to go on. If we tell them it's a kidnapping now, and it turns out she was just pleased to see the guy, we're going to look kind of stupid. For now, we need to concentrate on finding out who the guy in the black car is."

...

Upstairs in Jessica's bedroom, Carol had returned to her place on the twin size bed. Blaine sat beside her, gently rubbing her back.

"I don't understand this. Something doesn't feel right. I know our Jessie wouldn't do something like this. And I'm sure those detectives are keeping something from us." He stood up and paced around his daughter's room, contemplating every little thing that sat on a shelf or hung on a wall.

"So what can we do?" Carol asked.

"For now we just pray that she's safe."

43

Bleeding the Edges

Jessica lay flat on her stomach, as she had done for the past couple modeling sessions, her feet fidgeting in the air, her elbows propping her up as she read the book in her hands. Thomas had become increasingly diligent about improving his paintings, and as the quality increased so too did the time spent working on each one.

Once she finished a chapter she placed the ribbon between the pages, closed the book, and set it down it front of her. She turned and watched Thomas as he painted. He would only glance at her for a second before his eyes were back on the painting. To get his attention she picked her book back up, opened it, and closed it with a dull clap. Nothing. She reopened the book and slapped it shut. When he finally looked up at her she said,

"Don't think that your little acts of kindness will win you my consent, because you won't have it."

Thomas rested the hand he held his brush in on his knee, a grin playing on his lips, and said,

"We'll see."

"Yes, we will see," she returned his grin, defiant.

Thomas glared at her as she opened her book back up and resumed reading. He went back to his painting and tried to put her defiance out of his mind. As he painted, his eye twitched at each crackling sound as Jessica turned a page in her book. Unable to stand it any longer he blurted out,

"How can you stand reading those tissue paper pages? You go to turn one and five others stick together. Then you have to crinkle them between your fingers to try and separate them and…"

"Really?" Jessica replied, tilting her head as she deliberately rubbed the pages between her fingers.

Thomas got up, snatched the book out of her hands and placed it on a table beside a few others. He picked up a different one from his own library and handed it to her. She glanced over the cover – *Romeo and Juliet* - then waited for him to sit back down.

"Personally I think his comedies are better. His tragedies are too depressing."

"It's the tragedy that makes it so good. Can you image how boring the story would be if they hadn't died? Their coupled death is what elevates their love."

"Oh please. Their love? Those two spend the entire book lusting after each other from the moment they make eye contact. It's only because their love is forbidden that they find each other so desirable. Take that away and what foundation for a relationship do they have? Nothing."

"So you're saying if they had some more of a history together, other than their families' feuds, then their love could be justified?"

"Sure. I guess if they had known each other for some time before and not been so instantly hot for each other then it would seem more genuine."

"Like if Romeo had known Juliet for a few years and gradually developed a liking for her before he worked up the courage to express his feelings for her?"

"Yeah, that would make more sense."

"Then it wouldn't be a tragic love story, it would be some dumb suburban marriage." He shook his head irritably. "Just read it."

Once he resumed painting, Jessica turned her head straight toward Thomas, deliberately turned the pages as loudly as she could, not bothering to read any of it.

Thomas gave up. He stood up with his brush and the beaker in hand and said,

"You know what, that's good enough for tonight. You can go wait on the bed while I clean up."

Her playful attitude quickly evaporated at the word 'bed'. She stood up and shuffled into her room.

As she lay on the bed she could hear Thomas rattling around in the open room. She closed her eyes and focused on preparing herself for what was to follow.

Thomas came through the doorway carrying the same drawing supplies he did each night. However, this time he also brought the other bag, with the restraint straps in it.

"What are those for?"

"Just to make things more interesting."

She struggled as he restrained her hands, but only half-heartedly. A faint frisson of excitement flickered through her mind; she quickly suppressed it.

With the restraints in place, he tied a blindfold over her eyes.

"What are you going to do?" she asked nervously.

"You'll see. Or rather, you won't see."

Thomas propped the fold out stool at the edge of the bed and then sat there silently. He quieted his breathing and made no sound at all as he watched Jessica's torso rise and fall. When he could see goose bumps starting to form on her skin he began noisily sketching. She let out a short sigh of relief.

Lying there, she tried to keep her mind from the anticipation that threatened to overcome her. *I'm driving my car ... through the canyon ... in the fall, admiring the changing leaves.* It went silent again and she couldn't tell if he'd moved or not. Her breathing sped back up and she felt her face redden. *I'm in a park, or maybe sitting through a boring lecture on campus.* He blew air lightly over her stomach and hips; she felt blush on her face spread over the rest of her body. She turned her face away from where she thought he was and held her breath as she strained to focus her thoughts. *No, I'm in church.*

After minutes that felt like hours, the sound of the pencil against the paper resumed and she released her breath. Her blush slowly receded, but she still felt on edge and tense.

An extended period of drawing, erasing, and noises indicating that he was only at the side of the bed on the stool gave her time to relax. But then the sounds came to a halt.

"What are you doing?" she asked, blindly gesturing around the room. "Are you done? I'm, uh, getting a cramp in my leg."

There was no answer, only silence. Thomas sat quietly at the side of the bed, smiling at every little flinch or reaction to the slightest breeze or faintest sound. He poked the side of the mattress, inches from her ribs. A nervous laugh escaped her mouth before she stuttered, "I ... I, need to use the bathroom." Her whole body was covered with goose bumps.

He removed the blindfold and undid the restraints. Humming to himself he gathered up his drawing supplies. Jessica watched him suspiciously and asked, "What did you do?"

"Nothing." He grinned. "Don't you have to use the bathroom?"

He stepped out of the room and locked the door behind him. Jessica sat motionless on the mattress, waiting for her heightened senses to calm back down.

44

WHAT COULD BE MORE SHOCKING THAN GAS PRICES

Cindy shifted her phone to the other ear and propped it up with her shoulder as she turned off the Mountain Valley exit and into the nearby gas station.

"Yeah mom, I'll be there in a few more minutes. My car's thirsty. I gotta fill 'er up." She paused as she listened to her mother's voice again. "Yup. I'll see ya soon. Bye."

Cindy hopped out of her car and began filling the tank. She cringed at the rapidly rising numbers as she thought about the upcoming week. Valentine's Day was just around the corner and she'd wanted to ask Thomas if he had any plans. Even though she knew Jessica was back in his life, she felt she had a chance; she thought of his drawing, and goose bumps pushed at her clothes. Cindy had seen him the day before in the art department, but had frozen and walked away before he saw her. The coming Monday would be her only chance to ask him before the fourteenth.

Being back in her home town for the weekend, to visit her parents, gave her time to relax and think of what to do when she got back up to Vernal.

The lever on the nozzle clicked; the tank was full. Cindy replaced the gas cap and headed inside the gas station to pay. A forgettable pop song was quietly playing from the speakers in the ceiling. She bobbed her head unconsciously to the beat of the music as she waited in line.

When it was her turn she placed her cash on the counter and said, "Pump number three."

The cashier counted the bills, removed a few coins from the till and handed them to Cindy. "Here's your change."

Putting the coins in her pocket Cindy headed for the door, and stopped suddenly in her tracks. On the bulletin board next to the exit door, staring right at her, dark brown hair, brown eyes, and fair skin, wearing a navy blue shirt was Jessica Shawsen. Above the picture were the words *'Have you seen this girl?'* Cindy pulled the paper off the wall and rushed out to her car. Sitting in the driver's seat, she stared at the paper, her mouth hanging open. *Oh no, Tom?*

Below the pictures it stated Jessica's height and appearance; then came the information that she had last been seen at the Wal-Mart in Denver on January 13th. There was a phone number at the bottom as well.

Cindy stared silently at the paper for a few moments before she folded it up and stuffed it into her purse. She counted in her head. Not more than a week ago she'd seen a new painting of Jessica hung up in the art department display cases.

When she was able to steady the shaking in her hands she pulled out of the gas station, tires squealing, and drove off.

45

SINKING SINSATION

Jessica sat, curled into a small shape on the bed. She hadn't moved for some time. She twisted a strand of her hair around her finger, and stared blankly at the wall in front of her. She closed her eyes, trying to recall every detail of the evening before, trying to imagine what he'd been doing as she lay there, bound and blindfolded. She stretched out on her back, arms and legs spread-eagled, goose bumps rising on every surface of her flesh.

Damn you, Thomas King. Even as she tried to dismiss him from her fevered mind, the sensations he had awakened in her whispered under her flesh, sensual sirens calling to her. The truth was, she ached to feel those sensations again; she was lost in a sea of longing. She wanted him to take her again, to open that door to the sensual world. Her skin burned at the thought; every nerve sang with desire.

All the resolution that had carried her through the past weeks dissipated in an instant. She was weak. Her convictions melted into her warm flesh and sank without a trace. A still small voice inside her told her to hang on to what she believed, but the voice was quickly drowned under the flood of sensations.

It wasn't her fault, was it? After all, he had forced her, it wasn't as if she'd initiated anything, wasn't as if she'd consented, even. She had done nothing wrong. If he chose to force her again, what could she do? It wasn't such a sin if she let it happen; she was powerless after all, a prisoner. The more she justified it to herself, the more the still small voice cried out, from far far away.

She wondered if this was how St. Theresa felt, waiting in anguish for the arrow of desire to embed itself in her willing, wanting flesh. Bernini had made her into an erotic icon, and she could see why.

She knew now. She was his, his creature. He had made her from the ashes of her old self. There was nothing she could do. She curled up in the white comforter that he had brought her, ignoring the world outside her little white cloud.

46

TO FALL FOR
IS TO FALL WITH

In the art department hallway, Thomas walked past the display cases, assessing the new work that had been added to the wall. He heard someone coming around the corner, looked over and saw Cindy. He smiled and said,

"Hey you."

She gave him a faint smile and didn't say anything until she was standing next to him.

"Hey. So, um, you got any big plans for tomorrow?"

"Tomorrow?"

"You know, Valentine's Day."

"Oh right, yes. Yes, I do. I have a ... a date." Thomas looked like a person who'd just remembered his mom's birthday.

"Oh good. Good. Who ya takin' out?"

"Just a girl from my advanced painting class, you wouldn't know her."

"I might. What's her name?"

"Her name? It's … its Jen. Her name is Jen. How about you? You have any plans?"

Cindy made a false start followed by a nervous laugh. "Actually, I wanted to ask you …" She swallowed hard as her glossy, loving eyes stared into his. "But, somebody asked me before I could find you and even so … it looks like I'm too late." A small, sad smile flashed and then quickly faded. "If I'd caught ya sooner … maybe things could have been different."

"Can you take a rain check for now?"

"Of course. Yep. No worries. Plus, I've still got a date too."

"With whom?"

"His name is, uh, Wally. Yup Wally. Wally West."

"Well you'll have to let me know how it goes." Thomas turned to leave, suddenly busy, but Cindy placed her hand on his shoulder and said,

"Tom, I was … I was wondering."

"Yeah?"

"How do … how do you feel … " Cindy couldn't bring herself to ask. "… about the longevity of your paintings? Like, how long ago was it that you did these paintings of Jessica?" she pointed to Thomas' newest paintings hanging in the display case.

"Well, these two were sometime last week and that one there was from the week before. Why?"

"I just wondered how long the uh … color … stays that rich?"

"Oh, yeah. Well, I spray each painting with a protective coating to keep the color from fading. I figured it out after a couple of them started to brown more than I wanted. Luckily, I was able to stop that happening … so far. Only time will tell."

"Like a UV protective spray, sorta thing?"

"Yeah something like that."

"Okay, well that's all, I …" It was Cindy's turn to leave; but she hesitated for a moment, and then hugged Thomas, her arms around his neck. She pressed her whole body into him as he hugged her back. When she started to cry she let go and hurried away saying,

"I gotta go. Bye Tom. Love you."

Thomas stared as she disappeared around the corner at the end of the hallway. She'd been unusually emotional the last couple times they'd met. He thought he knew why; the drawing. He'd woken up some awkward feelings in her, feelings left over from their high school friendship. He shrugged, and turned to go, a wry smile on his face. *Women.*

47

CAPILLARY CONFESSIONS

Pretty women. Thomas worked at his latest painting, keeping Jessica in the corner of his eye. She kept glancing at him, then looking away immediately. He thought he knew why. But he asked anyway.

"Something on your mind?"

"No. Yeah. What are you going to do later?"

"Going to do?"

"Yeah, tonight."

"I don't know, but something. Yeah, definitely something rather than, uh, nothing." It was all he could do not to grin at her.

"What, specifically?"

"Why?" Now he let her see his smirk. "Is there something specific you'd like me to do?"

"No. NO, not at all. I was just wondering, is all." He could see her squirming, shifting in her pose. He was enjoying himself; his painting was almost forgotten.

Jessica sat on the stool, her knees tucked up against her chest. She was sure her desire was visible on her skin; she tried to hide it, push it back down where it belonged, but it marked her like a tattoo. She gritted her teeth and worked to suppress it.

...

It seemed like hours before Thomas put his brush down and said, "Alright, we're done for now."

Jessica got up quickly, and headed for her room before he said anything. She hurried through the door, and he watched her retreating back, his smile threatening to split the mask.

She slipped into bed, and listened to the sound of Thomas clearing up in the studio. *Hurry up.* The sounds subsided, and she heard him fiddling with something else by the corner units. Her anticipation grew, clamored.

Thomas came into the room with a tray in his hands. *Where's the bag?* He set the tray down at the foot of the bed. "Here's your dinner, enjoy. Have a restful night; I'll see you tomorrow." He stepped out the door, closed it behind him and locked it shut.

Jessica sat bolt upright, fuming. *He knows, dammit.* A half-swallowed scream of frustration escaped her; she grabbed the pillow from behind her, and hurled it as hard as she could at the metal door. It hardly made a sound.

48

FROM LIGHT INTO
DEEP CADMIUM RED

Jessica jolted awake. She was momentarily dazzled by the light. She heard a quiet tap on the metal door. The door opened and Thomas poked his head in, smiling, and said,

"Morning sunshine."

She glared at him spitefully for waking her so rudely. She remembered his teasing the night before. And she was sure he remembered it too.

"Go on, wash up."

He stepped away from the door, leaving it slightly ajar, and turned on the water for her. She defiantly burrowed deeper into the comforter and rested her head back on the pillow. When Thomas looked in to see why she wasn't showering yet, she glared up at him with one eye.

"If you don't go shower then the shower will come to you."

He stepped out of the room. She heard the sound of a running faucet and some other rattling noises in the next room. When he returned he had a bucket of water in one hand and an ice cube tray in the other. He set the bucket down on the floor and started tauntingly tossing one ice cube at a time into the bucket. She scooted into the corner of the bed and wrapped all the blankets more tightly around her.

After all the ice cubes were in the bucket of water, Thomas picked it up and drew it back, preparing to toss the contents on the little white mound with Jessica's head poking out the top. As he stepped forward to throw the water Jessica burst out of the sheets shrieking,

"Alright, alright! I'm going."

She quickly got in the shower and began soaking under the hot water. Turning her back to him she muttered under her breath,

"Pain in the ..."

A cold rush of water splashed over her backside and down her legs.

"Thomas!"

He strolled out the door and into the open room. Jessica growled her frustration and then carried on washing.

When she was nearly done washing she heard him come into the room. She moved to the far corner and shouted,

"Thomas King, don't you *dare* throw another bucket of ice water on me." She paused and waited for a response.

"Do you hear me?"

He said nothing and soon she heard the metal door shutting. The water to the shower turned off, so she knew that he wasn't in her room. She stepped cautiously around the corner, expecting another playful surprise, then stopped at the sight on her bed. She stared at the silky red dress laid out on the bed next to her breakfast. The strapless dress was a rich bright red and the highlights on it had an almost orange tint; the shadows turned it a deep crimson. Beside the dress was a single rose with two of its petals plucked off and placed next to it. Attached to the rose's stem was a note that read, *'Tonight my muse will be my Valentine.'*

49

CODE 1: 10-57

At the Mountain Valley police department, Detective Marshall sat at his desk speaking on the phone with a recent scam victim. He was losing patience; the scowl on his face was proof of that.

"Yes ma'am, I understand how upset you may be, but the unfortunate thing is that this overpayment scam happens all the time and it is difficult to catch the persons doing it, which is ... yes ... yes ... which is why they keep doing it."

Pressing his fingers into his forehead he rubbed along the length of his impressive eyebrows. He had a headache coming, he could tell.

"For now what you can do is go onto IC3.gov and file a complaint. We will contact you if we need further information. Uh huh; yes ... alright, have a good day."

Hanging up the phone, he leaned back into his chair as far as it would recline and let out an audible sigh. Detective Ramses sat down at the desk beside his and turned toward him with an open folder.

"I've got an update on the Shawsen situation."

Sitting reluctantly back up in his chair, Detective Marshall leaned forward over his desk and said,

"What's the news?"

"First thing, it doesn't get us any closer to an answer, but it lets us know what her parents' assumptions are." Detective Ramses pulled out a copy of a piece of paper with a picture of Jessica Shawsen on it, and a caption that read – *Have you seen this girl?* He handed it to his partner.

"Her father put 'em up around town with his personal cell as the contact number."

Marshall glanced over the poster and placed it on his desk.

"Okay, what else?"

"Denver got back to us about a second sighting of the black Intrepid. It turns out the same car returned to the exact place in the parking lot where it was last seen and the driver got out of the car."

"Could they get a decent look at his face?"

"No. He'd shown up in the middle of the night and was wearing a dusty black coat on top of a hooded sweater that was pulled low on his face; which he kept deliberately tilted toward the ground."

"So what was he doing there?"

"Video shows him stopping the vehicle with the front end facing the security camera and the headlights left on. He got out of his car, opened the trunk of Miss Shawsen's vehicle, and removed a few items before leaving."

Detective Marshall silently gestured for his partner to specify the known items.

"Looks to be a musical instrument case, like a viola or violin, plus a few books."

"Did they get a shot of the back license plate as he drove off?"

"No such luck. The guy drives out in reverse through the parking lot until he was out of the cameras' line of sight."

"Alright." Detective Marshall said as he stood up to stretch. "You mind calling the Shawsens and giving them the update? I need a break from my last phone call."

"Yeah, no problem."

50

Like Petals to the Floor

Jessica paced the length of her tiny cinderblock and concrete room. The whole day had dragged by; she wasn't able to focus on reading any of her books, nor could she play her violin for very long before the anxiety got to her and the notes got all mixed up with her scattered emotions. It was nearly dinnertime; she could hear some faint noises out in the large open room.

The rose Thomas had given her with the dress earlier that morning was stuck into a small hole at the top corner of the mattress. There it stood up tall and in full bloom; the second most colorful thing in the little room.

Jessica had done her hair up as best as she could while looking at her reflection in the two-way mirror. Grabbing the top of her snug fitting dress she shifted it back and forth, pulling it up a little. Having never worn a strapless dress before, she felt slightly uncomfortable; but she was glad to be wearing any sort of clothing.

There was a quiet knock on the metal door. Jessica's bare feet pattered across the concrete floor to the bed, where she sat down and placed her hands in her lap.

It was quiet. Jessica was getting up to glance through the small window when she heard a second knock. Gripping the handle, she pulled open the door, curious.

Thomas was in a full tuxedo with a bow tie and vest that matched the fabric of her dress. His hair had been cut short and he wore it in a messy spiked-up style.

"You look beautiful," he said as he held one hand out to her and with the other directed her through the doorway toward the modeling platform.

In the center of the room, on top of the platform, sat a table with two mismatched chairs; on the table burned two white candles beside two place settings.

He pulled out her chair and sat her down in the seat facing the bomb shelter. Orchestral music played quietly in the background. Stepping behind her, he grabbed a couple salads off the counter and placed one in front of her and the other in front of the empty seat.

Picking up the empty glasses from the table he took them over to the counter and pulled out a bottle of sparkling cider from the fridge, breaking the seal on the lid. He glanced over at Jessica and saw that she sat waiting with her back to him. Placing the freshly opened bottle back into the fridge, he removed another bottle two-thirds full of sparkling Champagne. He poured the contents into each glass and then placed them on the table.

"What's this?" Jessica asked.

"Sparkling cider," Thomas replied.

"Can you leave the bottle on the table?"

"Sure." Thomas placed the bottle on the center of the table then sat down in his seat. Jessica glanced over the bottle and looked over the ingredients on the label; she took a few sips and flashed a knowing gaze toward Thomas before starting on her salad.

When she was nearly finished with her salad Thomas stood up and went back to the counter for the entrees.

"It might have cooled a bit. I picked it up at the restaurant on my way here."

Taking the empty salad plate away, Thomas replaced it with a plate of salmon with a side of lentils and sautéed spinach.

"It looks delicious."

They ate their dinners quietly, occasionally glancing up at one another then smiling as they returned to their food. Whenever Jessica's glass was half empty, Thomas filled it back up to the top.

After they had finished, Thomas cleared the plates and brought out a small round piece of rich dark chocolate cake.

"Here you are."

"Oh that looks so good. Is it like a dense brownie cake?"

"Yeah, it's very rich; so you may want to wash it down between each bite." She smiled at him as he handed her glass back, filled to the top. "I know this isn't cider," she said before taking another sip. "But that's okay."

...

When they had finished their desserts, Thomas stood up and held his hand out to Jessica. Placing her hand in his, she stood up as he directed her off the platform and onto the warm concrete floor.

"Wait here a moment."

He cleared off the table and put it away along with the chairs. Then, after placing a few cushions on the platform, he draped a sheet over the entire thing.

"What's that for?" Jessica asked with a suspicious grin.

"For modeling tomorrow," he replied.

She folded her arms and looked around the room. There was a light sway in her step; she was floating.

Thomas went over to the stereo and made some adjustments to it. The music changed to a slow romantic song. He walked to the center of the room and held out his hand. Jessica came to him and put her hand in his. They danced slowly. She soon noticed that her feet were getting warm and asked,

"How is this floor always so warm? Is there a kind of underground heating to this place?"

"Yeah, it's radiant heating. There are tubes in the floor that circulate heated water."

"Ah, I see." She bit her lip as she struggled to think of something more to say. "It's nice." She shook her head at herself for making such a dumb comment. Then she asked something that had been on her mind for some time, "When you, uh, sketch me, in the small room . . ."

"Yeah?"

"Why do you always cover part of me with the sheet or comforter? I mean you've seen me completely naked while you paint."

"Well, it's like I've said before." He looked into her eyes. "Out here, when you're modeling, you are my muse and inspiration. I'm looking at your form, your contours, the lighting across your figure, and concentrating on accurately depicting you in my painting."

"So, you're not fantasizing about me the whole time?"

"It's not a fantasy if you can see it right in front of you."

"So that's when the sheet comes in?"

"Yeah, as beautiful as any person's body may be, it is more desirable when viewed within boundaries, where imagination can fill in the gaps and drives our desire to see more."

"Like a skimpy swimsuit or a barely there dress?"

"Right, yeah. It's in the presentation of almost being visible that the body becomes sexualized. Well, that and the pose or facial expression..." He went quiet as she gazed intently into his eyes.

They danced for a while; then a very different song came on. Jessica stopped dancing and gave Thomas a peculiar look.

"Are you serious? A Disney song? Mister sophisticated artist, who listens to classical music whenever he paints?"

As Angela Lansbury's voice played through the speakers Jessica started to sway again.

"I can still dance to this," she said.

She gave her hand back to Thomas and they continued dancing. As the song progressed Jessica drew nearer to him. Her head was swimming with emotion and alcohol, and her desire began welling up inside her. Letting go of his hand she leaned in and wrapped her arms around him. His arms soon followed. Their bodies were pressed close, so close, like two petals from the same rose.

When the song ended she raised her head from his chest and looked at him through tear-soaked eyes. Slowly closing them sighed and leaned into him. As their lips came together, his hand held the edge of her face, tenderly, while he gathered her closer to him. She leaned into him even harder and writhed against his body. Breaking from their kiss, her breath coming in short gasps, she looked into his eyes.

"Take me."

"Now?"

"Yes!"

Thomas looked around for a moment and reached over to a nearby table. He took a pair of scissor shears in his hands, placed one blade inside her dress, between her breasts, and the other on the outside. He slit the silky red fabric open, the dull side of the scissors running over her stomach and down her thigh.

When he had cut through the full length of the dress he looked up from where he knelt in front of her, and watched as the dress opened and slid off her trembling body, landing with a sibilant shudder on the covered cushions behind her.

51

LOST WAX LOVER

Jessica woke with a dull ache in her head. She was still in the open room on top of the modeling platform. Beside her, Thomas lay asleep. His clothes were scattered around them and her dress lay on the floor beside them. She stood up and stretched, rubbing her hands up and down her arms and over her torso; her body was still glowing. She strolled around the room.

The spotlights from the night before were still on, as was the stereo, silent after having played through all its programmed tracks. The candles had melted to stumps, and the drinks had gone flat.

On top of the mini fridge sat Thomas' sketchbook. She picked it up and began flipping through it. The first couple pages had sketches for a sculpture design, done in a technique where a mold was formed around a wax figure. When heated, the solid mold would retain the form of the figure as the wax melts out; which is then replace with a more permanent material.

Several pages in were drawings of two individual girls she could only guess were Rachel or Stacey. Not wanting to spoil her mood with dark thoughts, she quickly turned the pages.

Further in, she found drawings of herself. In many of them she seemed to be asleep. Over two-thirds of the book appeared to be sketches of her. Turning through them, she blushed at a couple drawings of her more intimate parts and flipped the pages, glancing up as if to see if anyone was looking, even though the only other person there lay asleep on a nest of cushions.

Closer to the back the pages went blank. She thumbed through to the end quickly to see if there were any other random sketches. Catching a glimpse of some upside down writing, she flipped the book around so the back cover was now the front and looked again.

A few pages in she came across several notes and some bold writing. The words '*Five Sirens*' were written in the top inside corner; underneath the phrase, a line had been drawn. Beneath the line was a list of names: '*Rachel Grute, Stacey Williams, Jessica Shawsen, Shannon Oldham, Amie Henrie.*'

A startled gasp escaped her and her heart began to race. Beside Rachel and Stacey's names there was a check mark; a line that had been crossed through both of them. Then to the right of each name was the @ symbol frequently used in an email addresses, as well as the # symbol. *Email and phone number?* Beside her name there were only a check mark and the two symbols. Just beneath her name was Shannon's, which also had the @ and # symbols beside it. The last name, Amie Henrie, had nothing next to it. *He must have already contacted Shannon.*

She closed the sketchbook and put it back on the fridge. She held her breath so as to make as little sound as possible. Tip-toeing over to the platform, she gathered up the remains of her dress. As she stood up she saw Thomas begin to stir. Clasping the crumpled dress in her arms she walked as calmly as she could toward her room. When she glanced back she saw Thomas looking at her. He smiled and watched as she stepped into the room and closed the door behind her.

She was shaking. Her pulse was racing. She felt panic building up inside her. The romantic delusion of last night came crashing down at the sight of Shannon's name.

She shook out the remains of her red dress. On to the mattress fell the pair of shears, which Thomas had used to cut the dress open. She picked them up in her shaking hands and stared at them. Hiding them between her folded arms, she went to the door and peeked through the window. She couldn't see anything or hear any noises. She went and flushed the toilet. While the water noisily refilled the tank she hurried over to the mattress, where she cut a slit along the seam on the side. She stuffed the scissors inside and placed the pillow over the slit. Wrapping herself up in the sheet and comforter, she curled up on the bed and tried to slow her breathing.

She soon heard the sound of bare feet on the floor. The metal door opened. Thomas stepped in, naked, his hair pressed flat on one side of his head and sticking out from the other. In the full light of her room she had a clear look at Thomas' body for the first time. He had a lean swimmer's build; her eyes stopped at the ominous scar that ran from one hip to the other.

"It's still a few hours 'til morning. Go ahead and go back to sleep."

She nodded her head and closed her eyes. As Thomas turned to leave she glanced at him and saw a couple circular burn scars that dotted his backside. He left and shut the door behind him. The light in her room soon turned off and there was just the faint glow coming from the small window outside the door.

A stifled sob broke into her pillow. *How could I be so stupid?* Jessica lay in her bed trembling; all thoughts of the night before forgotten, as she weighed in her mind what she would have to do in order to stop him from getting to Shannon.

52

RETALIATORY, EXCITATING WOLVES

The next evening, Thomas ended up working late at the veterinary clinic, with a little help from Roger, and yawned constantly as he painted. He was trying to refine the pose she had been in for what seemed like days now. Jessica sat with her arms wrapped around her knees, her knees tucked up against her chest. Neither of them had much to say during the modeling session; the few times that Thomas had tried to make conversation, Jessica gave short answers and said nothing more.

Thomas realized he wasn't making any headway; either he'd overdone the subject, or he was just too tired. He gave up.

"I guess that'll be all for tonight. You can go ahead and go to bed."

She got up and shuffled into the corner room and lay down on the bed. Throwing the bed sheet over herself, she stared at the ceiling. She didn't know if he was planning to come to her room. Anxiety gripped her, until she couldn't wait for him to decide.

"Tom. Can you come here?"

Thomas finished putting some containers inside the fridge and then went over to the doorway of the corner room. Inside, Jessica was lying on the bed, her hands above her head and the sheet covering the lower half of her body.

"Take me, like last night." Her voice was shaky.

Thomas' face lit up; without hesitation he stripped off his clothes, but as he grabbed for the sheet Jessica said,

"No, I ... I want you under the sheet."

He smiled and leaned down, lifted the sheet over his head, crawled forward and started kissing the inside of her thigh.

With as little movement as she could manage Jessica reached for the scissors she had stuffed into the mattress. It took a couple tries to wrap her fingers around them. As she struggled to remove them from the mattress, she felt her body flush and her head started spinning. *No, not yet.* She made another try at gripping the scissors, but her hands were made of rubber.

Shaking her head, she tried to clear her mind and reach for the scissors. But then Thomas grabbed her hips and pulled her toward him at the foot of the bed. She strained to reach the head of the bed, but the scissors were too far out of reach now. Placing her feet against his bare chest, she pushed as hard as she could, sending him stumbling backward, knocking the wind out of him as his back hit the wall.

Thomas had no idea what was going on. Did she want to, or didn't she? Jessica gathered the sheet closer to her and burst into tears.

"I can't do this!"

Thomas' struggled to catch his breath. He watched her, waiting to see what she would do or say next.

"I must have been crazy last night, or drunk. This fantasy can't possibly have a happy ending." She struggled to talk through the sobs. "This is wrong! As much as I've tried to convince myself that it's not. How can I possibly be with you?" Thomas was squatting at the foot of the bed now; his wounded eyes were fixed on her, trying to make sense of what he was seeing and hearing.

Cowering at the head of the bed, she reached behind her back and at last got a firm grip on the shears.

"After what you've done, what you plan to do. I can't *be* with you." She couldn't bring herself to meet his gaze. She tensed her grip on the scissors and readied her arm behind her as she spoke,

"So if you want me, then you'll just have to rape me," she swallowed hard and added, "like the coward you are."

She braced herself for the worst. He'd regained control of his breathing and his arms and shoulders were fully tensed. He looked as though he would lunge at her at any moment. But he didn't pounce; he shrugged his shoulders in defeat, in confusion. He picked up his clothes, left the room, and shut the door behind him; locking it.

Jessica struggled to put the scissors back into the mattress. The light in her room, as well as all the other lights, had gone out and it was pitch black. She rolled off the bed and knelt at the side of it, intending to pray, but all she could do was weep.

53

No Secrets Kept

as the Blood Cries out

The black Intrepid swerved drunkenly along the deserted blacktop; Thomas was driving fast, faster than he'd ever driven before. He felt out of control; instead of the quiet pleasure of nighttime driving, he felt like a kid trying a computer game for the first time. His hands, wet with his tears, slipped dangerously on the steering wheel. He narrowly avoided ending up in the ditch.

That bitch! She had hurt him, again; this time worse than before, worse than the humiliation of high school. His tears seemed to fly around him in the car. Before she had come along, his plan was running like clockwork. The five sirens; what had she said about there being only three? She knew all along. She had planned this, plotted to ruin him, just at his moment of triumph. And to think he brought her back from the brink of death.

He had truly believed that they could be together, that she would be his siren muse, his lover. *You're a fool, Thomas, a romantic fool; she's just the same as the others.* Well, he knew now. He would finish with this siren, and move on to the others. Shannon; ah, Shannon; he would enjoy bleeding that gossiping, lying redhead. He had saved a few choice experimental techniques especially for her. Now he'll get to try them out.

But first, he had to clear his head, figure out what to do about Jessica. He decided to drive up to college and collect his paintings; no one would suspect if he took them down, they'd been graded; he was free to do as he pleased.

...

The campus appeared to be empty. There were a few cars in the parking lot, and one or two lights on in the buildings, but Thomas figured they were just the cleaners. He pulled into the alleyway beside the art department, and parked the car. Normally this was a tow-away area, but at night he could get away with parking there. He could get away with anything; he felt a surge of raw energy coursing through him.

Up on the second floor, Thomas rounded the corner of the dimly lit corridor and headed for the painting studio. There was a single light burning in the room. Thomas walked over to the storage slots, where the students kept their work. He pulled out a few of his paintings and read the grades; they were good. *You're on the right track, Tom; this stuff is really original.*

He'd just finished stacking up his paintings into a pile he could carry when he heard a rustling sound behind him. Liam! He stood there with his usual supercilious look, lording it over Thomas.

"Well, if it isn't the pretentious blood guy, himself."

Thomas didn't answer; he glared briefly at his nemesis and turned to his stack of paintings.

"Don't ignore me, Thomas King. I have news for you. Your little charade with the animal blood? I know all about that."

Thomas stopped and looked back at Liam; he could feel himself shaking with rage, but still he said nothing.

"That's right, I figured it out. Plus I went to every butcher's shop in the county, and none of them have been supplying blood to an artist. Oh yeah, and I talked to Roger; very illuminating. Roger thinks you're a freak, Thomas. He isn't the only one."

Thomas felt his chest constricting with panic. No! Of all people, it had to be Liam who found him out. He had to do something, and he had to do it fast. His hand scrambled for something to keep his balance.

Liam backed away when he saw the heavy wooden picture frame in Thomas' hand. "Oh no you don't, Tom. It's too late for that. Now I know what you're up to, I think it might be a good idea to go public. What do you think, Tom? Any publicity is good publicity, right?"

As Liam spoke, he pulled a chair toward him, and brandished it in front of him to fend off Thomas' attack. Thomas couldn't wait any longer; with an animal roar, he launched himself at his adversary, swinging the frame like an axe. He saw blood spurt from Liam's head, heard the soft thud of a body hitting the floor. Then everything went black.

...

He came to in the car. He was aware of something wet on the side of his face. He ran his fingers over the area, licked them, the acrid taste of blood came to him. He tried to recollect what had happened. He had a fuzzy memory of hitting Liam, of dumping him into the cart he'd planned to use to carry his paintings; of loading Liam's inert body into the trunk of his car. "You should have minded your own business, Liam."

Outside, the rain was threatening to turn to snow. Thomas switched on the wipers, and kicked the engine into life. He pulled out of the alley with a squeal of tires, and sped back onto the country blacktop, heading for home; heading for Jessica.

54

Hemoscuro

Liam's eyes struggled to open as he awoke. A bright light shone in his face; as he turned away from it he felt a pressure around his arms and legs. Struggling to move, he realized that his arms were bound at the wrist, elbow, and shoulder to the wooden chair in which he sat. Looking down, he saw only his pale flesh slumped in the chair. His legs were bound at the knees to the chair. His ankles ached from lying, awkwardly twisted against the floor.

Panic began to overwhelm him. He was unable to take in a deep breath of air; his mouth had been taped shut.

A stereo to his left was playing really loudly; he arched his neck to see where the sound was coming from. He was puzzled to see that the speakers were turned away from him, pointing down a short narrow hallway that led to a metal door.

Suddenly a deep shadow loomed over him. Liam whipped his head around to see the silhouette of a masked man leaning toward him. From the mouth of the wrapped mask came a spiteful voice.

"Pretentious?"

Liam struggled against his bonds. The silhouette reached for the large upright object beside him and turned it around.

"Does this look like I'm pretending to you, Liam?"

The light that had been shining in his face shut off; it took a few seconds for Liam's eyes to adjust, to focus on the object before him. A large white sheet of paper came into view; on the paper, in various shades of red, sat a man in a solid black chair, his head slumped down. On either side of the chair were two large jars full of red liquid.

He looked from side to side and saw the same jars beside him. From each jar a thin tube rose up out of it and wound it's way up the chair and into the sides of his arms.

"Well, what do you think of your portrait?" Thomas grabbed the corner of the tape over Liam's mouth and ripped it off in one quick motion. "Come on. You've never been one to hold back an opinion."

Liam stared silently; his mouth struggled to move, but produced no words. Thomas ripped off his mask and crashed the hollow cowl against the side of Liam's head. "Speak!"

Liam's voice was ragged and hoarse.

"Tom, I ... I ... what's going on? Where are my clothes?"

"You just couldn't accept the fact that my work was better than yours."

"I ..."

"It's bad enough you stole Jessica from me in high school." Thomas cracked the mask against Liam's head again. "But then you had to stick your nose where it didn't belong, thinking you could somehow discredit my work."

"That's not what …"

"Well now you can see the full strength of my art; the sacrifice that each model has given to be immortalized by me. This painting, rushed as it is, is more a portrait of you that anything you could ever paint.

"I've kept all my other work; it's a tribute to my models, the tiny essential part of each of them used as material, rendered as the fragile and broken beauties they are. Your portrait, on the other hand, is only to prove a point. I'll likely piss on it before I burn it. I'd never hang such a dull subject beside my masterpieces."

Thomas turned and spat on the painting of Liam.

"A pathetic snob, stripped of his ego, and shown for the weak thing that he is; rendered in his own blood."

"Tom, I had no idea. I … I only meant to prove that you weren't using blood at all and … and that it was just a ruse to get attention."

Thomas glared down at Liam, his arms crossed over his chest.

"But now I truly see the … greatness and … and magnitude of your work." Liam forced the words out, wincing at every sound.

"I won't ever say anything to discredit your work again. I swear."

Thomas stepped around and behind Liam. "You're right. You won't." He slapped the tape back over Liam's mouth and wrapped his arm around Liam's head, tilting it to the side. Out of his pocket Thomas produced an extra-long needle, which he stuck into the side of Liam's neck. Adding a small piece of tape to keep the needle in place, Thomas watched as a rhythmic spurt of blood began to drip from the needle.

When he felt the warm liquid running down his neck, Liam jolted, and the flow rate increased. He watched wide-eyed as his blood ran down his torso and into his lap, mixing with the fresh puddle of urine.

Thomas was interrupted in his triumph by a sound from the narrow corridor. He glared at the metal door in the hallway.

"I image you'll be more selective about your comments, as this paintings is more a part of you than any other. Now I'll leave you to your final critique of your final portrait." Thomas pointed a remote toward the stereo and increased the volume even more. Liam's muffled screams were blocked by the duct tape, and only faint sounds escaped. He grew lightheaded and stared blankly into the painting before him. Thomas disappeared around a corner to the right, leaving Liam alone with the deadly image of himself still wet on the paper before him.

55

ALONE IN THE DARK

Jessica paced restlessly around her room, the sheet wrapped tightly around her like a strapless dress; its folds moved around her like sails. Occasionally stubbing her toe in the dark, she waved an arm out in front of her to keep from running into the walls of a room that felt even smaller in the dark than in the light.

Ever since she'd verbally attacked Thomas she had been left alone and in the dark. He stopped bringing her food and the light in her room had remained off the entire time. In fact the last time she could even tell he was there was when loud music had been played just outside the metal door. There were brief moments when she caught what sounded like a male voice, and possibly a second, but they sounded so similar she couldn't distinguish the two. She had banged on the door and yelled, hoping that perhaps someone would find her. But then the stereo volume got louder and she couldn't hear any other sounds.

Her stomach groaned in protest and she gripped her arms around her ribs. Without a clock or indication of night or day she was uncertain how long it had been. Based on the ache in her stomach she figured it had been at least two days since she'd last eaten.

The water from the sink in the shower corner was the only thing she could use to quiet her hunger. Without any light her books were useless, and she wasn't skilled enough to play her violin blind; all she could do to pass the time was try and sleep. But sleep began to fail her as a new worry grew in her mind. As much as she hesitated to think of what might happen when Thomas returned, she now feared that he might not return at all, leaving her there to starve to death, alone in the dark.

Stumbling in the dark, her arms in front of her, she found her way across the room to the edge of the bed. She dropped to her knees and prayed.

56

THE WORTH OF HER TEARS

Strolling down the hallway of the art department, Thomas carried only a sketchbook in his hand as he headed to class. Although he had presented his work earlier in the week for critique, he and the other students still had to attend the presentation of others' works.

He made an effort to keep his expression neutral, not wanting to draw attention to himself. Since his disposal of Liam, he felt a rush of anxiety whenever he stepped through the doors of the art department building.

At the opposite end of the hallway he saw Cindy come around the corner. She stopped short when she saw him. Thomas gave her a friendly wave, but she didn't wave back. Instead her eyes welled with tears; she glanced down at the books and folder full of papers she held in her arms, as if she was looking for something. Looking back up at Thomas she tried to force a smile but couldn't; she turned and ran back the way she had come.

Thomas headed up the stairwell next to the north entrance doors. He wondered if she might be upset because he hadn't gone out for Valentine's Day with her. When last they spoke it was clear to him she was just making up the name of her date. Thomas might not be as much of a comic enthusiast as

Cindy, but he doubted she had a date with *The Flash*. Plus she'd become strangely uncomfortable when he had told her that he already had a date. *Unless … could she suspect something? No. How could she have any way of knowing?*

Inside the painting studio Professor Foster began the discussion of the latest paintings presented to the class.

Thomas kept his head down, looking intently at the sketchbook, where he traced over notes he had previously written down. He concentrated on slowing his breathing and keeping a blank, somewhat bored expression on his face.

…

After the critique had ended, Thomas meandered down the hallway, reflecting on a rare critique untainted by the bile of Liam's criticism. He couldn't remember the last time a critique had been so relaxing. To his surprise no one seemed to notice, or rather care, that Liam was absent. He felt good, calm and in control, as he made his way down the south stairwell.

Around the corner, he glanced at the few of his paintings still hanging in the display case. Over the case someone had taped a sheet of paper. Thomas was mildly annoyed; couldn't they think of a better way to publicize an event than stick a flyer over someone's work?

Curious what the flyer had to say, Thomas walked up to investigate. He blanched, and staggered, as he saw the sheet of paper staring back at him; there, in black and white, was Jessica's face. Details of her appearance and last known whereabouts were posted below. At the bottom of the paper were tear-away contact information tabs, half of which had already been removed.

He looked over at his paintings. There, right beside the missing person flyer, was the exact resemblance of Jessica, painted in blood.

He ripped the paper off the display case and glanced around for any others. There was another one behind him. He ripped that one off the wall too. Five feet down the hallway were two more and then dozens more, all the way along the corridor.

He spun in circles as he decided what to do. With a quick swing of his elbow he shattered the glass of the display case and grabbed all of his paintings.

Down the hallway he heard a startled shriek. Glancing to his left, at the north end of the hall, Thomas saw a couple students talking and looking right at him, pointing. When his gaze met theirs they hurried away into the nearest classroom.

He gathered his paintings in his arms and burst out the nearest exit doors, running full sprint for his car.

57

Home is Where the Art is

The half-hour drive out to the country eased his mind; the closer he got to his hidden studio, the safer he felt. He rubbed the wound on the side of his head, and grinned ruefully at himself in the mirror. Oh yeah; there was the little matter of Liam to dispose of. That cheered him up even more.

Down in the open room Thomas hung the paintings he had taken from the campus, back in their rightful places, on the walls that surrounded him. There were so many now he was nearly out of space. *Enough room for one more*. And he knew exactly what that one would be.

He heard a faint high-pitched sound, shifting very slowly. It seemed to be coming from the bomb shelter. Making his way closer he realized it was the sound of a violin. He stood just to the side of the metal door and listened as she played. It was a hymn, one of the few hymns Thomas knew by name: *'Nearer my God to Thee'*. It had been burned into his mind when he had seen the movie 'Titanic', during the scene where a string quartet calmly played as many of the passengers awaited their inevitable death. Then it had been saddening, but hearing it now was heartbreaking.

Inside her tiny prison, Jessica swayed as she continued to play her violin. When a faint hint of light had shown through the little window of the metal door, she had picked up her instrument and begun pouring her heart out. As she began the fourth verse her tears made a tapping sound on the body of the violin, and rolled into the f-holes.

The light flashed on, and she covered her eyes from the intense brightness. She recoiled when she heard the door swing open. Instantly a damp rag was clamped over her face. She tried to swing her violin at him, but he was too close to strike a proper blow. Her grip failed her and the violin fell to the floor and split open; the bow landing beside it. She struggled for a moment longer, and then fell limp.

58

CODE 3: 207, POSSIBLE 187

After a long day filled with far too many phone calls, Detective Marshall pushed his chair against his desk and grabbed his coat off the nearby hook. Before he could get his arm into the second sleeve his partner came jogging up to his desk,

"I just got off the phone with the Shawsens," said Detective Ramses, a little out of breath, "They called while I was on my way back to the station."

Reluctantly Detective Marshall put his coat back on the hook and sat down at his desk. He could tell by the expression on his partner's face that this couldn't wait until morning.

"What have we got?"

"You know the flyers he put up?"

Detective Marshall gave a nod.

"Well, turns out copies of that flyer had made it to the Uinta State University in Vernal, Utah. Mr. Shawsen has received multiple calls this evening, from various people, all with the same story.

"The name Thomas King kept coming up again and again, and claims that he's been painting portraits of the missing Shawsen girl."

"So? He could be grabbing pictures off her Facebook page and using them for a reference in his oil paintings."

"Oh, but that's where it gets weird. The paintings aren't done in oil, they're done in blood."

"What?"

"Apparently King told the students and Faculty that they were done in animals' blood, but within minutes of the missing person flyer being placed up beside one of the paintings, with a model that matched the picture on the flyer, there was a lot of concern. Plus, the appearance of Miss Shawsen as a model in these paintings began a couple days after she was last seen in Denver."

"What I don't get is why would he paint with blood?"

"Simple answer; he's a psycho."

"But it's not that simple. Never is." Detective Marshall rubbed his eyes. "Contact the Vernal police and see if they can do a DNA test on the paintings."

"Mr. Shawsen mentioned that a couple people who contacted him had said the display case in which the paintings were in had been shattered and the paintings stolen."

Detective Marshall ran his hand through his hair and let out a deep breath. Straightening his shirt, he moved closer to his desk and grabbed for the phone, "Alright, let's call it in."

59

THE SILENCE THAT FOLLOWS

Jessica came to. Straining her eyes to focus, she found herself in a familiar but terrifying situation. Her hands were bound and needles in both her arms fed two overflowing jars on the floor in front of her. She was tied down in a kneeling position with her arms locked and pulled forward over the brown rectangular cube. She made to drop her head, but something was tied to her ponytail that kept her head upright. She sobbed as she strained against her bonds.

Thomas moved only his eyes as he glanced between his painting and the fragile, broken creature before him. His face remained cold and hard. His mind was fixed. This would be the last portrait of Jessica Shawsen.

Out of the stereo came a frantic cacophony of string music; the panicked tonalities filled the room.

Jessica shivered, and her teeth chattered. She stared at Thomas as she crouched and cried. Her head swayed slightly at each new wave of dizziness that came over her.

Thomas didn't attempt to meet her sorrowful gaze; he went about painting without looking at her face. She looked from side to side, trying to find some way to remove the needles. Pained by his refusal to look at her, Jessica made an effort to speak.

"Please, please Tom. I … I … Please, look at me, Tom."

She choked on her own sobs. Gathering her composure, she made another effort to get to him.

"Please, don't do this. I'm your model, your muse, your siren…"

"And what about Liam, huh? I saw the paintings he did of you." His voice rose quickly to a shout.

"What … what are you talking about? I … I've never modeled for anyone but you."

"Liar! You posed with drapery wrapped under your arms, and in that red dress. The same red dress that you wore to the dance!"

She recoiled under his shouting, "I've only ever been yours. I swear."

"Prove it. Prove to me you are mine." He nodded toward the tiny corner room. "Right now."

Just once more, with her willing and wanting. He had time. Yes, there was still enough time. His eyes drifted into the dark spaces of the studio; he was lost in thought. When they returned to Jessica, he got up and went over to the counter, where he picked up the bag with the restraints inside it.

"No, no," Jessica cried out. "I'll be good. I'll be good."

He put the bag down and picked up the bottle of chloroform and a dry rag. Placing it in his back pocket he gripped Jessica's arms and removed the needles; a small drop of blood beaded at each insertion point.

Cutting her restraints, he nodded for her to go to her room. He followed close behind her, watching her stumble and shuffle her way to the metal door. As she lay down on the mattress, Thomas removed his cloths and placed them on the floor by the side of the bed, the chloroform within easy reach.

Through a blinding mist of tears, she held out her arms to receive him. As he crawled into her embrace, the dry petals of the rose that had been stuck in the mattress at the head of the bed fell off on to the mattress and the floor.

Jessica raised her arms above her head as he burrowed his face into the side of her neck. With shaking hands she reached out and pulled the scissor shears out of the hole in the mattress.

She felt his body tense and stretch. She couldn't let him escape this time; she wrapped her legs around his lower back and crossed her ankles. Raising the scissors as high as she could behind Thomas' back she looked at the quivering metal in her trembling hands. He began to convulse, holding her tight. Jessica took a deep breath, trying to will as much of her remaining strength into her hands as she could. Then she noticed the thin band of silver on her finger and hesitated.

Suddenly her own body followed suit and she began to spasm with him. She was betrayed by dark pleasures. She pitched and rolled like a raft on a roiling sea. She wrapped her arms around the back of his head as she gasped and moaned.

When their two bodies slowed to a stop, Jessica broke into tears. Her arms were still wrapped around him as she sobbed.

"I can't do it, I just…" She swallowed hard. "I'm so sorry, Tom; I'm sorry for everything I did to you." Her head swirled and she blinked her eyes hard as she struggled to focus. "I should never have listened to … to those rumors, those lies. When you painted me in high school I … I was so nervous, but excited." She could feel her head growing heavier. "I never, ever modeled for anyone else. I don't … I don't know anyone named Liam. I swear I … I have only ever been your muse."

She wrapped her arms tighter around the back of his neck, pulling him as close to her as she could; his eyes were so close to hers she couldn't see them. Coughing on her tears, she tried to go on.

"I could have … I wanted to love you, the idea of you. But the reality of you … I, I just can't. I'm sorry. And I … I forgive you Tom." She lifted her head up and cupped her tear soaked lips into his. "I forgive you," she repeated, pulling him into her weeping kisses.

"But I can't let you do this. Forgive me!" With all her remaining strength she threw her arms up and quickly drove the scissors downward. He snapped back at the sudden movement; throwing his arms up reflexively. The blades glanced off his forearm and plunged into Jessica. She lurched forward convulsing frantically. Thomas' hands trembled around the embedded scissors, afraid to touch them as if they would burn him. Suddenly his hand was snatched in a cold grip. Jessica stared unblinking, terrified into his eyes. She squeezed his hand in rhythms of three. *One, two, three. I'm sorry. One, two, three. I love you. One, two, three…*

She pulled herself up, inches from his face and locking her final gaze into his shocked eyes she choked, "Tom… stop. Stop."

Everything seemed to slow down. Thomas watched her hair flutter slightly as her head descended back into the pillow. The soft skin of her arms and thighs gently brushed over his lower back and shoulders as they fell to either side. He stared, bewildered, into her glazed eyes as they closed.

He froze, staring at the scissors' silver blades, gilded in blood, his shocked expression reflected back at him by the paired blades driven in her core.

A flutter of movement out of the corner of his eye caught his attention. The last petal of the dried-up rose fell and landed in Jessica hair. He stood up and backed away from her until he could lean against the wall.

She lay there on her back, her legs awkwardly splayed, one arm dangling over the edge of the bed while the other lay bent across her chest. Both her hands stained with blood; one open almost reaching out. Bloody finger trails followed the other clasped over her heart. Thomas carefully, reverently straightened her legs and draped the sheet over her lower body, placing it just below the protruding shears.

Standing there, pale and in shock, looking down at her, he struggled to think. *What did she mean?* He felt the confusion and conflict raging inside him. *How could she not remember Liam? Wait . . . the painting.*

"No! Its not supposed to be like this." He frantically stuttered, "Her final portrait… I have to capture it! I need to…"

Thomas went out into the open room to grab his sketchbook and a pen, but then he saw the painting of the young man in the solid black chair. His legs wobbled and he groped for the nearest chair to sit down in. A chill crawled up his spine at the realization that the face in the painting was his own.

"What, where … where's Liam?" Thomas asked the painting. He desperately searched the room for any sign that Liam had been there. Nothing.

He went outside to search the septic tank where the previous sirens had been disposed of. The chilled air and icy snow was nothing to the cold of his bare skin; his body had gone numb. With his hand covering his mouth, he shone the flashlight into the dark tank. Searching over it again and again he could only make out two bodies, as he peered down the opening into the foul darkness.

…

Thomas sat dumbfounded on the modeling platform in the basement. Blood from the slash on his forearm began to dry. A cold chill crept through the house and down into the basement studio. Neglected doors left open in his stupor. *There's no Liam? Jessica is gone.*

He went back into the corner room. He gazed at Jessica's lifeless form as he scribbled frantically on the piece of paper. After rereading it over several times and rewriting it once, he tore it out and placed it between the scissors handle that still lay immovable in her bluish white abdomen.

Returning to the open room, the concrete warm against his bare feet, he paused. *Who painted these? Did I? Did Liam? Who am I?* He looked from one painting to another, his eyes darting from expressions of fear, sorrow, and weeping, then over to slight grins, peaceful sleep, and gentle smiles. He turned to the final portraits of Rachel and Stacey, both filled with terror and sadness. Then he looked at the portrait he had just been painting of Jessica; over to the painting that should have been Liam, and back to Jessica. His face cracked and the tears ran down his cheeks. Dropping to his knees, he wrapped his trembling arms around his shivering body and wept.

Looking up for a moment, he saw a full-length standing mirror behind a couple of modeling chairs. His sadness faded into determination; he got up and grabbed the mirror and placed it in front of his easel. Placing Jessica's final portrait on the nearby table, he picked up a fresh sheet of paper and clipped it up on the easel.

He took an empty jar in his left hand, and a length of tape between his teeth, and a large needle with tubing in his right hand; he punctured a vein on his left arm and taped the needle in place. Biting down on one end of the elastic tourniquet, he used his free hand to tie it into place around his bicep.

As the jar started to fill he sketched his reflection in the mirror onto the paper. Working fast, he began to paint. Though it didn't even come close to what he'd put her through for the past month or so, Thomas knew he had to inflict this punishment on himself. He tried to image how it had felt for her, for all of them. This self-portrait would be an addition to the letter, a further attempt to rectify his unforgivable acts.

...

Much of the face and body were nearly finished; but the eyes were still blank and empty. When he looked over at the dozens of painted Jessica's staring back at him, he felt the world whirling around him. *Am I painting me? Am I painting Liam? Or is Liam painting me?* Struggling to paint through the tears veiling his eyes, he swayed, feeling increasingly dizzy.

He was startled at the feel of his own warm blood, overflowing from the jar on to his hand. The large beaker slipped out of his hand and shattered on the floor beside his feet. He jumped as the glass scattered. When his feet touched back down, one landed on the broken glass shards, the other in the slick red puddle. Reflexively he reached out for anything to brace himself against, but he found nothing; his hand brushed against his sketchbook, which flipped off the counter and landed on the floor.

His feet flew out from underneath him, sending him falling backwards. The back of his head bashed against the metal pipe that protruded from the wall behind him. He collapsed onto the floor and felt a sharp pain shoot up along his inner thigh. As his dazed eyes slowly closed, he looked up at the painting; it seemed to stare back at him with a knowing gaze. A faint, distant sound of sirens whispered through his ears. His head drooped, and as it did he saw the bright red liquid, rhythmically pulsing from his inner thigh and out of the tube still stuck in his arm.

60

JUNIOR MINTS
AND MOUNTAIN DEW

Lying in bed at the University Hospital in Salt Lake City, their latest patient stared out the nearby window, a mind full of terrible acts and unthinkable loss, trying to loose itself in the city below. Two eyes leading troubled thoughts on a tour through the city; zigzagging through the Avenues, lingering in Temple Square, and climbing up to the Capitol Building just before taking flight across the Salt Flats and the escape beyond Salt Lake Valley.

A police officer stood outside the door and spoke with the doctor.

"I need to ask your patient a couple more questions."

"I realize that, but bear in mind that with these injuries and such an excessive amount of blood loss, it takes time for a full recovery. So you may want to keep your questions to a minimum."

"Are you kidding? After what he did to…"

"Trust me. Just try not to expect a lot right now. The shock from such a trauma will be debilitating."

"You got it doc."

The police officer tapped on the door and stepped in,

"Thomas King."

She turned at the sound of his name and looked up at the uniformed man standing before her.

"Miss Shawsen, I know in cases such as yours it can be difficult to talk about what happened, but I need to get a statement from you for the police report. Was your captor's name, Thomas King?"

"Yes, it is… or was. I…" Her hand cupped her mouth as she turned away to the window. Tears dripping from her nose crept down between her fingers.

"If you can tell me everything you remember from just before you were kidnapped up until you were rescued …" he trailed off, thinking he'd probably asked too much of her. But Jessica knew she needed to tell the story.

"Well I, I… had come home for the weekend to visit …" as Jessica retold her experience over the past five weeks, the officer remained quiet, and only asked her to elaborate on a detail here and there.

"… and then I woke up… here. I don't even know how I got here." Her tears were spent. A red nose and matching eyes stared blankly at the wall, forming imagery from the stucco texture.

He finished jotting down a few more notes then asked, "Are there any questions you want to ask?"

Rachel. Stacey. "Did you find the ... others?" Her gaze remained fixed on the textured wall, searching. Her words came slow and quietly.

"Victims? Yes we located their remains." The officer kept his answer short and hoped that she wouldn't ask anything more about the other victims. He was grateful enough that he wasn't the one who found the corpses; rotting inside a septic tank, in the barn beside the old house in which they had found her.

"Their names, along with yours, were written down in the sketchbook of your captor."

"Thomas," she corrected him in a distant whisper.

"Uh yes, Thomas."

"And what did they determine was the cause of his death?" Jessica asked slowly.

"Based on the evidence at the scene, it looked as though while he was painting he dropped the glass jar, and slipped on its contents, knocking himself unconscious against," the officer flipped through his notes. "...a pipe sticking out of the wall behind him. It was determined that he basically bled to death. Not so much because of the needle that was still inserted in his arm, but because of the base of the shattered glass beaker we found under him, with a ninety-degree shard embedded into his inner thigh. It had severed his femoral artery."

"So it wasn't suicide?" Her words were distant as she found the image in the texture; two lovers, dead in each other's arms.

Poison, I see, hath been his timeless end.

O churl! drunk all, and left no friendly drop

To help me after! I will kiss thy lips;

Haply, some poison yet doth hang on them,

To make me die with a restorative.

Thy lips are warm!

Yea, noise? then I'll be brief. O happy dagger!

This is thy sheath; there rest, and let me die.

As the stucco texture Juliet spoke her final words to her dead Romeo, Jessica's fingers cautiously wandered to the dressing over her own sheath.

"No. It was completely accidental." The officer's voice drew her attention back and her hand away from her abdomen.

A tight, half-smothered sob escaped her. "I'm sorry. I…"

"Don't worry about." He stood up to go, then paused and said, "This… letter was found on, uh… on your person." He cleared his throat as he offered her the letter. "Its from, him."

A shaking hand reached forward with dread and hope. Unaware that she held her breath, Jessica opened the folded paper and braced herself for Thomas' last words.

My Dear Jessica,

If only I had come for you first. Then things might have been dif-ferent. I want so much to be with you. To be beside you, not as a captor, but as a partner. But it's too late now. It wasn't so much what the other people said; it was the fact that you believed it that hurt me the most. You meant everything to me. But I never wanted to hurt you. Why did I hurt you? Now I don't know how I can ever forgive myself for the things I've done to you. I'm sorry. I couldn't think of any other way that I could have you and even when I had you like this, it wasn't real. It was a lie.

"Not all of it." Jessica whispered to the letter as she read on.

I swear I saw the paintings that Liam did of you, but when I looked at the painting I had done of him, just before I killed him, the only person there was me. Am I Liam? Or is he me?

I have to get away from you. From the things I did to you and the others. I have to escape from this. You meant everything to me. I can't be-lieve I hurt you like this… and now you're gone. I'm sorry. I'm sorry. I'm sorry for all the cruelty and everything I've done. Know that I love you. I love you, but I think I wanted you to love me more. My siren muse.

Thomas

Sensing a pause as she refolded the letter, the officer continued, "The families of the other victims are requesting the uh, paintings of their loved ones be destroyed after they have been documented for evidence. I assume you'd like the same."

"No! I want them."

"Excuse me?"

"Every painting of me, every drawing; I want them all!"

"Okay." He wasn't sure what to make of the request, but he kept his cool.

"I also want his self-portrait, if I can."

"I'm pretty sure we can get you the pictures of you…"

"Paintings."

"Ah, right, paintings of you, but I will have to find out about the self-portrait."

"I'd appreciate it."

"Alrighty. Get well and try to have a better day," the officer said as he left the room.

Jessica turned back to the window and stared blankly out of it. Her eye caught by the glint of a golden figure perched high in Temple Square. The angel reflected the morning sun with his trumpet held high. It was such a relief to see the sky and the trees, even if they were still bare of leaves. Light flutters of snow occasionally drifted past the window. She was running out of distractions to stop the tears.

...

Jessica turned her head at the click of the door latch to see her attending nurse enter the room. The kind-hearted woman saw the new sadness on Jessica's face instantly and hurried to her side.

"I'm sorry Jessie. Is there anything I can do for you?" The nurse asked as she switched out the I.V. bags.

"Tell the hospital to use some fabric softener." She joked, thinking to herself that she would almost rather have the old bed sheet wrapped around her than the rough, flimsy hospital gown. "Actually, I'd like to hear more about your daughter's horse shows. And your son sounds like quite the creative one… if you have time?"

"You sure I'm not boring you with all my stories?"

"Of course not. You speak so highly of your kids. They must mean the world to you."

"They do." A tender smile reflected fond memories. "It will have to wait though, dang it. My shift is almost over and I've errands to run before I can go home to get some sleep, but I'll see you again tonight."

"I look forward to it. Thank you, Lori." She reached out her hand, the attached I.V. line following, and squeezed her nurse's hand.

"I brought you a little treat." Lori enthusiastically pulled a box of chocolate mint candies from the pocket of her scrubs and placed it with a florescent green soda on the table next to Jessica. "These'll make you feel much better than this." She tapped the fresh I.V. bag sarcastically.

A fresh smile scrunched on Jessica's face. "Thanks."

"Feel better Jessie. I'll see you soon." Lori exited the room, but left a comforting peace behind.

A tap on her door took her mind away from the quiet scene outside. In the doorway, under a mop of curly red hair, stood Shannon.

"Oh Jessie, I'm so glad you're okay. How are you feeling?"

"Fine, I guess. Better now that you're here."

"Are your parents here too?"

"Not yet. I talked to them on the phone earlier. They should be getting here soon."

"Well, it's over now. You're safe now that … that monster is gone."

"Monster?" Jessica's voice was sharp. "I created that so called monster. If it weren't for me…"

"No Jessie. He chose to do those things, not you."

"But I put the choice in front of him." She turned away to hide her tears. "He was a good person, but through the cruelty of others, including me, he was made into…"

"Don't ever believe that you're responsible for what he did. Because you're not!"

"I'm sorry Shannon. I just don't really want to talk about it right now."

"Hey, it's alright Jess. I'll be here when you need me." Shannon pulled out a piece of paper and pen from her purse.

"Here. Here's my real number. I'll have to get yours later, unless you really did lose it with that ski hunk." She winked, "Oh and speaking of hunks, I ran into someone downstairs that you know."

Another knock came at the door; Jessica turned, a look of irritation on her face. *Who is it now?*

"Hey pretty lady. Watcha in for?" said Eric Matthews.

"Eric! What are you doing here?"

Eric Matthews leaned over and gave her a hug, being extra careful of all the equipment and monitors she was hooked up to.

"I've gotta run. Call me later," Shannon said as she followed Eric's hug with one of her own.

"Thanks Shannon." Jessica called out to her friend as she left the room.

"Seriously, what are you doing here Eric?"

"I told you on our last date, back in … too long ago, that I was looking for a residency position in Utah."

"Yeah, to follow your rock climbing and kayaking buddies." She teased with a coy grin.

"Hey, all work and no play…"

"But still, what are the odds?"

"I know, right? Lucky for me they flew you out here from Ashley Regional."

Eric pulled up a stool with wheels on it and scooted up to the edge of the bed. He looked at her with big sad eyes.

"I've missed you."

A tearful smile formed on Jessica's face. "I've missed you too."

"How are you doing Jessie? I mean really… how are you feeling?"

"I'll be fine," she said, glancing back at the window. Every person that had come to see her made her reopen a wound that still hadn't even begun to heal. Every thought of Thomas threatened to bring her to tears.

"I want you to know that whatever happened, you will always have a place in my heart, and nothing can take that away." He smiled at her affectionately. "Just know you can talk to me, when you need to."

"Thanks." She placed her hand on his, and he encased her hands in his.

"Do you mind if I take a peek at your chart?"

"Go right ahead, doctor," she said with a grin.

"Oh …" he made an exaggerated expression of distress, "I see they have nurse Error checking in on you."

"Error? You mean Lori?"

"I'm only kidding. Don't let her last name fool you. Lori's an excellent nurse. In fact…" He picked a single chocolate mint out of the little box on the table and popped it into his mouth. "… I'm certain these little delicacies are a gift from her."

"What makes you say that?"

"That's all I see her eat through her whole grave shift. I swear she runs on these things. Seriously I don't know how she does it." He kept skimming through the chart. His eyes slowed over the words - *exhibiting symptoms of strong emotional attachment to her captor.* The pleasant smile he wore shrank a fraction then faded the more he read on.

"You're lucky to be alive Jess. Well no, that's not accurate enough. Blessed! You are very blessed to be alive." Eric's face was a mixture of concern, relief, and gratitude. "Had he stabbed you a faction of an inch in any direction..." He swallowed hard. "You might not be here."

"It was me." She whispered as her gazed drifted back to the wall.

"What was?"

"I stabbed myself... by mistake," Jessica swatted the tears off her face. "...when I tried to stab him."

Eric said nothing as he sat on the edge of the hospital bed and wrapped Jessica into his arms; rocking her slowly, like a gentle breeze.

Reluctantly, Jessica pulled herself from his warm embrace and tried to regain her composure. "I've ruined your shirt." She let out a teary laugh at the tears and snot marks on the shoulder of Eric's scrubs.

"Eh, this is nothing. I've had a lot worse things get on me."

There was yet another knock at the door. Jessica's doctor came back in and held out his hand for the chart, grinning as he said, "Thank you Doctor Matthews. I'll take it from here."

"Yes, of course." Eric briskly stood up and handed over Jessica's file. "Oh, hey Jessie…"

"Yeah?"

"If you're feeling up to it later or you need something a little more than the Lori Special; they've got a pretty decent cafeteria down stairs."

"Sure. Thanks Eric."

"I'll see ya."

"Bye."

Eric closed the door behind him as he stepped out of the room. Turning her attention back to her doctor, Jessica listened as he went over her chart.

"Let's see; everything is looking good. We'll keep you on the antibiotics for a while to fight off the infection from your perforated intestine. Let your nurse know when you start feeling any pain and we'll make sure to keep it at a manageable level." He skimmed the latest update to her chart. "We're still waiting for the results on a couple other tests. Just relax and keep drinking those liquids. Juice or water is fine. You'll definitely want to keep it to a minimum with your neon soda. Then later you can probably have a bite in the cafeteria.

"If you don't mind my asking, where do you know Doctor Matthews from?"

"Oh, we dated for a little while before he graduated and moved here for his residency."

"Well it's nice that you know somebody here. I must warn you though, the cafeteria food really isn't that good, but the right company can always help."

"Yeah, it can."

61

HEMOSTASIS

Two months later

"I've tried so hard to let go of you, but I ... I just can't." Jessica struggled to read the words on the letter that shook in her trembling hand. "I know you've become an irrevocable part of me that I have to accept."

Jessica stared tearfully at the empty leather couch in front of her. "I'm going to take what you've given me, what you've made from me, and treat it with the love and understanding that it deserves. The same understanding that I should have given you. I'm sorry; I'm really sorry."

She turned the letter face down on the coffee table and wiped the tears from her eyes. Sitting beside her on the same couch, her father asked,

"Is there anything else you want to tell Tom?" Dr. Shawsen gestured toward the empty couch across from him and Jessica. She paused and swallowed hard. Struggling for a silent moment to will the words from her mouth, she could only manage the faintest whisper as she spoke to the empty couch.

"I did love you." She choked on her sob. "I still don't know ... what form of love, but for a brief moment, I did ... and still do."

Dr. Shawsen placed his hand tenderly on his daughter's back as he spoke,

"You did good sweetheart. I know it's a difficult exercise to do, but I can see that it has helped you. Do you feel that it has helped?"

"Yes." She cleaned the remaining tears from her cheeks.

"Good." Dr. Shawsen returned to his usual place on the couch opposite his patients. Repositioning his iPad on his lap he continued with the session.

"Now getting back to your decision with the paintings. You said you want to turn them into a strength, correct?"

"Yeah, I feel it will be better for me than to hide them and be ashamed of them."

"Right, you have nothing to be ashamed of."

"I feel like it will be my own version of Powers' sculpture."

"The Greek Slave?"

"Yes, although I was in a circumstance of … of enslavement or bondage…" She paused to search for the words to adequately describe her complex web of thoughts. "When I look at those paintings I feel a sense of hope, of empowerment; and with some of the latter ones, affection."

Dr. Shawsen nodded. "I understand."

Jessica contemplated the glass chess set on the coffee table between the two of them. Dr. Shawsen glanced at the clock above the roll-top desk at the opposite side of the room.

"Well that's all of my doctor/patient time for today." He stood up and held open his arms for Jessica. "But I still have some father/daughter time."

A comforted smile formed across her face as she hugged her father.

"How are things with Eric?" Mr. Shawsen asked.

"They're good. He's so patient and understanding. I'm very lucky to be with him."

"We're looking forward to the big day next month." Mr. Shawsen's smile of endearment threatened a tear or two as he spoke. "My little girl. You'll make a beautiful bride."

They embraced once more before Jessica gathered up her things. Dr. Shawsen's secretary paged over the phone. "Dr. Shawsen, your next appointment is here."

"I better go." Jessica placed her hand on the door, but paused before opening it. She turned back to her father and said, "Thank you, dad, for everything."

"You bet, sweetheart."

"And about mom; don't tell her, at least for now. I will talk to her about it when I'm ready."

"Sure thing."

EPILOGUE

In a small home located near the Sugar House Park area of Salt Lake City, Utah; a doorbell rang and instantly a little yellow puppy went bolting towards the door. Slipping and sliding on the hardwood floor it came to a stop with a thud against the front door.

"Honey, can you get that?" Jessica called out from the kitchen table; she darted from oven to stove to microwave, her left hand covering the mouthpiece of her cell phone. The light dancing off the diamond of the ring she wore on her left hand balanced the one with the chipped blue shield on her right. When she heard footsteps on the back porch, she turned her attention back to the phone.

"Yes, Hi. Thank you so much for taking my call today? Like your assistant probably told you, my name is Jessica Matthews and I'm looking for a gallery to hold an exhibition…"

Shedding off his layers from snowboarding earlier that morning, Eric placed his snowboard atop the rack on the back porch, just beneath where his kayak hung. Rubbing his hand rapidly through the damp of melted snow in his hair he shook it up into a messy spike before leaning over to kiss his wife on the cheek. Jessica brushed the side of his face affectionately as she continued speaking on the phone. "Wow, really? That far in advance? No, no that would be great. Then I will have plenty of time to get everything ready."

Eric paused to look at his strong, beautiful wife and thought how proud of her he was, for taking control of what happened to her. By finding the tiny bit of good amongst all the bad and nurturing it to deal with the pain.

He grabbed a dry shirt to put on as he walked down the hallway, passing the print of Jesus Christ that had once hung in Jessica's old bedroom, before going to answer the door.

. . .

Blaine signaled as he steered the car onto the I-80 West exit for Salt Lake City. He and Carol had been discussing the events of several months earlier. Carol continued to talk.

"I still don't understand why, after all she went through, why she would want to keep something that links her back to that nightmare."

"Now darling, you have to believe me." Blaine coaxed her in his best 'doctor' voice. "I have talked with her a lot about what happened before, what happened during, and what to do now. I know it upsets you that she doesn't want to talk to you about what happened, but that's her choice and you need to re-spect that. It took a lot for her to tell you as much as she has.

"Those paintings are hers in every way possible. They hold very complicated and conflicting emotional connections for her and she feels that what she is doing is for the best."

"How can she want to show those paintings of herself, completely naked and exposed, to the world?"

"Darling…" Blaine smiled, "Our bodies are works of art all on their own, and the nude figure isn't something to be shunned. Yes, there are people out there who perversely use the body for immoral purposes…"

"Which is what he did with Jessie's."

"Actually, that has been one of the major issues Jessie and I have discussed. Although the means by which the paintings were created were unorthodox, so to speak, the way she is presented focuses so much more on her form, her likeness, and who she is as a person. The paintings have become more empowering to her than anything else.

"I'm very proud of the strength she continues to have as she gets over that ordeal. Furthermore, she and I have been doing a lot of analytical discussion about him."

Carol scowled at the mention of Thomas, but bit her tongue as she listened to her husband's insight into discussions she wished she could have been a part of.

"There is so much more to it than we had first thought. She hadn't been entirely honest about the incident back in high school when we'd originally dealt with it. There are very complex emotions and deep-rooted meanings in why he chose to paint with blood. By exhibiting the paintings she wants to shed light on those possible meanings and open discussions. She wants to rehabilitate his memory by focusing on his talents and the good aspects of the paintings, in spite of how they were created.

"Many people in that same situation would fester with hate and fear inside, but the way she's taken back her life and sifted the little gold flecks of good out of all the dirt is really quite admirable."

"I know. I just want to be part of what helps her," Carol said as they pulled into the driveway.

"You can best help by not talking about what happened unless she brings it up and by not criticizing her about what she is doing now. One of the most wonderful things in her life has come of it." Stepping out of the car and making their way up the front steps they rang the doorbell. "Though it may take extra sifting for some to see it."

Most important is the reason we're here today." There was a thud at the base of the door. Blaine looked down toward the sound with a smile.

"Today we get to meet him."

The door swung open and the yellow puppy enthusiastically greeted the two visitors that stood before him.

"Sorry, you can just nudge him aside with your foot." Eric said with a grin. "Thanks for coming. How were the roads?"

Picking up the little puppy, Carol said, in a sugar-coated voice,

"Oh, no snow or number of hours of driving would stop us from coming to have Thanksgiving with you, you sweet little puppy doo. Yes. Who's a good boy? Who's a good boy? That's right, you are."

"Oh mom! You're just getting him all wound up," Jessica called from the kitchen as she pulled the turkey out of the oven.

"Sorry poochie, but I need to see the person I came here for." Carol put the excited puppy back down and brushed her hands off on the sides of her skirt.

Jessica stepped out of sight somewhere down the small hallway, and came back into the front living room and sat down on the couch. In her arms she held a small bundle of blankets.

"Mom, Dad," she said, tilting the bundle toward her parents. A dark-haired, pink-skinned baby boy lay sleeping soundly, with his tiny thumb in his mouth.

"I want to introduce you to your grandson; Tommy."

THE END

T. M. PRINCE

was a recent college graduate with a Bachelor of Fine Arts degree when he stepped away from the safety of the academic shelter and out into the real world. He had gone above and beyond the expectations of his instructors when he developed, through his own tireless efforts, a technique comprised of painting with his own blood. Aided by his nurse mother and phlebotomist wife; he regularly has his blood drawn to continue his art. His handling of the figure results in a softer, more humanistic approach to blood art. He takes a substance that is so impactful, so visceral that its presences screams outs, then through his technique transforms it into a whisper.

During the winter months he took to writing a short story to add further narrative to his paintings. He envisioned his opposite; an evil twin and what form of blood art would come of it. The short story *Dark Artist* grew and grew until it became the novel *Leeching the Sirens*. The ten paintings he had planned grew to thirty paintings. This project also presented him with the opportunity to develop a new technique. The learning and refinement that the antagonist of the story goes through is shared with Mr. Prince's own progress with the new materials.

T. M. Prince is an artist, with an emphasis in figure painting, known for his works done in blood. He earned his BFA in drawing and painting from Utah State University and studied abroad in Germany. Mr. Prince lives with his wife, three young sons, and dog in Utah.

His website is www.trevinprince.com

www.ingramcontent.com/pod-product-compliance
Lightning Source LLC
Chambersburg PA
CBHW050903250626
47155CB00001B/77